IF YOU
DON'T
KNOW...

AN ACT OF LOVE BETRAYED

JEREMY BENDING

First published by Cranthorpe Millner Publishers (2023)

ISBN 978-1-80378-118-1 (Paperback)

www.cranthorpemillner.com

Cranthorpe Millner Publishers

Other books by Jeremy Bending:

A Listening Doctor
In the Shadows of the Birch Trees

For Rachel
and her work for human rights and gender equality

"Men become mortal the night their fathers die."

"Moonbright", *Speak, Old Parrot.*
Dannie Abse, 2013, Hutchinson.

Chapter 1
August 2014

'If you don't know, I don't know… things not discussed can never be recorded and therefore have never taken place.'

Those were the last words his father said to him on the night before he hanged himself.

They never knew he was depressed. In truth, he had never seemed to be depressed. He left no suicide note or any other piece of evidence, written or otherwise, to explain what it was that had led him to take his own life. His mother found the body hanging from a rope in the garage at six thirty a.m. that Sunday, already stone-cold dead. The ambulance crew arrived in minutes, but all they were able to do was to certify the fact of his death. The police team came and went, concluding that there were no suspicious circumstances but, as was clear, having no more idea about what had led to his father's death, and why it had occurred, than they had themselves. The coroner recorded a largely narrative verdict. In other words, he summed up the inquest into his father's death by describing what had happened and what they knew already, without being able to throw any further light whatsoever on the "who", the "how" and the "why". In spite of these outstanding questions, with no real evidence as to the affirmative or the negative, the coroner's conclusion was that his father had taken his own life by hanging himself.

The pain was indescribable. And this referred not only to the pain of the first few days and weeks and months, but to the pain that they were all left to endure for the rest of their lives. The tears and handwringing, the self-recriminations and "what ifs?" not only overwhelmed his mother, but also his brother, his sister, the cleaning lady, his father's friends and colleagues, and himself. Not so long before, suicide had been a criminal offence. It had been against the law for a man or woman to take his or her own life. He would never forget the sheer weight of pain he'd felt in those early days, but he had also had to live with the belief which was to remain with him for a long time after: that suicide was indeed a criminal action for any person to undertake. What Jeff Butler had felt most of all, however, was a deep-down and immovable conviction that the act of suicide leaves such unbearable pain for those left behind that for anyone to even contemplate their own self-destruction is unforgivable. An act of love betrayed. Added to this was the lingering question, which hung over them all following the inquest and for many months and years thereafter: was their father really responsible for taking his own life?

Chapter 2
Three years earlier
September 2011

Paolo stood on the steps of the open doorway of one of the fleet of coaches the Red Cross had sent to evacuate the Roma families. He was in charge of the evacuation. He looked up the road to where he could see a river of Roma families – men with fear on their faces, women and children in tears – streaming down from the streets of Göspata towards the buses. For weeks this town of two thousand eight hundred residents located northeast of Budapest had been the focal point of conflict between right-wing activists and the Roma who lived there. Last month a uniformed radical group had marched through the town several times, striking terror into the hearts of the Roma community. The previous day, fascist thugs had started to throw stones at a number of Roma houses there in Göspata. Three people had been injured in fights between the extremists and Roma men who were defending their properties. Then, earlier that day, dozens of men had flooded into Göspata in an organised demonstration against the Roma families living in the town.

Several other Hungarian towns with large numbers of Roma residents had likewise seen right-wing marches, protesting, the marchers said, against "gypsy criminals". Five protestors had been arrested during one of these marches for disturbing the peace, but were released two days later. The mayor of one of the towns had accused the group of creating an environment of fear in which Roma women and children were afraid to go out onto the street. In defiance, a member of parliament from the far-right Tovabb party had said that the group would continue their marches "in the name of public order and security".

A short distance up the road Paolo could see a young Roma woman with a baby in one arm and two small children cowering behind her skirts.

'Help us, please help us,' he could hear her screaming, pleading to the man he knew as Michael Butler, gripping his shirt with her free hand as she did so.

He saw Michael gently take the baby from her and hold out his hand to the little girl, leading them down the road through the crowds of milling, scared people towards the safety of the coaches. He reached the first coach and helped the mother up the steps to where Paolo was standing, passing the baby up into her arms and lifting the little girl and her brother up after them. Paolo saw that Michael was wearing an armband on his right arm with "OSSE" printed on it. Michael had already told Paolo that he had been sent by his organisation as an observer of these events and was there to record what he saw. Paolo was touched by this one small humanitarian act the man had made.

By the end of the day, Paolo had helped Michael record the fact that two hundred and seventy Roma residents of Göspata had been evacuated, nearly two-thirds of the four hundred and fifty Roma who lived in the town. When questioned by the media about the event the next day, the Hungarian government responded by saying the coaches had been hired as part of a "holiday trip" which had been arranged for the Roma families.

Chapter 3

A few days later Paolo received a message from Michael, asking if they could meet up. He walked to the small café on Vaci Street, arriving at eleven a.m., just as he had been invited to. Michael was sitting at a table at the back of the café.

He stood up as soon as he saw Paolo and shook him by the hand. 'Hello Paolo, nice to see you again. How are things in Göspata now?'

'OK, I suppose,' Paolo replied, as he pulled his long scarf slowly off his neck and sat down at Michael's table. 'We managed to find all of the families accommodation elsewhere by that evening, and now it seems they are being allowed back into their town again. Most of them are moving back slowly, but they are all still very anxious about what happened and frightened about the possibility that the intimidation and violence might start up again.'

After they had ordered coffee, Michael sat forward and looked straight at Paolo. 'I have never seen anything like that before. I've worked for the UK Foreign Office in different European countries for more than twenty years, but have never seen that degree of racial violence and intimidation close up. It was appalling. But all I could do was to stand and watch; I felt ashamed that I was impotent to intervene in any meaningful way because of my organisation's remit which, as an observer, barred me from becoming "involved".

I'll never forget the fear and panic I saw on the faces of the Roma families as they were driven out of their houses. I felt sick at what I was witnessing. I haven't stopped thinking about it since. I would like to help you.'

'What can you do to help?' Paolo asked, unsure what it was the man was offering.

Michael went on to explain that he worked for The Organisation for Security and Safety in Europe (hence the OSSE armband he had been wearing that day) which was a pan-European inter-governmental organisation, with offices in most European capital cities. He had influence not only within Hungary but also throughout Europe. He would like to put this influence to work to do whatever he could to help the plight of the Roma people there in Hungary.

Paolo relaxed as he realised that Michael was genuinely on their side. He really did seem sincere in his wish to support the Roma people living in Hungary.

'This is nothing new, Michael,' he explained. 'My people, Roma gypsies, have suffered discrimination and subjugation across Europe for many centuries, not least alongside the Jews in their mass extermination by Hitler and the Nazis during the Second World War Holocaust. What you learnt the other day is that discrimination and subjugation is still being practised in present day Hungary – as it is to varying degrees in other parts of Europe – including against our Roma population here. At an estimate, our Hungarian Roma people constitute about ten per cent of the country's population of about ten million people, yet they are still shackled by poverty and illiteracy and are the victims of neglect and discrimination, by the population in general and the state itself.'

Paolo and Michael sat discussing the political situation in the country further. Hungary had become worryingly right wing in recent years, as far as Michael was concerned, and Paolo agreed. The far-right Tovabb party and its members were so ultra-right in their beliefs and actions as to be frankly fascist. The party members may not have worn brown shirts but they had their easily recognised uniform: white shirts with black coats, black trousers and black leather boots. They seemed to operate quite independently and outside the written law, apparently completely unchecked, as though the party had the right-wing Fidek government's blessing for their activities.

'What you saw last week was just one more example of all this,' Paolo said. 'Tovabb have been associated with many disturbing events in recent months including the eviction of families of Roma from the city of Debrecen and in late-night brawls and the defacing of Roma properties in a number of other cities, for example. As far back as 2008 and 2009, six Roma were killed in sectarian attacks.'

Before they left, Paolo had accepted Michael's offer of help in whatever way he could, and they agreed to meet up again from time to time to discuss in what form this help might be needed.

Chapter 4
April 2014

Paolo jumped off the Metro and emerged from the subway into the daylight at Deak Ferenc Square. He was making for his weekly appointment with his friend Michael Butler, now the First Deputy Director of the Organisation for Security and Safety in Europe. He strode across the busy, wide-open square, navigating his way around three or four islands of buskers surrounded by their circles of appreciative audiences. He waited patiently for the pedestrian lights to turn green at the long diagonal pedestrian crossing, to cross over the wide boulevard to the beginning of Andrassy Avenue.

Andrassy Avenue was the main thoroughfare of Budapest, sweeping up from the elegant river Danube and through the centre of Pest, the downtown part of the city of Budapest. At the far end of the Avenue the road opened onto the wide expanse of Heroes' Square, where the Museum of Fine Arts and the Palace of Arts were to be found facing each other imperiously on either side of the vast square. No more than three centuries before, Pest had been the infected disease-ridden swamp (from which its name derived) on the eastern banks of the Danube, sitting opposite the dominant Buda with its castle, palace and churches arising from the hills on the west bank of the river. Now, in the present day, Pest was the thriving social, commercial and lively part of the city of Budapest. As Paolo walked up the lower part of the Avenue he stared into the windows of the art galleries, cake shops, cafés and expensive international stores selling goods such as furs, *haute couture* gowns, designer handbags and so on. It was like being on the moon, as far as he was concerned. He had absolutely no desire to acquire any of this merchandise, and in any case could never afford to shop in any of these places if he had. He therefore rarely had occasion to visit this part of the city.

After Andrassy Avenue crossed the Oktogon intersection, the buildings gave way to the upper part of the Avenue with its large, elegant buildings; these included the embassies of many different countries, the headquarters of multinational companies operating in Hungary, and the palatial residences of the very rich. Halfway up on the right-hand side of this section of the Avenue, he entered the iron gates of the grand nineteenth century building occupied by the OSSE, nodding to the security guard as he did so. Paolo rang the bell of the impressive shiny black mahogany front door and waited for it to be opened.

Michael's PA Angie opened the door to Paolo with a smile and preceded him through the hallway with its grand high ceilings and ornate mouldings, up the stairs to the first floor and Michael's office. She knocked once on his door and walked straight in, in her usual efficient manner.

'Paolo Crusesco is here to see you,' she said, placing a file on the desk in front of him.

'Good. Send the Big Bear in,' Michael said, laughing.

Paolo, who had hesitated politely behind Angie, strolled in through the door smiling broadly, having heard what Michael had called him. It was true, he *was* a big bear of a man, tall and muscular but also thick set and hirsute, with dark brown skin, long black sideboards and long, jet black hair falling over the back of his bull neck.

'Hi, Michael!' he said, extending his huge bear-like paw across the desk towards Michael.

'Hello, Paolo. Good to see you,' Michael said in return as he shook the out-stretched paw. 'How are things?'

'Not good,' replied Paolo. 'There was a serious house fire in Pecs last night. The parents and five children only just escaped with their lives. Two of the children including the baby are in hospital suffering from smoke inhalation, although I have just heard that it appears that they are going to be alright. The police have said that they suspect arson, but have found no proof. I bet nothing more will be heard of that theory. Meanwhile, we have re-housed the family in temporary accommodation in part of the old paper mill nearby.'

Paolo was by now the leader of the Roma council in Hungary. To call it a "council" was perhaps overstating the body. In practice, it consisted of Paolo and a group of his trusted friends who were working together to protect the rights of their Roma community in the country. Paolo knew that Michael was well aware that he was a self-elected leader of a group of poorly organised and mobile people, but Michael had indicated at their first meeting that he recognised that Paolo was deeply committed, and that he was respected and trusted by the other Roma people who Michael came across regularly. As far as he was concerned, he told Paolo, this fact alone gave Paolo the authority to represent his peoples' interests, and that was all that he required to enable him to do business with Paolo. Michael had also told

Paolo that he was perfectly aware that, at some time in the future, he may face a challenge by his own secretariat or, more likely, by the present Hungarian government, who would come to the OSSE demanding to know what he was doing colluding with "this man", and on whose authority? But Michael told Paolo that he had never been interested in such sham challenges from those in opposition to his work, whether in authority or not. Paolo had come to learn that this approach was what made Michael a somewhat alternative civil servant and government officer, but it was also an important reason why he was invariably an effective one, as far as he was concerned.

Paolo and Michael got straight down to business.

'Since I saw you last, we have been able to set up five soup kitchens in different places around the country and I have so far been able to obtain forty-three residency permits from the applications you presented me with last month,' Michael told him. 'I have also been in private discussion with three opposition members of Parliament to talk about the discrimination on the ground which your people are suffering. They were keen to hear my views and I think they have understood the size and significance of the problem facing the Roma in Hungary. They told me openly that they are sympathetic with the plight of the country's Roma population. I believe they will be good allies for the future and hope they will form a nucleus of support within the opposition from which we can expand. I am sure you will understand, however, that they are not able to express their opposition views openly at the present, for fear of being discriminated against themselves, whatever the government would have us believe to the contrary. We do need to be careful not to name them publicly or call on them to talk out openly at the moment, for this reason.'

'Thank you, Michael. I already know about the soup kitchens and the residency permits, for which we are very grateful. And trust me, I shall keep in strict confidence what you have told me about any political allies you may be able to establish,' Paolo said.

This man has a good heart and a brave face, Michael thought as he bowed his head in acceptance of the thanks. They continued their business together, spending a further fifteen minutes discussing other issues which had recently come to light. After they had agreed on the next priorities, Michael stood up, opened the door for Paolo and shook him by the hand.

'Angie, please show Mr Crusesco out,' he called to his PA who was in the outer office.

Chapter 5

Paolo strolled along the banks of the Danube, the sun on his back. It was a beautiful summer day and the waves caused by the wake of the many pleasure steamers carrying tourists up and down the river sparkled in the sunlight before they slapped into the riverbank at his feet. On an impulse, he decided to turn inland and walk the couple of hundred yards to Vörösmarty Square. He wanted to say hello to his Roma friends were selling their wares at the outdoor market there.

As he entered the square, he could see that the street market was still in full swing. He could hear the hum of conversation, as the bustle of tourists and locals negotiated prices with the traders, and he could smell the frying of sausages and onions coming from the food stores. He heard someone call his name.

'Paolo, Paolo – over here!'

He had reached the Gerbeaud Café and, as he looked over the people sitting out in the sunshine on the pavement tables drinking and eating ice cream, he saw his friend Michael. He was standing up at a table at the back of the pavement part of the café, with his hand raised, calling to him. Paolo pushed between the tables towards where Michael was standing. As he drew near, he saw that there was a very pretty woman sitting at Michael's table, a glass of beer in her hand.

'Paolo, welcome, welcome,' Michael said, shaking Paolo's hand. 'Do join us, Paolo,' waving at a spare chair rather over-expansively.

'Let me introduce Zita.' Michael opened the palm of his hand towards the woman sitting next to him.

Paolo shook the young lady's hand with a friendly smile. Michael had told him that he had a new "girlfriend", but actually meeting up with her made Paolo feel just a little uncomfortable, having already got to know Michael's wife Marion – who was back in their family home in England at present – quite as well as he did. He also had the impression that, in spite of his ebullience, Michael was a bit embarrassed himself to be seen in public with his girlfriend by Paolo.

They sat and talked for a while. Paolo accepted a cup of coffee, but did not join Michael and Zita in the meal they were eating, finishing up with large, tall glasses of the café's famous ice cream sundaes.

Michael looked at his watch. 'Hey, is that the time! We really must be going. We're off to see *Don Giovanni* at the Opera House this evening. We need to go back to the flat and get dolled up.'

Paolo stood up to leave. 'Pleased to meet you,' he said, shaking Zita's hand politely.

'See you again soon, my friend,' Michael said.

With that, they left the café and Paolo headed back towards the river again to catch the last of the early evening sunshine.

Chapter 6

These days Paolo and Michael were meeting up to discuss Roma affairs on a more or less weekly basis. At their most recent meeting, Paolo told Michael that he would like to take him on a visit to the Roma community in the southern city of Pecs, and would Michael be in agreement to this suggestion?

'That would be great!' Michael replied at once. 'To be frank, I have been in Hungary for over three years now, working in Budapest, but I've had very little time to explore the rest of the country. Marion and I did spend a short summer break last year staying at a lakeside lodge on the northern shore of Lake Balaton. We spent a beautiful sunny day walking around the small Tihany peninsula which stretches out into the lake, and took some time out to visit Badascony and the Balaton wine making region. But, apart from that, I've not had much opportunity to visit other parts of Hungary.'

Angie booked the tickets for them and they left on an early morning train on a Tuesday from Keleti station, one of the three mainline stations of Budapest. It was true that the view out of the window of the outskirts of the city was not very exciting, but Paolo found Michael in a good mood and he was pleased that his friend already seemed to be enjoying the day out. They started to talk about Hungarian politics and the ruling right-wing Fidek party.

'Bloody Fidek,' Michael said. 'I thought it was the

Hungarian word for a dog when I first arrived in the country! But I soon found out that their bite is even worse than their bark.'

Paolo couldn't help laughing, even though they were sitting in an open train carriage.

Paolo relaxed and started to tell Michael about himself. He had been born into a Romanian Roma family who were at the time living in northern Romania near the Transylvanian border with Hungary. They had moved to Hungary when Paolo was an infant, his parents settling in Budapest with himself and his seven siblings. His father had been a lock maker, hardworking and reliable. With time he had established his own business, working from a small room which fronted onto the main street of Terez Korut. In size it was really not much bigger than a cupboard under the stairs, but was close to Nyugati main line railway station and a good place to attract plenty of business. His mother brought in some extra money with part-time cleaning jobs. Life for the family was always hard, his parents working seven days a week from dawn to dusk, and the children handing down clothes to each other until each piece of clothing or footwear finally literally disintegrated. But they were happy.

In spite of the friendly mood they were in as they left the city, Paolo had not invited Michael on this trip as a merely social outing. The train arrived at Pecs-Kulvaros railway station around midday and Michael invited Paolo to have lunch with him at a busy restaurant just down the road from the station. They were both hungry and enjoyed a good Hungarian meal washed down with a glass of draught Hungarian beer. When they had finished the meal, rather than linger longer to chat over a cup of coffee, Paolo wiped his moustache and upper lip with his napkin and stood up from the table.

'Thank you very much for this kind meal, Michael,' he said. 'Now let me show you one or two things which I think will be of interest to you.'

Michael paid the bill and they left the restaurant turning in the opposite direction from the station and into the centre of the city, towards what was already a poorer residential area.

They turned into Janos Kiraly Street, a street of badly maintained tenements which were clearly, even from the outside, housing for deprived families. The traditional Hungarian buildings were a number of stories high, with very sharply steeping tiled roofs above them. The corrugated tiles of the roofs were an orange colour, the walls of the buildings painted yellow or green or other pastel shades. Except that in this street the outsides of the houses had become dirty with many decades of weathering and grime from the atmosphere. The painted plasterwork was cracked and the colours dulled by the years. The buildings were of an impressively large size, but stood quite close in opposition to those facing them on the other side of the street, which appeared by modern standards to be unusually narrow for the size of the houses it contained. Three boys were playing an excited game of football, punting an old half-inflated plastic ball enthusiastically between them backwards and forwards across the street. They had placed threadbare pieces of clothing and a dirty rag on the pavement at each side of the street to act as goal post markers.

Paolo came to a stop outside number 27, hesitated, then walked towards the front door. 'Come on, Michael, let me show you inside.'

Inside, number 27 Janos Kiraly Street was virtually a shell of a building. There were no carpets or curtains across the windows, let alone recognisable soft furnishings. The plasterwork in the hall and stairwells was crumbling, with large holes in the walls at frequent intervals representing places where the plaster had fallen away completely. They walked from room to room. Every room was full of people, mostly women and children. Mothers were sitting breast feeding babies as they attempted to supervise dozens of other children at the same time. Not only were there no curtains across the windows, only pieces of cardboard or rags in places, the rooms were cold and damp without exception. If there was a means of heating these rooms in the coldest weather, this was not evident to Michael. The one or two fireplaces which were to be seen appeared to have been blocked off by pieces of hardboard in an attempt to prevent the cold air and weather entering the room by that route. There was no sign that the fires had been lit recently.

'I have lived in Hungary long enough to know how severely cold the winters can be,' Michael whispered to Paolo. 'God knows what it must be like in the winter living in a house like this with no heating or insulation.'

Paolo moved on freely about the decaying tenement building, showing Michael around downstairs. He did not bother to knock on the doors of those rooms that had doors, but his presence was clearly accepted by the inhabitants, underlining the fact that he was considered one of them.

Occasionally, he came across a man or woman who knew him personally: "Szia, Paolo" they would greet him. Michael followed Paolo at a respectful few steps behind, not wanting to intrude or to impose his presence on the families inhabiting the place.

Upstairs, the dilapidation was repeated. The floorboards were in poor repair, and frankly dangerous with seriously hazardous gaps present in many places. As they stood on the top landing, having seen enough to understand the degree of poverty and deprivation which existed, Paolo turned to Michael.

'These people have done nothing to deserve their fate. Many of the parents of these families are well-educated and skilled workers who have lost their previous employment and been chased out of their family homes. The family in the last room we were in have come here after being rescued from the fire that burnt down their house here in Pecs, which I told you about. At least the room they now have here has a dry ceiling, unlike the old mill that we had to house them in temporarily. That had large holes in the roof and more leaks than buckets which could be found to catch them.'

As they picked their way slowly back down the dangerous staircase, Michael laid his hand on Paolo's arm, pausing on a middle landing as he did so. 'You know, I've had the feeling that I have seen all this before: this house could have been a replica of one of the safe houses commandeered by the Swedish diplomat Raoul Wallenberg, who set up such refuges in an attempt to protect the lives of the Hungarian Jews in Budapest in 1944.'

Paolo looked quizzically at Michael.

'At that stage of the war,' Michael continued, 'Hungary had been taken over by Adolf Eichmann as the next step in his "Judenfrei" policy of ridding the German Reich of all Jews, committing them in their tens of thousands to a mass death in the gas chambers in Poland. Wallenberg was successful in helping thousands of Jews escape deportation to the death camps, by the use of fake Swedish documents. Eventually he himself disappeared and was almost certainly killed, either by the Nazi occupiers or, more likely, by the invading Russian armies, only a short time before the War came to an end. Have you seen that statue in memory of Wallenberg which is situated on the central reservation of the Hüvösvölgy Road leading out from the city to the suburbs?' Michael went on. 'It depicts a shadowy man in an overcoat peering through the gaps between two upright granite stone columns. I've always found it particularly moving. I had heard from others that places like this still existed in Hungary, but before now I could not believe that the extreme deprivation we have just witnessed here in Pecs could still be found. It may not be part of such an evil institutionalised genocide as that orchestrated by Eichmann, but at the very least this degree of depravity amounts to a serious and inhumane social indifference to these Roma families!'

Paolo could only nod in agreement.

As they stepped outside number 27, they were apprehended by a man wearing a black overcoat and black boots who had been observing them from the other side of the street and who strode across the road towards them.

'Papers, please,' the man demanded, holding out his palm straight at them.

The command was not so much a request as an order. He looked at Michael's papers first, raising one eyebrow at the sight of a British passport and European Union diplomatic credentials. He then turned his attention to Paolo.

'What are you doing here in Pecs?' he demanded of Paolo in Hungarian, examining Paolo's identity card in detail.

'Visiting family and friends,' Paolo replied.

'Humph!' snorted the man. 'As for you, Mr Butler,' he said in English, turning his direction back to Michael, 'I suggest you take your nose out of Roma affairs.'

With that, he thrust their documents back at them, turned on his heel and strode away up the street. He left without giving them the courtesy of introducing himself, let alone an explanation as to under what authority he had demanded to see their identity papers.

Paolo looked at Michael, as the man marched off down the road. 'Tovabb,' he said, shrugging, confirming what Michael had assumed from the fact that the man was dressed in the unofficial uniform of the ultra-right party in Hungary. Paolo could see that Michael was shocked and upset by this intrusion. 'Come on, Michael. I think you have seen enough? We might as well make our way back to the station.'

The train ride back to Budapest was not surprisingly a little subdued. But without discussing further the visit they had just made to the Roma refuges, Paolo and Michael used the five-hour journey to conduct a longer business meeting than they had ever had before, while sitting either side of Michael's desk in his office in Andrassy Avenue. Paolo set out a long list of problems, practical and political, small and seriously large, that faced his Roma community, but all of which he had been meaning to bring to Michael for some time. For his part, Michael listened carefully, made detailed notes, and had a positive discussion with Paolo as to how his organisation, and himself in particular, could set about providing further help.

Chapter 7

'What's the matter, darling?' Zita asked.

Michael was pacing round his apartment bedroom seeming very agitated, even though a few minutes ago they had just made love.

'Things at work are bugging me,' he replied.

'Come and tell me about it,' Zita invited him, patting the side of the bed where she was still sitting, partly dressed.

Michael sat down beside her and sighed. 'Work problems, that's all.'

'What kind of work problems?' Zita asked. She knew enough about what his job involved to avoid being in the habit of asking questions about the specifics of his work. She was aware that a lot of what he did included sensitive political business, things which would make it difficult for him if she were to pry into the details. But, not for the first time during her relationship with Michael, she felt the need to calm him down, to put whatever it was that was bothering him into perspective.

'This stuff I've been doing to help the Roma. Looks like I'm being targeted by people who don't like it,' Michael replied. 'One of those Tovabb guys stopped me and Paolo during our trip to Pecs yesterday. Intimidating fellow. Gave me a warning about not interfering in Roma affairs.'

'Don't be silly, darling, I'm sure you're imaging things.' Zita said, doing her best as usual to help him out of these moods he frequently got himself into. She was getting used to Michael's bouts of anxiety and depression. 'Anyway,' she said, 'I'm sure they wouldn't dare do anything to harm a man in your position. They'd be scared of the political consequences and the likelihood that the law would come down hard on them.'

'Don't you believe it, love,' Michael said. 'I've seen what these fascist bastards can do! As for the law, they consider themselves above it, and to all intents and purposes, they are.'

Zita jumped up and finished dressing. 'Come on,' she said, taking Michael by the hand, 'let's go out for a drink.'

They walked round the corner to a basement bar they liked and sat drinking and talking for the rest of the evening. Even though Michael had calmed down a bit, Zita could sense that he was still anxious about what had happened the day before, although he did not mention his concerns to her again that night. But, to tell the truth, his bouts of anxiety and depression were beginning to get her down a bit as well. As it got late, they went back home to his flat and no more was said.

After they had made love again, Zita lay awake for some time considering what Michael had told her. Despite her words of reassurance to him earlier, she was all too aware of the precarious political situation that Michael was in. It seemed the government was determined to curb the influence of the foreign agencies that were working in Hungary. The recent elections had swept the government back to power following a campaign they had run that had encouraged anti-Roma and anti-immigrant sentiment. There had been large billboard posters all around the city openly targeting one particularly prominent Hungarian Jewish citizen as part of the government's election campaign. A high-profile education foundation had been forced to relocate to Vienna and former employees were finding it impossible to get jobs in Hungary. Doors were closing, newspapers were silenced and even the judiciary were unable or unwilling to oppose the government edicts. Hostility towards immigrants was also being promoted in new legislation aimed at keeping the Roma in ghetto-like conditions and making it difficult for them to receive decent health care and education. And now a law was being considered that would criminalise anyone found to be helping refugees. Anti-Semitic attacks on Jewish citizens were also becoming increasingly common.

Worse still was the tolerance shown to mafia-type gangs that now openly operated in areas of the city. This situation had deteriorated since Hungary joined the EU in 2004 and particularly since the Schengen treaty of 2007. Free movement of people across the European Union, with no border checks, had facilitated drug- and people-trafficking across the continent. Zita's friends had told her that gang leaders paid huge sums of money to their minions to ensure their loyalty in order to enable unfettered passage of trafficked persons across Europe, which included making bribes to unscrupulous border officials and police officers.

Budapest was fast becoming a city of two halves, Zita reflected. The green suburbs peopled by the well-paid expatriate communities and wealthy Hungarians, with their international schools and private health care facilities, were in stark contrast to the bleak, urine-stained streets of the less salubrious areas of the city. The tourists marvelled over the gracious and grandiose buildings that lined the beautiful Danube. They were impressed by the smartly dressed, polite police officers in the tourist areas who responded to their requests for directions in excellent English. But they never saw what should not be seen. Zita loved her city of Budapest but was cynical about its Janus identity–the Roman god with two faces. One did not have to stray far from the tourists to witness the city's darker side.

As Zita lay next to him, unable to sleep, she also reflected on her relationship with Michael. She loved him passionately. Despite the difference in their ages she felt him to be the perfect partner for her. He was a sensitive and generous lover. She was proud of her beautiful young body and of the pleasure it gave him. She saw the glances that men gave them as they walked hand in hand to the opera or concert hall. They envied him his good fortune in having such a woman by his side. Women envied her too. Michael was tall and carried his fifty-six years with authority and dignity. He was handsome and intelligent and she could match him with sparking wit and knowledge of music and literature. The fact that he was married caused her some discomfort, even though his wife was back in England with their children most of the time. But she continued to hope that Michael would one day have the courage to tell his wife that the marriage was over and that he intended to marry her, Zita.

She rolled towards him and kissed him. His hand reached for her breast, stroked the nipple gently at first and then more demandingly. She moaned slightly and guided his fingers down between her thighs. She was still wet from their previous lovemaking.

'You really are a hot little witch,' he murmured as he pulled her tightly towards him and lost himself to her.

Chapter 8

A few weeks after their trip to Pecs together Paolo came to see Michael again. He walked straight into his office unannounced and without knocking – Angie must have been away from her desk dealing with other business. As he entered, Paolo hesitated when he saw that Michael was working at his desk with his head down, concentrating. Michael looked up from the paperwork he was correcting, somewhat surprised.

'Sorry for walking in unexpectedly, Michael,' Paolo said. 'There was nobody at the door, so I assumed you must be on your own. I hope you don't mind this intrusion.'

'No, no – not at all,' Michael reassured him.

Paolo sat down hard in the chair in front of Michael.

'How are things, Paolo?' Michael asked. He sensed that Paolo seemed a little agitated.

'We've got a problem,' Paolo replied.

Michael sat back in his chair and put his pen down on the papers he had been working on. 'Tell me about it,' he said, looking straight at his friend.

'Some of our girls are missing,' Paolo said.

Paolo explained to Michael that in the last two weeks eight or nine young Roma girls had disappeared from home without trace, leaving their parents and families distraught. The girls were all in their teens or early twenties. Initially, two young girls who were friends had gone missing on the same Saturday evening. While this was quite out of character, their parents had assumed that they must have gone away for the night, perhaps with a couple of boys, although neither of them was known to have a boyfriend. When they had not returned by the Monday morning, their parents had become seriously worried. One of the fathers had gone to the police, but had got no information from them and precious little practical help. He'd been told "we will ask our patrol cars to look out for them", but they had heard nothing since. The other father, who was known to Paolo and was a friend of his brother, had come to see him. The man had been in tears, and shaking with fear, pleading with Paolo to do what he could to help them find Maria and her friend Christina.

By this time it was Wednesday of the first week. Paolo had started to make enquiries and by the end of the week had learnt through the Roma council network that three other girls had also gone missing, two in Debrecen and one in Györ, not so far from the border with Austria. All of the families he had spoken to were distressed by the disappearance of their girls, but none of them had any idea where they had gone or knew of any reason why they might have left home without a word. None of the disappearances could be explained by a family argument or any other such reason which the girls might have had for running away from home. Not one of the girls had made contact with anyone since they had disappeared, not even with their closest friends. Their family and friends had tried repeatedly to raise them on their mobile phones, but they had found the phones switched off and their daughters unreachable. Even as he was leaving to come and discuss the situation with Michael, Paolo said, he had received a telephone call to say that there may now be three or even four more Roma girls also unaccounted for within Hungary.

As Paolo related these events to Michael, he stood up and started walking around the office. He was using one hand to count on the fingers of the other hand as he catalogued the disappearances of the girls, one by one. As he heard Paolo's story, Michael began to understand why his friend was so agitated and distressed. He indicated to the chair in front of his desk.

'Do sit down Paolo. Let's talk this through.' After Paolo had settled himself in front of his desk, Michael continued. 'I do agree it all sounds very worrying. The disappearance of so many girls in the same way in such a short space of time seems to be more than one would expect by chance. There does seem to be a pattern to all this, but goodness knows what it might be. Can you leave this with me for a while, Paolo? I know you would not have come to discuss this issue with me unless you had a very good reason to be concerned. I'll do my very best to see if I can find some information for you.'

'Thank you, Michael, I knew you would agree to help,' Paolo said, acknowledging that he knew Michael was on his side. Shaking Michael's hand in thanks, he got up and started for the door. He hesitated. 'It's just that all the families are getting more desperate by the day. And they feel they have nobody else to turn to for help,' he added over his shoulder as he left his office.

As soon as Paolo had left, Michael got straight onto the phone. He called his contact in the Hungarian emigration office; the border offices in Austria and Slovakia; as well as the OSSE offices in Prague, Vienna and Berlin; his friends in the Europol Headquarters in The Hague; and the Foreign Office in London. Everyone he spoke to was perfectly polite and told him they would make a note of his call and make whatever enquiries they could from their end. Michael got the feeling, however – although nobody ever said as much to him – that his calls were viewed as rather a routine everyday matter and that they were all having to deal with many much more serious political and international events than a few missing persons. As he finished his last call of the day, Michael put the phone down and sat there at his desk feeling dissatisfied and uneasy. He was quite sure, he said to himself, that the parents and families of the missing girls were not finding the disappearance of their daughters to be a matter which was either routine or everyday.

Chapter 9
July 2014

It was Saturday evening and Christina and her friend Maria were sitting at an outside table of a cafe on Margit Island. This small cigar-shaped island situated in the middle of the River Danube in the centre of the city of Budapest was a popular place for people to get away to and relax. After a beautiful late summer day, crowds of people were still arriving through the entrance gate of the island. They had walked over to the middle of Margit Bridge, which met with the entrance to the island, or alighted from one of the Number 4 or 6 trams which stopped every few minutes at the dog-leg bend in the middle of the bridge. From where they sat the girls could still hear the rumble of the trams as they thundered across Margit Bridge above them in both directions.

Maria and Christina frequently came to sit on the island and watch the world go by. They were both in their mid-teens and, in spite of the fact that they had no boyfriends and were not particularly looking out to attract one, they always went onto the island well-dressed and made up. This was all part of the social occasion which a visit to the place required, as far as they were concerned. Not far away, they could see families with children watching the kids playing in one of the many playground areas or sitting having picnics in the grass clearings between the trees. One group was sharing a candy floss stick between them. Others were riding around the paths on the for hire pedal cars or heading off to visit the small zoo at the end of the island.

Running right round the five kilometres perimeter of the island was a brick red synthetic asphalt running track. Hundreds of people chose to exercise around this track every day, especially on warm days such as this, from where they could look out on to the River Danube as they sweated around the periphery of the island. People of all ages, young and not so young, were walking, fast walking, jogging and running around this popular exercise area for the city. Some were out for a social stroll, others taking themselves and their exercise programme much more seriously, in a variety of designer running kits. The girls enjoyed being amused by the crowds of exercising people passing by. Some of these were content merely to get their daily exercise and go home; for others, exercise appeared to be a form of posturing to gain attention. This second group were not unlike the exotically plumed male peacocks on the grass in front of where the girls were sitting, who were announcing their magnificent display to the rather ordinary female peacocks that stood a little way off. The lady peacocks appeared less than impressed by the display the male peacocks were putting on for them, the girls thought, laughing at the performance they were watching. The posturing group of exercisers were part of the theatre, dressed as they were in every possible brand of designer sports apparel, supplemented of course by similarly expensive accessories including designer shades, earphones, iPhones, headgear and the like. They surely had no idea that they were being compared by the two girls to the vain male peacocks on the grass in front of them.

'Hi girls! How are you?'

The question came from a young man who appeared standing right in front of them. He was not much older than themselves – perhaps seventeen or eighteen – but handsome and confident, as well as friendly. The girls looked up, interested but with expressions pretending distain.

'Where did you come from?' asked Christina.

'What's your name?' Maria said.

Both of the girls giggled to each other, ready for a bit of innocent teasing.

'I'm Andras,' the boy replied. 'I couldn't help noticing two such pretty girls! Please believe me!'

He sat down on the bench seat beside them. The conversation ambled along between them, the usual topics being discussed. Both Christina and Maria were aware that they were enjoying this unexpected attention. When Andras turned to look at them both and express his appreciation of their looks again, they were unashamedly flattered.

'Two girls like you should both have successful careers in modelling or on the stage,' he said.

Christina and Maria looked at each other amazed. Was he having them on, or did he mean it?

'Oh, yes?' said Christina, 'Why should we listen to you?'

'As it happens,' replied Andras, looking down at his shoes, 'I work as a scout for the entertainment industry.' He did seem genuine and believable as he provided them with this information. 'That is the reason I chose to talk to you both.'

The two girls looked at each other, in some disbelief but also a little excited.

'We don't believe you,' said Maria. 'Prove that you are

34

what you say you are.'

Andras smiled from one girl to the other, amusement in his eyes. 'That's not difficult,' he said, putting his hand in his jacket pocket and producing his business cards, one of which he gave to each girl.

They stared at the cards in awe and had to admit to themselves that they appeared impressively genuine, printed as they were in artistic multicolours.

'As it happens,' continued Andras again, 'I am in the process of arranging a coach for a group of girls who are going on a trip to Bratislava to attend an audition being held tomorrow by a major international film company of which I am an affiliate. If you would like to join in, come and meet us at the coach stop next to Nyugati Station at ten p.m. You'd be welcome to join the party, and it would be a really great experience, even if you were not successful on this occasion. Although I have to say, being a good friend of the casting manager, I think you both have a very good chance of fitting his requirements. Hope to see you at ten!' With that he jumped up and with a wave disappeared into the crowds.

The two girls could not hide their excitement from one another. 'Why don't we go along?' said Christina. 'There is nothing to lose. If the whole thing's rubbish and we don't like the look of it all, we can just turn around and go home.'

They sat discussing their luck at this opportunity for a while. They both agreed that it would be better not to say anything to their family or friends at this point, in case the promise turned out to be a scam, so that they would not have to lose face if that proved to be the case. They agreed that it would be better not to phone home until after they had made their decision about whether to go along with the invitation. They could always telephone their parents from the coach if they decided to go on the trip.

Chapter 10

They arrived at the coach stop in good time to find that there was already much activity. There were about thirty other girls lining up to board the coach, all as excited as they now felt. Andras was there, making jokes and handing out free bottles of cold lager. The coach left on time and very soon they were nearing the Slovakian border.

As the coach approached the border, Maria and Christina realised that they did not have their passports with them. When they walked to the front of the coach where Andras was sitting next to the driver, to raise their concern with him, Andras responded with a laugh.

'Don't worry girls! We have a group pass. You are all VIPs!'

True to his word, the coach seemed to be more or less waved through by the two Slovakian border guards on duty and very soon they were driving off into the dark towards Bratislava. Andras had offered to look after all the mobile phones on the coach, in case there had been a problem with the border customs, but this did not seem to have been the case. The two girls had not had the opportunity to phone home, but it was late by then and they decided that it would be better to ring in the morning.

It was the early hours of the morning when the coach pulled up in front of a small hotel in the downtown area of the city of Bratislava. Andras addressed them all from the front of the coach.

'You must all be very tired,' he said. 'Don't worry about anything tonight. Have a good night's sleep. We can talk about the arrangements for the auditions and your other duties in the morning. Sleep well!'

Maria and Christina were helped off the coach along with all the other equally tired girls. They were led up the stairs of the hotel and found themselves in a room with two small single beds. The place did not appear all that salubrious, the furniture that there was being rather basic with tired looking brown linoleum covering the floor and crude hessian curtains covering the windows. But at least they were together and agreed that they could decide what they wanted to do in the morning after a night's sleep.

That night neither of the girls slept well. The beds were uncomfortable, with hard wooden slats under rather thin foam mattresses. Outside on the landing they could hear noises as doors opened and closed and people moved about for reasons that were not clear. Every ten minutes or so heavy footsteps passed outside their bedroom door, paused for a few seconds and then moved on down the corridor. Significant doubts were developing in both girls' minds about what they were doing there and whether they had made a mistake to come on this expedition.

'Are you alright?' Maria whispered to Christina after they had been lying awake for about an hour.

'I suppose so,' Christina replied, but not very convincingly. 'Let's try and get some sleep. We can see what things are like in the morning and, if necessary, catch an early train back to Budapest. I think I've got enough money on me.'

The next morning they were woken early by a hammering on their door.

'Up! Get up!!' A man outside was shouting in Slovakian as he moved down the corridor, hammering on every door as he went.

The two girls dragged themselves out of bed, pulled on their clothes and splashed some water on their faces from a chipped jug that stood on a chest of drawers in their room. As they tentatively opened their bedroom door, Christina and Maria looked at each other. What they saw was that they were both rather dishevelled, poorly slept and afraid. They said nothing.

Downstairs there was mayhem. All of the girls who had crowded on to the coach the night before were there, but they all appeared unhappy and agitated. There was no sign of the young man Andras. Instead, in charge of proceedings was a hard-faced older woman who was flanked by two tattooed muscular men who stood next to her with their arms crossed, chewing gum with aggressive grins on their faces. The men were rather roughly ordering the girls to sit in the rows of upright chairs in front of them.

'Sorry to tell,' the woman who was now in charge of them stepped forward and announced in broken English, 'auditions are postponed. In meantime, we have a program of duties for you all which will keep you busy and repay cost of coach trip and visas.'

Maria and Christina looked at each other. They both knew at once that they had been tricked. They were in a foreign country with no passports, no money and no mobile phones or other means of communication. The threat of "a program of duties" was already quite clear to them both. They had got themselves into this hole, and it was not going to be easy for them to get out of it.

Chapter 11

And so it began. The threats, abuse and beatings. Every morning they would be ordered out of bed at about seven a.m. and given the minimum amount of time to wash and dress. Their bedroom doors were then thrown open and they were marched in a crocodile line downstairs to the dining area next to the kitchen. There they were sat on two benches either side of a bare wooden trestle table. They were served a very basic breakfast of a sort of watery porridge, which was slopped with a ladle into bowls which would then be thrown on to the table in front of each girl. With this "porridge" they got a glass of water and only dry black bread to accompany it. The meal was the same every day, never altering in any way and barely enough for them to live on. They received no other sustenance for the rest of the day, apart from water which they could drink from a drinking fountain in the corner of the living room.

Maria and Christina had no opportunity to talk to each other during the course of a day. If they attempted to talk to each other or with or any of the other girls, this would be met with the threat of physical violence or actual beatings from their minders. They were at least still in the same room together at night and would whisper to each other from under their blankets once they were sure that none of the guards were still patrolling the landing and listening for noises outside their room. They both felt intense shame about how naive and stupid they had been to have become duped and then imprisoned on a promise based on flattery and their own gullibility. A feeling which was very quickly replaced by fear, in the knowledge that they were now engaged in a situation which was so very serious it might indeed threaten their lives.

A few days went by, during which the girls were marshalled backwards and forwards by the two tattooed strong men. After the basic breakfast each morning they were ordered to undertake menial jobs such as washing the dishes, scrubbing the floors and cleaning the toilets. Maria and Christina were never in a position where they were able to have any meaningful conversation with any of the other girls who had been brought with them on the coach. Nevertheless, it was clear that all the girls lived in fear, as indeed they did themselves, and that their morale was also at rock bottom. They were quite literally imprisoned in the building and it did not take them long to realise that there were no obvious routes through which they might escape. The windows were all barred from the outside and even internal doors securely locked, restricting movement from one part of the building to another, let alone providing any possible exit from the place.

One afternoon after their morning cleaning work they were called to assemble in the lounge downstairs. The hard-faced woman who had become known as "Anna" addressed them.

'Pleased to tell,' she began, 'we have party tonight. Please to go to your rooms, wash yourselves and dress nicely for this reason.'

With that, they were ushered upstairs to prepare themselves for the "party". Once in their room, looking stone-faced at each other, all Christina and Maria could do was to follow the instructions they had been given to make themselves look "nice". They did not have to speak to each other to know what was planned as the next sinister step in their exploitation.

At about seven p.m. the doors to their bedrooms were thrown open by the tattooed guards and they were marched downstairs to the living room area. There the girls were seated on the red velvet sofas and armchairs in groups of twos and threes. Maria and Christina sat on a small sofa next to one of the other Roma girls. They heard the hotel main doorbell ring and then the door being opened and slammed behind the visitors as they were let in. A couple of minutes later, a group of men were ushered into the living room, where they stood leering at the girls in front of them.

Christina and Maria had never been so frightened in their lives. Christina could feel Maria shaking in fear next to her and was aware that she was also trembling in the same way.

Suddenly Maria let out a groan. 'I can't do this!'

With that she fainted head-first on to the floor, vomiting all over the carpet as she did so. Unconscious, she was immediately pulled to one side of the room by one of the guards while the other guard threw a towel over the pool of vomit on the carpet. Christina was not so lucky. One of the visiting men lunged forward and dragged her by one arm to her feet.

'Leave me alone!' she screamed, tears pouring down her face.

At that instant, she was hit by a heavy blow across the side of her face by the open hand of one of the minders. She reeled back, stunned and dizzy from the impact. Before she could recover herself, she was dragged by the other arm out through the door and up the stairs, receiving another vicious blow to the head as she went.

What followed was something that she could not have imagined, even in her worst nightmares. The man who had dragged her up the stairs tore her clothes off her almost before he had got her into the room, threw her on the bed and proceeded to rape her. The pain was indescribable, but she had already been beaten down to the point where she knew that she should no longer resist. Some basic instinct had come in to play, urging her not to fight back and risk putting her very life in jeopardy. She lost all sense of time, and had no perception of how long the ordeal had lasted. Eventually, the man let out one last grunt and rolled off her, breathing heavily. Christina lay still on her left side in an embryo position, her knees pulled up under her chin, facing the wall with her back to her attacker. She could feel the man's semen mixed with her own blood oozing out between her thighs. She was dizzy with the shock and pain of the attack and lay praying for the man to get up and leave, which eventually he did.

But that was not to be the end of Christina's ordeal. Only a few minutes after the first man had left the room, two other men entered and the whole process was repeated again. Before long, a point was reached where she had been repeatedly raped by an unknown number of men an unknown number of times. With each attack she willed herself not to resist actively, to do her best to just lie there submissively. In spite of her attempt at passivity, she was receiving more and more bruises to her body with each attack. She had got to the point where all she could do was to pray to be dead. Eventually she passed out and was therefore spared further knowledge of events by her state of unconsciousness.

The next thing Christina remembered was coming to on her own bed in their room. Maria was sitting next to her, gently bathing her wounds and bruises with an old piece of cloth soaked in water. As soon as Christina opened her eyes and looked at her friend, Maria threw her arms around her, relieved that she had at last come to, and both of them broke into deep, sobbing tears.

Chapter 12
July 2014

The day after Paolo's visit to see him, having received no practical help from the numerous telephone calls he had made the previous afternoon, Michael decided to investigate matters further for himself. He got into his car and drove west out of Budapest on the M1 motorway towards the Austrian border. The traffic was heavy, but most of it was flowing against him into Budapest early that weekday morning. The journey of more than a hundred miles to the border took him a little more than two hours.

When he reached the Hungarian border post, Michael parked outside the border office and walked in. There were three border guards inside drinking coffee and chain smoking, with the result that the wooden cabin they were in was like the inside of the smoke box he had once seen being used by a man they had got round to get rid of a wasps' nest. He had found the nest under the eaves of their house in Ealing. From it, literally hundreds of wasps had been invading the garden as well as getting inside of the house on a regular basis. The smoke from the smoke box had emptied the nest of all the wasps completely within a matter of minutes. Michael found it difficult to imagine that these men were able to survive in this smoke-filled atmosphere from one day to the next, in a way in which the wasps had not. Apart from smoking and drinking coffee, the men appeared to have little else on their hands. One of them was sitting with his boots on the table and did not remove them from there when Michael walked in. The eldest of the three men, whom Michael took to be the one in charge, did at least stand up when he walked in and shake him politely by the hand.

Michael explained to the older man that he was making enquiries about a number of young Roma girls who were missing and handed him photos of five of the missing girls that Paolo had given him. The man looked at the photos one by one, before handing them over to his two colleagues who looked at the faces in the pictures themselves. Having done so, the two younger men handed the photos back and shrugged at their boss, who turned and addressed Michael.

'I am sorry, but I and my colleagues do not recognise any of these girls. We will certainly keep an eye out for them and give you a call, if you would like to leave us you card. But you must appreciate, Mr Butler, we do have thousands of people crossing this border on a daily basis.'

Michael acknowledged this fact, left some spare photos and his address and contact numbers with the man, shook him by the hand and left the border office. He did not feel that this visit had achieved much and was not particularly optimistic that he would hear from the man again. Nevertheless, he showed his diplomatic card and drove the few hundred metres across to the Austrian side of the border.

The Austrian border office was quite different from its Hungarian neighbour. It was clean, well-organised and business-like. The border officer was on his own in the office but appeared very smart in his dark green uniform and cap, efficient and professional. He beckoned politely to Michael to take a seat and sat behind his desk himself, listening attentively to the story that Michael was telling him and making notes as he did so. After looking carefully at the photographs which Michael showed him, the officer sat back and looked at Michael.

'I cannot say that I recognise any of these girls individually, Mr Butler. But I should tell you that I and my Government have been concerned for some time that there has been the trafficking of people across our borders. Three or four times a week we come across young women who are travelling in vehicles – usually in eight- or ten-seater minivans – who seem frightened and tearful but who are accompanied by escorts in the presence of whom they are clearly not able to speak freely. Their escorts provide us with documents for all the passengers which are completely legal. They usually give us some story to explain the girls' appearance, saying something like they are part of a college trip or sports team who are understandably very weary and exhausted by the many hours they have been on the road. It is impossible for us to apprehend them at the time on the basis of suspicion alone.'

'Thank you very much Herr Grossman,' Michael said. 'I very much appreciate your helpful information, off the record of course. Can you tell me anything else which might help me in my search for these particular missing Hungarian Roma young women?'

'The evidence that young women have been brought across this border to be sold into prostitution or human slavery has been gained from statements made by women who have subsequently presented themselves to police stations in Austria and elsewhere claiming such maltreatment. You must understand that the volume of human traffic passing across this border is immense, and we are physically unable to interview and vet each person individually. Even if we had the personnel to do so – which we haven't – it would be practically impossible to conduct such a system and still maintain normal European social movement and commerce. We believe that most of this human traffic passes on through Austria into France, Belgium, The Netherlands and the UK. Nevertheless, the Austrian Government would be keen to co-operate in putting a stop to this miserable traffic if it possibly can. If you are successful in finding these girls, I would be very keen to receive any feedback from your investigations which you might be able to give me.'

'Thank you very much, Herr Grossman,' Michael said again. 'Do you have any suggestions as to what my next step should be? Where I should look next?'

'That is difficult,' the man replied, 'but you might try taking a look at the Slovakian border north of Budapest as well.'

Michael thanked the Austrian border officer, left him his contact details, shook him by the hand and got back into his car. He drove more slowly back to Budapest, on the way contemplating what he had heard.

As he approached the outskirts of Budapest, rather than drive back into the city, Michael took the road north to the Hungarian border with Slovakia, on the route that Herr Grossman had directed him. It took him less than an hour to travel the fifty kilometres or so before he reached the Hungarian border near the Slovakian town of Sturovo. He again stopped and talked to the border control officers on the Hungarian side at Esztergom, before driving across the bridge over the river Danube and once more showing his diplomatic papers at the Slovakian border point. Even in this short distance, he had a clear impression of the change in circumstances between the two countries. The farms he could see on the Slovakian side were enough to make him aware of the poverty that still existed in this country since it had split from the Czech Republic in 1993. The border office was shabby and only very basically equipped. After talking to the border officers here, he realised quickly that they were not interested in the disappearance of a few Hungarian Roma girls. Nevertheless, Michael thanked them politely and got back into his car.

As Michael turned his car around at the Slovakian border point, he saw in front of him a rather battered old coach which was being waved into the inspection bay by other border guards. He pulled into the parking area on the opposite side of the road and sat and watched, as inconspicuously as he could. Out of the front door emerged a man carrying a sheaf of documents which Michael guessed were the papers of the coach passengers. One by one behind the man, a line of rather bedraggled girls emerged, being coaxed out by the Slovakian border guards. He could see that the girls looked tired and hungry. He could not put his finger on it, but he was sure that many of them looked distinctly frightened as they were marched into the border office for immigration checks.

On an instinct, Michael jumped out of his car and walked with purpose towards the first group of girls who had emerged from the coach, intent on talking to them if he possibly could. As he got within a few metres of the party, however, an arm was thrust across his chest, barring his way. Michael spun round to see who it belonged to.

'Can I help you, sir?' The uniformed man asked in English. The question he posed to Michael was clearly more like a command than an enquiry.

'I am looking for some girls who are missing from the families of some friends of mine,' Michael replied. 'It occurred to me that one of the girls coming off this coach here might be able to help.'

'I am sorry, sir,' the man said looking straight at Michael. 'This is a Slovakian border post and out of bounds to foreign nationals.'

Michael saw that there was no point in arguing with him, so he got back in his car and watched as the young women were ushered back on to their coach. He realised that there was no point in his remaining there and that he would not be allowed further information, even if he were to show his diplomatic papers to the man in charge of the immigration point. He did, however, take a piece of paper from his pocket and write down the Hungarian number plate of the coach – HOE 652 – before it pulled away into Slovakia. As soon as the coach had disappeared up the road, Michael started his car and drove back towards the Hungarian side of the border.

As Michael drove quite slowly back towards Budapest, he was clear in his mind that he had confirmed his belief that the young women he had just seen were being moved across the border with Hungary as part of a human trafficking business. They were obviously not tourists or even college students on a vacation trip. He would take this information back to Paolo and his international contacts and decide with them what should be done about it next. He knew that this was a serious issue which he was determined to do his utmost to investigate further. He would also put this information in to the hands of his friends in Europol at the earliest opportunity.

Chapter 13

The next morning Paolo's phone rang and he answered it straight away, seeing that it was Michael who was calling.

'Any news, Michael?' he asked at once.

'No news yet about your particular girls, but I think I'm on to something,' Michael replied. 'Are you free to join me on a trip to Slovakia today?'

Paolo agreed to the trip without hesitation.

When they met up, Paolo could see immediately that Michael was excited by what he had learned the day before. He told Paolo that he had woken up determined to follow up the leads he had been given. He felt he had been "on the scent" and was anxious to investigate further what he had seen and heard during his border trips without delay. He had been asked by Paolo and his community to do whatever he could to intervene in the case of their missing Roma girls, and was impatient to do so.

Before long they were travelling together on the way to Bratislava. This time Michael had borrowed one of his organisation's cars with its CD number plates. They crossed the Hungarian-Slovakian border on the motorway and very soon found themselves entering the outskirts of Bratislava, the capital city of Slovakia which had at one time been the capital of Hungary. Paolo was the perfect guide. He knew the city well, having lived in Bratislava for some years in the past. As they entered the city Paolo directed Michael confidently through its outskirts and into the centre.

Once in the city centre, Paolo directed Michael away from the main roads and into the part of the old town which he guessed would be the place to start. Michael found himself driving around the back streets of the city, away from the commercial and tourist centre, on Paolo's instructions. Paolo directed him backwards and forwards across run-down areas which Michael could see would never have been visited by any tourist or casual visitor. They started to conduct their search as systematically as a search-and-rescue team scanning a wide expanse of ocean for a single survivor might have done.

The search was initially quite exhilarating, as they realised how much of the back street areas of the city they could cover in a relatively short space of time. With Paolo's careful directions, and by a logical system which involved visiting half-mile sections over a number of blocks at a time before moving on to the next area on the imagined grid, they felt that they really were making progress. Occasionally they came across a one-way street which meant that they had no choice but to follow it in one direction to its end. But inevitably, with Paolo's street knowledge, they were able to navigate back around again to start searching that part of the area which they might have missed when locked onto the one-way system.

The process of searching for a needle in the proverbial haystack was eventually wearying and not a little emotionally tiring, however. They had both known at the outset that their chance of finding the missing girls was probably slight at best, although they had not admitted as much to each other.

After a couple of hours, Michael sensed that Paolo was getting tired and fed up.

'Let's stop for a beer,' he suggested, and Paolo agreed eagerly.

After about thirty minutes sitting at a table on the pavement outside a small bar, having consumed a couple of glasses of beer each, Michael urged Paolo not to give up.

'Come on, my friend,' he said with as much enthusiasm as he could manage. 'We've come this far – let's give it a bit more time!'

Paolo hunched his shoulders, emptied the rest of his glass, and agreed rather wearily. 'OK, Michael. If you say so.'

By now they were both aware that they were tired and pretty demoralised. But Michael in particular was not prepared to give up yet and did his best to carry Paolo along with him.

They found themselves cruising round a particularly seedy part of the city. Michael could see that the down-at-heel hotels they were passing were almost certainly brothels and that the area was altogether unremittingly depressing. He was driving east along one of these streets when Paolo suddenly shouted.

'Stop!'

Michael jammed on the brakes and reversed back a few metres to the side street which they had just passed and to which Paolo was pointing. He turned left and drove slowly into the street. He saw at once the reason Paolo had stopped him.

Parked halfway onto the pavement about fifty metres down the right side of the street was the beat-up old grey coach with the Hungarian number plate he had remembered from the day before: HOE 652. Michael parked the car on the same side of the road as the coach and pulled on the hand brake. They looked at the entrance to the Hotel Avalon that the coach was parked outside of and then looked back at each other.

'Leave this to me,' Paolo said, looking at Michael. 'Wait for me here.'

He opened the car door, straightened up to his full height, and marched towards the front door of the hotel, disappearing through it.

Michael waited at the wheel of the car with the engine running. After about ten minutes he was becoming increasingly anxious for Paolo's safety. A further five minutes passed and he decided he should go in after his friend. Just as he was opening his car door to do so, Paolo re-emerged running from the hotel entrance, pulling a distressed young woman after him. Paolo opened the back door of the car and threw her in, jumping into the front passenger seat himself almost in the same action.

'Drive!' Paolo screamed at Michael.

The car wheels screeched as Michael roared off the kerb and down the narrow street. As he did so, he saw in his mirror two men run out of the hotel front door from which Paolo had just emerged with the girl. They were sprinting after the car, waving and shouting aggressively. For a second Michael expected to hear the sound of gun shots, but he wrenched the steering wheel to the left as they skidded onto a busier road at the end of the street and accelerated away. They were free and, as Michael drove fast to put distance behind them, he could see no evidence that they were being followed.

Michael slowed the car to a more legal speed as they merged with the road taking them out of the city. Through his mirror he could see that the girl on the back seat was still shaking in fear, tears running down her face.

'Is she alright?' he asked Paolo, noticing from the mirror that the girl appeared to have bruises all over her face and neck.

'I hope she will be,' Paolo said, 'given time. It's Christina.'

Chapter 14

Paolo and Michael continued to investigate the people trafficking and sex exploitation trade together. They did not have to look far. It soon became clear that a lot was going on on their own doorstep in Budapest. Paolo would ask around people he came across in bars and clubs, especially those in the Roma community, for bits of information. He and Michael would then follow these leads up together. This usually entailed paying a visit to the places that Paolo had heard about. It was always Paolo who would enter the building, while Michael sat in the car nearby, just as they had done when exposing the Hotel Avalon in Bratislava.

Most of the time the tips Paolo had been given turned out to be correct. The entrance to the hotel or house always had one or more heavy men guarding the door and, once inside, there was usually a hard-faced woman in charge of the place. All exactly as it had been in the Hotel Avalon. Paolo would play the game, choosing a suitable girl and going upstairs with her. As soon as he was in the room, he would explain that he was not a "client" but had come to help. Invariably, once he had gained her trust, the young woman would break down in tears, relieved to hear the reason Paolo was there, and would be desperate to tell him about her plight. Many of the girls he came across in this way were Roma, which made it easier for Paolo to secure their cooperation.

The stories Paolo heard had a depressing similarity. All

the young women he met had been tricked – either alone or with others, as had been the case with Maria and Christina. Once the girls realised their mistake, it was too late. They found themselves imprisoned with no access to their families or the outside world. Passports, mobile phones and everything of value to them were taken from them. They were held against their will, constantly threatened and regularly beaten, not because they had complained in any way – they were all too frightened to do that – but just as a way of keeping them obedient and in fear of their lives. As well as recording the girls' stories on his mobile phone, with the girl's permission, Paolo would document her name, the date and address of the pace and take some pictures of her, including close-ups of some of the many bruises which they all had. Once Paolo had gained as much factual evidence as possible, he would reassure the girl that he would do everything he could to help get her freed and leave without confronting the management.

After each visit, Michael would drive Paolo back to his office and there they would enter into their folder the details of the place, the names and facts which Paolo had collected. They built up a comprehensive file on each establishment as they went. The more places they visited, the more it became evident that there were links between each of the hotel-brothels and different groups of traffickers.

The name of a man called Mirgo Varga emerged as a significant figure in the investigations Michael undertook with Paolo. His network of brothels and massage parlours had spread across Europe and into the UK. He was of Romanian-Hungarian parentage and without doubt his empire had profited from the relaxation of border controls created by the Schengen Treaty. Girls could be ferried in convoys across Europe without checks on their documentation. Michael's contacts in the UK had explained that once they reached UK airports, for instance, it was a simple matter to produce EU passports to gain entry and then disperse the human cargo across the country to service brothels and massage parlours. Alternatively, they were loaded onto boats and crossed the Channel by night, in the hope of evading the border controls altogether.

The next step was to take the matter to the police. Michael recruited Alistair, the OSSE security attaché, to help with this. Michael had worked with Alistair for a number of years and he knew he could trust him. Alastair had been very wary of their project initially, but once he had heard the evidence Paolo and Michael had accumulated, he became as committed as they were to bringing this scandal to light and ending the trafficking cartels if they possibly could. He did caution Michael, however, that once he and Paolo had visited a place they should not return. He made it clear that under no circumstance should they try to take matters further into their own hands.

Alistair was also insistent that, once they had collected as much information as they could, they had no choice but to hand the evidence over to the Budapest City police and trust that they would act accordingly. When they were ready, Alistair set up meetings with the police chief of each Budapest district that the hotel-brothels had been in. Usually these meetings were cordial, but almost always they could detect an unspoken resistance to what was being discussed.

Either they were met with disbelief or, more disturbingly, a degree of hostility. Alistair could see that that Michael and Paolo were not optimistic about trusting the police to act in this matter, and he began to fear they might be right.

Chapter 15

Two weeks later, Alistair came into Michael's office looking serious and shut the door behind him. Michael looked up from his desk.

'Everything all right?' he asked.

Alistair sat down opposite him. 'I've some information that we need to discuss,' he said. 'Szolt Lukas has just been to see me. Remember him? He's the deputy police chief from District V who we went to see last month to tell him about the sex trafficking ring you had found on your visit to the Hotel Vac. He's one of a few police chiefs that I trust. I've had dealings with him on other matters and he's clearly honest. Apart from that, he is not a supporter of the Fidek party, although he can't admit as much in his professional capacity. He came to see me in his civvies, on his day off duty. He was anxious to make it clear that his visit was "off the record".'

'What did he have to say?' Michael asked.

'He wanted us – and especially you – to know that the information we have been uncovering about these sex trafficking rings is very dangerous. He has heard from an informant whom he trusts that the ring leaders have found out who you are and what the real purpose of your visits was. Maybe one of the girls told her minder, probably under duress, that Paolo hadn't been visiting as a client. Somehow they have also obtained information that you have been working with Paolo on Roma affairs, and that you are in a position of influence in the OSSE. Furthermore, this information has been shared with the members of the trafficking rings running the other brothels that you visited. He believes the situation is very dangerous. He told me that the men involved are violent – which we know already – and that they will not stop at anything to prevent their illegal rackets being exposed and shut down. He told me specifically that you are in danger. That they want to,' Alistair hesitated, 'to "take you out" before their activities are exposed publicly.'

'What do you want us to do, Alistair? Drop the whole thing?!' Michael panicked, suddenly agitated and alarmed about his safety because of what Alistair was telling him. He started sweating profusely. But he was trying not to admit his fear to Alistair. 'We can't just let it rest there. Anyway, we have already discussed our findings with the police chiefs of most of the city's districts.'

'That's part of the problem,' Alistair said. 'Many if not most of the district police are already aware of what is going on and certainly in some cases are actually involved in the illegal sex racket themselves. I feared this might be the situation when I saw the stony-faced reception we received during some of our visits to the different district police chiefs' offices. Szolt has only confirmed to me that this is definitely the case, even in his own district, although he would not give me any names of his colleagues that are involved.'

'So what do we do?' Michael said. 'Just sit on our hands and suppress our evidence?!'

'I am not suggesting that,' Alistair replied. 'But perhaps we should let the matter rest for a bit to allow the air to clear, Mike? While we give the ringleaders some time to think we have lost interest, we can work out who we should take our evidence to next within Budapest. In the meantime, I will also share our dossier with my colleagues in Europol, who will be very interested in the information. As we know, this sex trafficking is not just confined to Hungary but is taking place across many borders. Cracking it from a European perspective might be the best way of ending it.'

Chapter 16

Michael turned the corner into Eötvös Street on his way back home from work and stopped in his tracks, wondering what had hit the street. Piled high along both sides of the road, and taking over much of both pavements, were the piles of discarded items, large and small, that the inhabitants of the apartment blocks, small shops and hotels wanted to get rid of.

This was Throwing-Out Day. Once a year at the end of summer everything and anything the citizens of Budapest no longer wanted was ejected onto the streets, district by district, for the City Council refuse department to take away. This provided an opportunity for Roma and others to rummage through the cast-off items and salvage what they could to repair and sell. During the event, often whole families camped out in the streets to appropriate their pitch and claim territorial rights of salvage.

He looked along the street and all the way down it he could see there were tables, chairs, sofas, old electrical items, sideboards, mirrors and more sofas. The piles were high and growing fast. Occasional bits of furniture were in reasonable condition, but most of the pieces were badly damaged and the rest frankly broken bits of wood, metal and glass. On one section of the pavement along which he walked a wall of discarded books had been constructed, hardbacks and paperbacks, about ten metres long, enough to start a small library. In other parts of the street there were piles of rubble and old paper sacks of cement and other building material which had burst open and spread their dust across the gutter. Cars were still parked along both sides of the street in the usual way, but there were many fewer than normal. Those that remained were at risk of damage from the debris and broken glass around them. The numbers of unusual gaps between the cars still parked in the street had developed as a result of a particularly threatening pile of metal or glass spilling over onto the road which drivers were understandably literally steering clear of.

Parked outside the entrance to his apartment block was a rusty old Trabant. The Trabants were a very basic, bottom of the range economy family car which had been manufactured in their thousands in the former East Germany during the communist era and exported to the rest of the Soviet bloc countries. These days, because the car had achieved something of an iconic status, they had now become collectors' items in some circles, in much the same way that some old Morris Minors were lovingly preserved and still kept in mint condition at home in the UK. This relic was definitely not one of the collectors' items, however. Dented and rusty, it had seen much better days and, looking at it, it was difficult to believe that it was still able to function as a motor vehicle at all. Camped inside was a family of Roma gypsies, settled down for the night. Large pieces of cardboard had been stuck over the windscreen and windows to block out the street lighting and allow the mother and children within to get some sleep. From time to time, however, the men folk would jump out like ferrets and inspect every bit of the next lot of rubbish being deposited by a householder onto the pavement, removing absolutely anything which could be considered of any value, either to mend and use or, more likely, to be sold on as scrap or antique.

The Roma man sorting through the latest pile of junk to have been ejected from Michael's own apartment block looked up at him with a mixture of challenge and defensiveness on his face. Michael smiled back at the man as he passed. On receipt of Michael's friendly and encouraging smile, the gypsy's expression turned to one of incredulous disbelief. With the Roma man staring after him, Michael put his key into the lock of the huge wooden door leading into the vestibule of the aging block of flats and passed through the door which then clanged noisily shut behind him. He walked across the courtyard on the ground floor which was attractively decorated by plants and window boxes of different kinds. The courtyard was surrounded on four sides by five floors of apartments which looked down onto the courtyard below, wrought-iron railings protecting the sides of the walkways which led around the floors at each level. Michael smiled to himself. This Roma man could have no idea that much of his working days at the moment were taken up attempting to improve the lot of his people and in defending the Roma from further discrimination whenever he could. Of course he had said nothing of that to this particular man – why should he?

On his way out very early the next morning Michael handed two cardboard cups of steaming fresh coffee to the man and his wife who were just emerging from the old

Trabant car as he left for his office, as well as a two-litre plastic bottle of milk for their children. The silent look in gratitude he received from the man was even more incredulous than the look he had received when entering the building the night before.

Chapter 17

Michael turned right into Aradi Street. At that instant, he felt a sudden searing painful blow to the back of his head. He lost consciousness immediately. The next thing he remembered was coming to. He was lying on his back in a pile of rubble in one of the disused building sites in what turned out to be District V, about a mile away from where he had been when he was attacked. He could hear voices, but his hearing was distorted by a high-pitched whining sound in both ears and his vision was blurred. Suddenly, a face appeared above him, moving in and out of focus but staring menacingly into his field of vision.

'This is a warning to you, my friend. You are a visitor in this country. Stop your meddling with the Roma in Hungary and go back to England. If you meet up with us again, I promise you, the result will not be so kind!'

The next thing Michael remembered was a terrific pain in his right loin, where a metal toe-capped boot had been kicked into his right kidney, lifting his whole body a number of inches into the air and causing him to shriek in pain as his body thudded back again onto the rock-hard ground. He lapsed back into unconsciousness amid the rubble for a second time.

When he regained consciousness again, Michael lifted himself up painfully on his right arm and looked around. He was still in the disused building site, of the sort that are often cleared and used as car parks by day and temporary bar-restaurants by night in the summer months. He had a severe throbbing pain in the back of his head where he had been knocked unconscious. It was as if somebody was drilling into the back of his head with a pneumatic drill. He also had a pain in his right loin that felt as if a red-hot poker had been thrust into it. When he managed at last to bring his vision in to focus, Michael realised that the place was empty and that he was on his own. There was no one else around, although he could hear the sound of passing cars in the road outside. He sat up for a few minutes and then, very gingerly, raised himself to his feet. Once upright, he experienced a sudden rush of nausea and promptly vomited over the ground. Having been sick, he felt a little more settled, although the pain in his head throbbed on incessantly. After a few more minutes, he edged forwards hanging on to the wire mesh fence for support and made his way slowly to the site exit. Reaching the street, he found he was able to walk slowly along the narrow road towards the main thoroughfare Erzsebet Korut, and from there with difficulty, stopping every few hundred metres, to his office.

When he reached the office at last, Michael stood in front of the entrance and reached into his pockets. He searched them all, and searched again. He realised he had lost his keys as well as his passport and wallet which he normally carried in his inside jacket pocket. He had to ring the bell of the outer door a number of times to gain entrance, while he stood slumped over gripping the handrail of the steps up to the front door. After an agonising wait, the door was opened by Angie herself.

'My God, Michael!' she cried. 'Whatever's happened?' Angie's voice was marked with both concern and undisguised fear.

She pulled him through the door and managed to sit him on one of the chairs in the office waiting room. When she had satisfied herself that he could sit there and support himself without falling back onto the floor, she went to get a flannel soaked in warm water and leant over him gently wiping the dry blood from the side of his face with it.

Fifteen minutes later Alistair appeared. By now Michael was sitting up on the chair and sipping a cup of warm sweet tea that Angie had placed in his shaking hands. Angie wanted to call a doctor, but Michael said that he did not want to make a fuss, he'd be all right. Alistair sat down gently beside him.

'Tell me what happened, Mike,' he said quietly.

Slowly and in pain, Michael recounted what he knew and what he could remember. There wasn't really that much to tell, not much more than the facts of what had happened. He had been attacked without warning and without provocation by person or persons unknown who were clearly intent on giving him a warning to keep his nose out of Roma affairs in Hungary. They made it clear to Michael that his life would be in danger if he did not stop interfering.

'Christ,' Alistair said, when he had digested what Michael had to tell him. 'I never thought the bastards would actually be so crude! I'll brief Conrad, who will want to talk to you when you are fully recovered. For now, if you are quite sure you don't need a doctor, let's get you home for some rest.'

Angie called a taxi and went with Michael to help him home to his apartment. When he was safely back inside his flat, she poured him a stiff glass of whiskey and left him to call Marion in the UK. But with the parting instruction that he should call her at any time, either before or after nightfall, if he needed her help. After she had left, Michael sat in his armchair for a while, feeling bruised and battered and unable to move. Eventually he decided that that he would see this off on his own and that there was no point calling Marion at home in Ealing. This would only cause her alarm and distress when there was nothing that she could do to help immediately. Zita was away visiting her parents in their home in a small town outside of Budapest. He poured himself another stiff whiskey, swallowed a couple of the codeine tablets Angie had left with him and got into bed, still fully clothed. For the rest of the day and that night his sleep was intermittent and he was constantly awoken both by pain and dreams which were flashbacks of the events of the day before.

The next morning Michael awoke feeling absolutely shit. He still felt nauseous and had a severe headache right across the back of his head. As he stood at the toilet to have a piss, he was alarmed to see that his urine contained bright red fresh blood. He flushed the toilet, pulled off his clothes and got himself into the shower. As he showered himself down, he saw in the mirror that there was a huge black bruise in his right loin, where the boot had gone in. He dried himself off, had a cup of strong black coffee and was determined to get into the office, in spite of his injuries. He couldn't face his usual few hundred metres walk up Andrassy Avenue to the office, let alone a ride on the Metro, so he rang for a taxi.

When he arrived at the office, Conrad James, the Director

of the OSSE Hungary, was there with Alistair. Angie was busy answering the phones in between making them all coffees. Conrad was sympathetic but direct. Leaning forward in his chair, he was not exactly interrogating Michael, but was clearly anxious to get as much information about the attack as possible. For his part, Michael sat there with his head and his side throbbing in pain, and was only really able to repeat what he had told Alistair the day before. He had no new details that he could add. They agreed that there was nothing more to be done at present. They also agreed tacitly that this was not a matter for the local Budapest police.

'We'll get you fixed up with a replacement passport,' Conrad said, 'and we will also ask your bank for new credit cards. They should all be with you by tomorrow.'

Conrad said that he would send an urgent email with a report to the OSSE Head Office in Brussels and, when they had finished their discussions, thanked Michael for coming in that day and sent him back to his apartment in a taxi to rest again.

Chapter 18

Alistair did not allow the implications of the attack on Michael in Aradi Street to be ignored. He had not been appointed as Security Attaché to a major international organisation like the OSSE without an impressive pedigree. Indeed, his previous posts had included twenty years in the British Police, latterly as a Chief Superintendent in the Manchester force, and subsequently a stint as a senior Security Enforcement Officer at the United Nations Headquarters in New York. Following the attack, once he was sufficiently recovered, he spent time with Michael taking a meticulous statement from him and recording each item of the events which had occurred in his notebook. He went into every detail with Michael concerning not only the attack itself, but also all the preceding events of Michael's visit to the Austrian and Slovakian borders to interview the border guards there. Finally, and crucially, he wanted to detail every bit about the trip by car Michael had made with Paolo to Bratislava where they had uncovered the Hotel Avalon, found the Roma girls imprisoned against their wills and managed to rescue one of them.

So concerned was Alistair about the occurrence of the attack on the First Deputy Director of the Budapest office, and the very high possibility that his personal safety if not his life remained at risk, that it was on his recommendation that Conrad sent Michael back home to England to recuperate.

All of these deliberations were of course kept top secret at the time, known only to Conrad and one or two of the senior executives in Brussels. Nothing about Alistair's enquiries was shared with the rest of the Budapest office employees, including Angie. So secretly was the whole incident treated that the organisation also chose not even to discuss the issues with Michael's wife and family.

The day after Michael returned home to the UK, Alistair flew to Bratislava where he had a pre-arranged meeting with a senior Slovakian Police Inspector at the City Police Headquarters. He was able to share with Inspector Tomas Stefanik the dossier that Paolo and Michael had compiled, following their trip to Bratislava, concerning their investigations into the sex trafficking ring that was also operating in Budapest. Stefanik told Alistair that Michael had informed him about the impromptu raid he and Paolo had made on the Hotel Avalon and their freeing of the girl Christina. Immediately he heard this, Stefanik had placed the Avalon Hotel under discrete surveillance. He'd now gained all the evidence he needed and a search warrant. That day he had primed a squad of twenty armed officers ready to enter the building.

So it was that at five a.m. the morning after Alistair's arrival in Bratislava a hit squad, commanded by Stefanik and accompanied by Alistair, took up positions in three police vans, two at each end of the road near the front of the Hotel with one van at the rear. On command, the place was entered by force. There was much shouting and screaming from the girls, but no firearms had been discharged, as far as Alistair was aware, and no one had been injured.

When the commotion had died down, the perpetrators were led out one by one, handcuffed to police officers. Those arrested included the hard-faced Madam Anna and the two tattooed male guards, all looking singularly defiant, as well as a couple of kitchen staff. Following them out a little later came about fifteen girls, each of them shocked and physically and emotionally traumatised. They had all been repeatedly abused and raped by parties of men visiting the hotel on a daily basis. The group of girls set free included Maria, the friend of Christina. But only about half of the number of girls who had been kidnapped by coach from Budapest under false pretences that Saturday evening and imprisoned with them in the Hotel Avalon still remained there. The girls who had been freed were put up for a few days in a residential police training centre outside Bratislava, where they received help and support from a team of experienced female police officers while they recuperated sufficiently to enable them to be put through a detailed debriefing process.

When the released girls were able to start giving statements a few days later, the Slovakian police learnt that the other girls who had been imprisoned in the Hotel had been driven away in a minibus very shortly after Michael and Paolo's visit. It was likely that they had already been taken over the border, perhaps west through Austria or north into the Czech Republic. Stefanik ordered a race to search for them at once, in case they were still in Slovakia, and also alerted both the Czech and Austrian police forces.

The arrest of the woman and two male guards was only likely to have been the capture of small fry involved in a much wider people-trafficking organisation, perhaps even linked with that which was operating in Budapest. But Stefanik was confident that, when they started to talk to save their own skins, they would lead his investigation to the more important people involved in this international trafficking ring. With luck, perhaps, the national police forces would at last gain enough information to crack the whole of this particular outfit, at least.

Alistair was invited by Stefanik to sit in on the interview process with Madam Anna and the two male guards. He did so long enough to satisfy himself that the information that these three were starting to provide, in exchange for a possible reduction in their own sentences, would indeed very likely lead to the arrest of more important people involved in this trafficking racket. To the capture of the biggest fish of all, the powerful Mirgo Varga perhaps.

Alistair returned to Budapest two days later, pleased with the outcome of his visit to Bratislava and looking forward to bringing Michael up to date with events when he returned to the office following his leave in England.

Chapter 19

As fate would have it, Alistair was not going to have the opportunity of bringing Michael up to date with these events. The news of Michael's death by suicide while on leave in London two weeks later hit the office in Budapest like a bombshell. Everybody was equally shocked and saddened, not least Alistair himself. But he was not prepared to accept at face value the reassurances he had received by phone, following Michael's death, from the police in London and Europol that no foul play had occurred. He immediately booked a flight to London for an urgent meeting with his police colleagues at the Met.

The London Metropolitan Police Deputy Commissioner Albert Turner and the Head of Europol, Philippe Lloris, who had travelled from The Hague to be at the meeting, laid out to him in detail the results of the extensive investigations that had been made into Michael's death. He had been found hanging in his own garage by his wife Marion early that Sunday morning. They explained that no evidence of foul play had been found and that there was no reason not to believe that Michael had taken his own life.

But Alistair was completely unable to accept their reassurances about the absence of foul play. Indeed, he made it clear to them both that, as soon as he heard the news of Michael's death, he had been certain from what he already knew that his death could not have been self-inflicted. He assumed that they were both aware of the serious attack on Michael in the street only a few weeks before his death? The two senior policemen nodded in assent. As a senior respected colleague, they listened patiently to what Alistair had to say, but could only respond with raised open hands, indicating the simple fact that they had no proof whatsoever that there had been an attack on Michael at his home in Ealing. The three men sat looking at each other across the desk.

'I don't suppose there was… any question of mistaken identity here?' Alistair was an intelligent police officer, always prepared to think laterally and consider alternative possibilities.

'What on *earth* do you mean?' said Turner, staring straight at Alistair.

'Who identified the body?' said Alistair.

Turner flashed a look at Lloris and opened the file on the desk in front of him. 'Formal identification was made by Andrew White, the Butler's gardener, long term employee and a family friend. Mr Butler's body had of course initially been found by his wife hanging by a rope in their garage.'

'What was the evidence?' came back Alistair.

'What evidence do you mean?!' demanded Deputy Commissioner Turner, starting to exhibit his considerable irritation at being cross-questioned by a security officer who was not even a current serving police officer, let alone a member of his own force. This tendency to a lack of calm whenever Turner was put under pressure had already been noted by his superior, the Metropolitan Police Commissioner himself, and not a few reporting journalists.

'What *evidence* do we have that Michael actually took his

own life?' Alistair was still pressing. 'As far as I am aware he left nothing, such as a suicide note, to explain what might have led him to end his own life.'

'Who knows what leads a man to end his own life?' Turner replied. 'Probably only the members of his own family and his close work colleagues,' he finished, smiling at Alistair perhaps a little unnecessarily sarcastically.

'Well, that really is *just* my point,' Alistair said, undeterred, sitting back in his seat as he crossed his arms across his chest. 'It is the case that not one member of Michael's family or work colleagues know of any reason why he should have taken his own life or felt that he had recently been depressed or withdrawn. On the contrary, his PA Angela Mills has told me that Michael had been working at home in London very hard and productively right up to the day of his death. She had been in contact with him on a more or less daily basis, either by telephone or email, and not once, she said, had she had occasion to think that Michael had been depressed or under strain.'

The only reply Turner and Lloris could give in response to Alistair's statement was to shrug their shoulders in unison at him.

Alistair left the Metropolitan Police Deputy Commissioner's office singularly frustrated and dissatisfied by the outcome of their meeting. Before he left, he had at least extracted a promise from the other two men that, should any new evidence concerning Michael's death come to light, they would of course re-open the case and pursue it further. In the meantime, it was to be put on hold.

And so it remained.

Chapter 20
25ᵗʰ August 2014

Marion Butler woke early on Sunday morning in their house in Ealing. As soon as she was awake, she had a strong feeling that something was wrong. Michael was not in the bed next to her. Assuming he must have got up early, she got up herself and threw on her dressing gown, stepped into her slippers and paddled off onto the landing to look for her husband. Michael was not in the bathroom, and there was no sign that he had recently been in there and taken a shower. She assumed he would not have gone into any of the upstairs spare bedrooms for any reason, and did not bother looking into them.

Michael was nowhere to be seen downstairs either. The kitchen was empty and there was nothing to suggest he had prepared or eaten breakfast. She opened the back door to take a look at the back garden, just in case he had decided to step out there for any reason. Everything outside the back looked as it always did. Starting to feel concerned, she came back into the house, doing another round of the rooms on the ground floor, including the living room and dining room. There was no sign that he had been in any of those rooms, such as the Sunday paper discarded on the sofa, perhaps. Walking into the hall, she noted that the front door was still locked. Michael's study was in a bit of a mess, with books on the chairs and papers all over the desk and on the floor. But that was as it usually was, and how she remembered it had been when she had gone into the study to kiss him good night the previous evening. She went back into the kitchen and walked through to the utility room to open the inside door to the garage, to see if his car was there.

Michael's legs were dangling right in front of her. She knew at once exactly what had happened. Looking up, she saw the back of his head lolling onto his right shoulder, a thick rope around his neck extending up to the beam above. He was already dead.

She slammed the door. She stood in the utility room shaking and felt the sweat glands prickle across her forehead and palms. Somehow she moved back into the kitchen. The immediate sense of panic she had felt was already starting to be tempered in a strange way by an acceptance of the finality of the situation. She was too numbed to cry. After a while sitting at the kitchen table – was it five minutes or fifty minutes? – Marion picked up the phone and called Andy, the gardener.

Andy had been working for the Butlers for fifteen years. In addition to taking care of the garden, he did all the odd jobs around the house. He was not only adept at mending most things that had broken down, such as vacuum cleaners and washing machines, but also with time had proved to be equally proficient at small carpentry jobs as well as painting and decorating. Marion particularly liked him and found him easy to have around. Michael was grateful to have somebody to take the house and garden off his hands, not least during the time when he was working away abroad. They had become good friends with Andy and would trust him with the keys of the house when they both went away abroad together.

Andy came straight round in his beaten-up pickup truck, even though it was only seven a.m. on a Sunday. He was already awake when Marion phoned and, although he was unable to understand what the problem was, he could hear from the extreme distress in her voice that he was needed, and needed now. He had never before received such a call from Marion and understood at once that this was some kind of emergency. He knew that Michael was back from Hungary and working from home at the moment. He could only assume that Marion was calling him because there was a problem with her husband. He drove the mile and a half between his house and the Butler's house faster than he had ever done before. As he pulled up onto the Butler's drive Marion was standing in front of the opened front door, her face white and her dressing gown cord pulled tightly around her waist. With a trembling arm she pointed him to the garage.

Andy jumped out of his truck and swung the unlocked garage door up and over. He saw the reason he had been called immediately. Hanging on a thick rope attached to a beam at the back of the garage was Michael's dead body. His body was already stiff and contorted. There was a pool of urine on the floor and a strong smell of faeces. His head was lolling on to his right shoulder and his head and neck were a purple red. His face was swollen and unrecognisable, with his eyes, lips and tongue bulging forwards and distorting his features. Andy had no reason to doubt, however, that it was Michael. The dangling legs below the distorted face and body were dressed in trousers and shoes that he was familiar with. It was clear to Andy that Michael must have been dead for some time.

Andy slammed the garage door shut. A reflex action not so much out of shock – although his own hands were by now also trembling and his knees felt weak – but because he did not want Marion to walk in front of the opened garage door and see her husband like this, even though he knew that she had already seen him hanging there, which was why she had called him.

'I'm so sorry, Marion,' he said, as he walked over and touched her on the arm.

She said nothing in reply. Very gently, he held her by her left elbow and guided her back through the front door and sat her down on a chair in the kitchen, putting his arm around her shoulders. She was not crying, merely staring blankly right in front of her.

'Leave things to me,' he said softly, squeezing her hand tightly and looking with dismay into the ashen face of a friend.

He walked into the hall and dialled 999. After making the emergency call for the police and an ambulance, he walked back quietly into the kitchen, pulled up a chair next to Marion and sat there holding her hand as he waited for the police to arrive.

The ambulance crew arrived in minutes and pronounced Michael dead at the scene. The first police arrived a few minutes later, two uniformed officers in a patrol car. They walked straight in through the opened front door and into the kitchen where Andy was still sitting holding Marion's hand. About fifteen minutes later a non-uniformed officer followed, went into the garage and started taking some measurements, making chalk marks on the floor and looking around the scene. A police photographer followed him soon after and began taking photographs of Michael's body and the appearance of the garage, before moving on to take pictures of the whole house, inside and out.

Once the detective had given the ambulance men the nod, one of them carefully lifted Michael's body up with his arms around the upper legs while the other stood on a pair of steps and cut the rope with a sharp knife. They laid the body down on the ground carefully and with respect and then lifted it on to the stretcher and into the ambulance. Within the space of only about half an hour Michael's body had been removed from the house and taken away to the mortuary.

During all this time Marion had not moved from her chair in the kitchen. A female police officer arrived and said a few words of sympathy to her, standing next to Marion with her arm around her shoulders. Andy stood in the front room and gave a statement to the senior of the three non-uniform policemen who had now gathered at the scene, telling him what he knew and confirming Michael's identity. The detective inspector took down Andy's statement in his pocketbook, asking a number of questions of Andy as he did so. While this was going on, the other police officers were inspecting the house carefully, looking forensically at the window and door frames for any evidence of forced entry or anything which might raise the possibility of foul play. Two other officers were doing a search of the garden, paying particular interest to the shrubs and borders under the downstairs windows, looking for footprints or evidence that an intruder might have approached the house from the outside. Having found nothing to interest them outside the house, they then joined their colleagues who were now focussing their attention on the inside of the house.

Between them, the police carried out a detailed and systematic search of all the rooms in the house, paying particular attention to Michael's study. They were obviously looking for the presence of a suicide note or any other paper evidence which might be important to their enquiry at a later date. Without asking for permission, they disconnected Michael's computer with gloves on, placed it in a large plastic bag and carried it to one of the police cars now in the drive, to be taken away for examination by one of the police IT specialists. After the detailed search of the house and gardens had been completed, and having found nothing to suggest that this might be a murder case, the police did not attempt to speak to Marion at this time or take a statement from her.

The police finished their work and left. The woman police officer remained to pass on some further comforting words to Marion and leave her card and contact details with her. She told Marion that they would need to come back and take a statement from her, but that this could wait for a day or two until Marion felt able to do so. After she too had left, Andy was alone with Marion again. He called his wife Judy and asked her to come over and be with Marion. Leaving Marion still sitting in the kitchen, Andy sat down in another room to telephone the Butler's three adult children from an address book he had found on the hall table. Martin, Sophie and Jeff (who was away on holiday and on his mobile) all answered their phones personally in response to his calls, and all remained in silence at the other end of the line as he broke the news of their father's death to them one by one, as sympathetically as he was able.

*

The next morning Andy had a telephone call from Ealing police station asking if, in the absence of any of the Butler children and Marion's understandable distress, he would be prepared to formally identify the body. He agreed immediately, although he did not anticipate the task with great relish. He was accompanied to the mortuary in Ealing Hospital – where a post-mortem was to be held – by one of the uniformed policemen who had been at the Butler's house the morning before. The body was lying on a mortuary table covered by a white sheet. When he was ready, the mortuary attendant lifted the sheet back to expose the head and neck. Andy had trouble not to wince. The whole head and neck area was bloated and purple. He could see the marks that the rope had made cutting deeply into the right side of the neck. The facial features were even more distorted than they had been the day before when he had seen the body hanging from a rope in the Butler's garage. The tongue was bulging out of the mouth whose lips were grotesquely swollen, in a gargoyle-like appearance. The eyes were protruding from their sockets. This wasn't the face of the man he had known for many years, but he had no reason to doubt that it must be the face of Michael, hugely distorted by the violence of his death.

'Can you confirm that this is the body of Mr Michael

Butler?' the police officer who had accompanied him to the mortuary asked.

'I can,' Andy replied without hesitating. With that, he was led back out of the mortuary.

Chapter 21

The inquest into Michael Butler's death took place only a couple of months after the event. When the date set for the hearing was known, the Butler's eldest son Martin spoke to his mother Marion on the phone.

'Would you like me to stand in for us, mother?' he asked, offering to represent the family in order to save his mother further grief.

'I would appreciate your support on the day Martin,' Marion replied, 'but I have to be there.'

On reflection, Martin knew that it was necessary for his mother to attend. As necessary as attending the funeral at the crematorium, which they were all to do a few weeks after the Inquest. So Martin travelled down from Newcastle by train on the Monday and accompanied Marion to the inquest, which was to be held the next day, on the Tuesday afternoon.

Ealing Coroner's Court was situated in the County Court in a not very pre-possessing area of west London, just behind the police station. They arrived in good time and were shown into the relatives' room. They were joined there in a few minutes by Alice Bourner, the Clerk to the Court. She was a woman in her fifties, business-like and efficient, but understanding and practised in supporting the bereaved through this most traumatic part of the grieving process. She limped into the room carrying a weighty bundle of documents under her right arm. She introduced herself in a friendly fashion, sat down next to them and apologised for her limp which she explained was due to the fact that she had recently had a fall and damaged her right knee. It appeared that she might have torn a cruciate ligament and that she was waiting for surgery to repair this, which she was not looking forward to. All this seemed to go above Marion's head as she sat staring into space. Martin was aware that the woman was not meaning to be personal but was discussing her recent injury with them as a way of trying to help put them at their ease. He smiled back wanly at the clerk.

Mrs Bourner explained to Marion and Michael the course that the hearing would take in a clear and understandable way, describing the manner in which the inquest would be conducted and the order in which the coroner was likely to call the witnesses. She stressed that they were fully entitled to ask questions of any of the witnesses, and indeed the coroner himself, at any point in the proceedings, should they wish to do so. The clock on the wall indicated that it was time for them to go in, and she led them through the back of court number five and sat them in the relatives' seats at the front of the court. Having made sure that they were comfortably settled, and providing them with a decanter of water and two glasses, she disappeared into the coroner's chambers.

Looking around, the coroner's court was much as Martin had expected. It was a medium-sized hall with walnut panelled walls. The coroner's desk was situated on a raised dais at the far end of the hall, with a walnut witness box to the side on the left. A number of members of the public drifted into the seats behind them as the time approached: the case had received front page prominence in the local paper at the time of Michael's death. Sitting at the back of the Court were a handful of members of the press, hacks from the Ealing Herald and one or two other local papers as well as a couple who turned out to be from the national press. Marion was seated on Martin's left in the second row from the front. Sitting there motionless, she had not uttered a single word to Martin since they had entered the building.

Exactly at two p.m. the door to the right of the coroner's dais was opened and Mrs Bourner came through wearing a black gown.

'All stand!' she ordered, holding the door open for the Coroner to enter as she did so.

All those present in the court got to their feet and the coroner himself came in, walking forward to take up his place behind his desk.

'Please be seated,' he said politely to the assembled, before placing a folder of notes on his desk and taking his seat at the desk himself.

Mr Alan Cruse, the West London Coroner, was an avuncular man in his sixties. He was dressed without undue formality in a tweed jacket, shirt and tie. Martin had expected something a little more exotic, an expectation which was based on an inquest into a good friend's death he had attended in Southwark many years before, when the coroner in question had been a Knight of the Realm, with flamboyant facial whiskers, a gold watch chain and a pink and white striped shirt with starched white collar worn under a black tailcoat. He had found that coroner's appearance somewhat unexpectedly threatening at the time. This coroner seemed at first sight to be much less confrontational.

Mr Cruse was a solicitor by profession and a senior partner of a well-known family firm of solicitors in Ealing. He was known for being an intelligent man. He could be sharp with witnesses, especially if they had come unprepared, but was always compassionate and supportive, especially to bereaved family and friends of the deceased. He opened the file that he had brought into court under his arm and smiled benevolently at those assembled.

'This is the inquest into the death of Michael John Butler,' the Coroner started. 'May I remind the court that it is my duty to establish the person of the deceased, the mode of his death and also the cause of his death. This is not a Criminal Court, and it is not my duty to arrive at any conclusions concerning guilt or blame, should such questions arise. Now, I know we have a number of Mr Butler's family present: Mr Butler's wife Mrs Marion Butler and son Mr Martin Butler, is that correct?'

So saying, Mr Cruse leaned over his desk and smiled kindly at Marion and Martin. Martin nodded at the Coroner and Mrs Bourner interjected:

'That is correct, sir.'

'The family knows,' the coroner continued, addressing the rest of the court, 'that I am happy for the family to ask any questions of myself or any of the witnesses during the inquest hearing. I would, however, ask that questions to witnesses be directed through me in the usual way.' Mr Cruse again smiled kindly at Marion and Martin as he made this point. 'Now,' continued Mr Cruse, 'Michael John Butler was born in Ruislip on 6th March, 1958, is that correct?' again looking at the family.

Martin nodded in the affirmative.

'He died on 25th August, 2014, at 24 Eversfield Road, Ealing, the family home. Is that also correct?'

Again, Martin nodded assent on behalf of his mother and himself.

'Mr Butler worked as the First Deputy Director of the Organisation for Safety and Security in Europe, based at their offices in Budapest, Hungary, and was a British citizen with a family home here in Ealing? He was back at home in Ealing when his death occurred?'

Again, Martin nodded in assent to both these questions of fact.

'Then I call the first witness, Mr Andrew White.'

Andy appeared from the right side of the court and was guided into the witness box by Mrs Bourner, who asked him if he wished to swear on the bible or to affirm. Andy indicated that he wished to affirm, and the clerk handed him the text printed on a small board, from which he read:

'I do solemnly affirm that the evidence I shall give will be the whole truth...'

After he had been sworn in, Mr Cruse asked: 'Mr White you are a long-term employee and family friend of the Butler's, is that correct?'

Andy nodded, 'Yes, sir.'

'I understand from the statement you made to the police at the time that you received a telephone call from Mrs Butler at about seven a.m. on Sunday 25th August, 2014, and were asked by her to come quickly to the house.'

Again, Andy nodded: 'Yes, sir.'

'Please tell the court what you found, Mr White.'

Facing towards the body of the court, Andy gave his account of that awful morning, reading from a copy of the typed statement he had made to the police at the time. He was obviously nervous at undergoing this ordeal, but spoke clearly and without hesitation. He described how he had been phoned by Mrs Butler and asked to come round urgently. He told the court how he had found her standing in a very distressed state on the drive on his arrival and how, at Mrs Butler's direction, he had thrown open the garage door and seen Michael's body hanging by a rope from a beam at the back of the garage.

'And I understand that you also attended the mortuary the next day, at the request of the police, to formally identify the deceased?' Mr Cruse asked Andy.

'Yes, sir,' he replied, 'I did.'

'And was this the body of Mr Michael Butler, Mr White?'

'Yes, sir, it was,' replied Andy. 'Obviously, when I first arrived at the house he had been hanging there for some hours and' – he looked over to where Marion was sitting at this point – 'his facial features were significantly... affected.'

'But you were nevertheless able to formally identify the deceased?' Mr Cruse asked.

'I was, sir,' Andy replied.

'Thank you, Mr White. You may step down.'

Andy left the witness box and returned to sit next to his wife Judy, who had come with him to support him.

Andy's witness evidence was followed by those of two of the police officers who had attended the scene – one of the uniformed police constables who had been first to arrive at the house followed by the senior Detective Inspector who had arrived a little while after. Mr Cruse questioned each of the police officers as they gave their evidence, essentially to clarify the statement of facts for the court that they had already recorded in detail in their written statements.

Finally, Dr Arthur Gilmour, the Home Office pathologist, took to the stand. During the pathologist's systematic description of his post-mortem findings, including the precise features of the external and internal bruising to Michael's neck, the fracturing of his cervical vertebrae and the fatal disruption of the spinal cord within, Marion bent forward in her seat, staring at the floor, understandably finding the details very difficult to bear. Martin, who experienced a surge of nausea himself during this part of the proceedings, thought that his mother may be about to pass out and reached his arm across her to support her. The pathologist continued to list in detail his findings concerning his examination of Michael's heart and lungs, liver and kidneys and adrenal glands, his brain and all the other organs. Marion remained pale and impassive during this but at least found the strength to avoid fainting forward onto the floor, with Martin's support.

In due course, Dr Gilmour reached the end of his statement. 'In conclusion, I found that death was due to asphyxiation and cervical spinal cord dissection caused by hanging from a rope. I estimate that the deceased had been dead for approximately eight hours by the time he was found.'

'Thank you, Dr Gilmour. You may step down,' said the coroner.

The pathologist left the witness box and Marion sat back in her seat again. Gilmour had been the last witness called to appear.

Mr Cruse looked over his spectacles to the second row. 'Do the family have any questions that they wish to ask?'

After a slight hesitation, Martin replied: 'No, thank you sir.'

Mr Cruse nodded in acceptance and then sat looking at his papers for a few minutes, during which there was complete silence in the court. Looking up from his papers, the coroner started to sum up. He went through the details of the case, reviewing the evidence that had been heard, and giving a narrative step-by-step summary of the facts which had just been presented to the Court.

At the end of his summing up, Mr Cruse arrived at his conclusions: 'I am assured by our Metropolitan Police colleagues that they were unable to find any evidence to suggest that breaking and entry to the Butler's house had occurred. Nor did they find any other signs of possible foul play. I am also informed in a written statement I have received from Mr Conrad James, Mr Butler's Director in Hungary, that Mr Butler had been allowed home from his office in Budapest a few weeks before his death to recuperate from stress at work.'

Martin could hear the hacks at the back of the court scribbling furiously at this point.

'Taking all these facts into consideration, it is therefore my conclusion that Mr Butler took his life by his own hands. Accordingly, I have arrived at this verdict.' There was a pause while Mr Cruse waited to allow his verdict to be understood by the family and the whole court. 'I would like to express my condolences to Mrs Butler and her family at this juncture,' the coroner then added, smiling sympathetically over his desk towards Marion and Martin. 'I do believe from what I have heard that there was nothing leading up to Mr Butler's tragic death which could have alerted them to this possibility and also nothing that they could have done to have prevented it. I do hope that my assurances about this fact will provide just a little comfort to them with the passage of time,' Mr Cruse concluded.

With that, the coroner closed his file and got to his feet.

'All rise!' ordered Mrs Bourner.

The court rose and Mr Cruse picked up his papers and walked off the dais. As he left through the exit at the back of the court Mrs Bourner held the door open for him, bowing slowly as she did so. The coroner bowed briefly to her in return as he disappeared into his chamber. The public and press started to shuffle out at the back of the court. Mrs Bourner came over to Marion and Martin and led them out of the court and back to the relatives' room.

Once they were sitting back in the relatives' room, the coroner's clerk asked them whether they had understood and were content with the conduct and result of the inquest. Martin did not feel all that "content", as Mrs Bourner had called it, but he did not want to say too much in order to avoid upsetting his mother any more than she was already.

He did say to Mrs Bourner, however, 'If indeed my father's death was by suicide, we as his family are at a complete loss to explain what might have caused him to take his own life.'

'I do understand,' replied the coroner's clerk sympathetically but without passing further comment, which she clearly was not at liberty to do.

She then went on to complete the necessary bits of paperwork and to explain to Marion that she would be receiving a death certificate in the next few days which would enable them to proceed with the funeral arrangements. Marion looked away in distress at this thought, but Martin thanked her, and left supporting his mother who was clearly still too upset to talk.

Chapter 22
November 2014

Michael's funeral took place on a dull November Wednesday afternoon about three weeks after the inquest into his death. There were about one hundred and fifty people present, filling the Chapel to capacity with some having to stand at the back during the relatively short service. Representatives of all aspects of Michael's life had attended. In addition to the close family, previous friends and colleagues from the Foreign and Commonwealth Office were well represented, from the embassies in Warsaw, Prague, Brussels, Berlin and Lisbon, as well as more recent friends and colleagues from the OSSE and especially the Budapest office.

Angie was seated in the second row, accompanied by her husband Mark, as well as Conrad and Alistair and other members from the office in Budapest. Alistair, the OSSE security attaché, was looking particularly grave. Ever since the news of Michael's death had reached him he had been extremely uneasy. The conversations he'd had with the Metropolitan Police about Michael's death had got precisely nowhere and further discussions with his colleagues in Europol had been met with a bemused silence. Behind Alistair and Conrad sat an under-secretary from the British Embassy in Budapest who had been sent by the British Ambassador to Hungary as his representative. As well as a host of other friends he had worked with in Budapest and had known well, there were other acquaintances from the OSSE offices in Brussels and other parts of Europe.

Marion arrived dressed all in black, her sons Jeff and Martin walking either side of her, one on each arm to support her. Her daughter Sophie came behind them with her husband Guy to give her support. The coffin was brought in by four pall bearers, all colleagues from the OSSE, who placed the mahogany cask reverentially on the receiving catafalque. At the back of the crematorium chapel, coming in late as the chapel organ finished the voluntary which accompanied the coffin, appeared a swarthy dark-haired man dressed in a poorly fitting black suit. This was Paolo Crusesco.

The service was simple and unpretentious. In spite of Marion having specifically requested that the proceedings be secular – Michael was a life-long self-professed humanist and atheist – somehow the resident chaplain had become involved and was leading the proceedings. Marion was too weary to object in public and, as the service progressed, she sat back in her seat in the knowledge that all those present were well aware of Michael's beliefs and convictions and the kernel of the event was that they were all gathered there to celebrate and mark his life as they knew it. Martin gave a moving account, as the oldest son, as to what his father had meant to him and his brother and sister. Conrad read an extract from the works of Ali Krasnici, the Roma author who has depicted the life of the Roma in all its facets: dealing with suffering, privation, poverty and need, but also describing the longings, the happiness and everyday pleasures of the Roma peoples. Jeff played a piece of a Hungarian Roma dance tune on his violin, accompanied by two of his friends on piano and bass. Next, Michael's daughter Sophie, an actor, stepped forward. Speaking confidently and without notes to the back of the auditorium, she recited the poem by Dylan Thomas, *Do Not Go Gentle Into That Good Night*:

'And you, my father, there on that sad height...
Do not go gentle into that good night...'

Finally, Angie stepped up to the lectern and read a short poem from *The Roads of the Roma:*

'Ode to the Twentieth Century

Twentieth Century,
What did you hold in store for the sad Roma people?
Did you bring the sun into our dark lives?
Did you dry the tears from our women's eyes?

Did you lighten our songs and dances with joy?
Twentieth Century: listen to our songs.
Can you hear from the notes
how our hearts have been drowned in tears?

Look at our dances:
Our women's steps may seem as light as birds',
but in reality they are trying
to cast off a bitter burden
from their aching shoulders.

That burden is you,

Twentieth Century,
and the sorrow you brought into each of our lives.'

As Angie walked back to her seat a brief single round of applause broke out from someone at the back of the chapel. That someone was Paolo Crusesco. The congregation were restrained enough not to look back to see where the clapping had come from and sat with heads bowed in an appropriately reverential moment of silence.

The congregation filed slowly out around the side of the chapel at the end of the service, where Marion stood with Martin, Jeff and Sophie shaking each person by the hand, receiving their kind words of condolence, friendship and support, and being provoked into laughter or at least a smile by the occasional anecdote or remembered joke from memories of Michael's life. This process took about thirty minutes, with friends and colleagues old and new waiting patiently and all wanting to say a few words at least to Marion. She in turn reciprocated all their kindnesses, not wanting to miss greeting and thanking each one of those that had been kind enough to attend, for she knew some had travelled a long way to be present and at no little expense or inconvenience to their day-to-day lives.

The sky was grey and the air turning to drizzle as Marion turned away from having shaken the last visitor's hand. Standing in front of her was a tall dark weather-beaten man. He wore a black suit, but this and the rest of his clothes were old and rather shabby, as well as being poorly fitting. He had been waiting patiently and unobtrusively to one side of the funeral line. Paolo stepped forward, and delivered his address to Marion.

'Misses Butler, my name is Paolo Crusesco. I am here to represent the Roma people of Hungary. I have been sent by my Roma family and friends to pay our deepest respects to you for the life and work of your husband. We want you to know how much we loved Michael and how grateful we are for the help and support he gave to us over the last few years.' Paolo bowed low, and then held out his hand to Marion as he stood tall again.

Marion hesitated, surprised and somewhat confused by this unexpected tribute. She had no idea what Michael might have done in the past to deserve this heartfelt emotional appreciation. She regained her composure, looked at Paolo straight in the eye and took the hand which he had offered her.

'Thank you so much, Mr Crusesco,' Marion said, shaking Paolo's hand. 'I can't tell you how much this means to me and the rest of my family. We are very grateful to you for your kind words and thank you immensely for taking the trouble to have come all this way to pay your respects to Michael. I know he would have been so proud to hear your tribute to him. Please take my reply back to your people.'

Paolo bowed low again in respect and shook Marion's hand once more before turning and walking away across the garden of remembrance and out of sight into the rain of the damp November early evening. Marion stood still, looking after him and wondering who he was and what it was that Michael could have done to engender such lasting love and respect.

Chapter 23

When the news of Michael's death while on leave in England came through, Paolo had had no hesitation about wanting to travel over to the funeral. Since returning from the funeral he had felt deeply depressed. During their time working together he had not only come to trust and appreciate Michael, he had also started to value him very much as a friend. For a senior diplomat working for an international organisation Michael had been unusually unstuffy, with integrity as well as intelligence. Paolo had had experience of people in such positions over the years, both in Hungarian governmental departments and with similar officials in the other countries he had lived in, including Romania and Slovakia. He had come to appreciate that Michael was different from most of them. Not only was he easy to get on with personally, once you got to know him he exhibited a wicked sense of humour. On their train trip to Pecs together and at other times, he would crack jokes about the Prime Minister and the ruling Hungarian Fidek party which Paolo knew, if these got out, could have put Michael in a professionally vulnerable position. Paolo also acknowledged that the fact that Michael was prepared to share with him his philosophy and thoughts about the unpleasant nature of Hungary's governance – which Paolo agreed with completely – was in itself an indication that Michael had grown to like and trust Paolo equally.

A few days after returning from Michael's funeral in England, Paolo sought and was granted a meeting with Conrad James, the Director of the OSSE Hungary, in the headquarters in Andrassy Avenue where Paolo had regularly met with Michael in the months before his death. Conrad wore an expensive smart suit and black tie, the latter Paolo supposed as a mark of respect for his recently departed colleague. His demeanour was much more formal than Michael had ever been with Paolo, even in their early meetings together, and Paolo was unsure whether this was Conrad's normal professional manner or perhaps a reflection of the recent events that had occurred in the organisation. As Conrad shook his hand, Paolo also sensed a degree of tenseness in the man. He noticed how Conrad's facial muscles were taught, the regular contracting of the muscles forming lines around the skin of his mouth and eyes. The fact that Conrad sat and fiddled with a pencil as they talked, in a less than relaxed way, also indicated that he was a man under strain.

They sat in Conrad's office, just along the corridor from the office that had previously been Michael's, and talked about the events of the last few weeks. Conrad was polite but non-committal. If he had more information than he was admitting to, he certainly was not prepared to discuss this with Paolo. But Paolo was pretty sure Conrad was as much in the dark about the reasons for Michael's death as he was. He had got to know and like Michael well and could not believe that he was a man with the personality or indeed the reasons to take his own life. Paolo said as much to Conrad and, although Conrad made no comment on Paolo's point of view, Paolo took Conrad's silence as being confirmation that Conrad himself was inclined to agree with this assessment of his deceased colleague.

Michael had confided to Paolo the events surrounding his attack in the street a few weeks before his death. But when Paolo mentioned this episode to Conrad, while he acknowledged that he was well aware of the attack, he made no comment as to whether he considered this might in any way have had a bearing on Michael's subsequent death. After about ten minutes the two men had run out of things to discuss – Paolo certainly was not of a mind to use this meeting with the OSSE Director to bring up Roma issues as well – and they said goodbye politely to each other. As they shook hands Paolo undertook to contact Conrad if he received any intelligence which might be of help, and Conrad thanked Paolo for this offer.

*

Later that Friday evening Paolo was sitting by himself in the corner of a restaurant in the Mariaremete District of Buda. He was thinking over his meeting with Conrad that morning and going through the events leading up to Michael's death in the hope that there might be something which Michael had said or done which might provide an important clue. The *Nagy Neni* was a very popular, moderately expensive and rather up-market restaurant set in a prosperous dormitory district of Budapest, stretching up over the Buda hills to the west of the River Danube. Open seven days a week, right the way through lunch and into the evening dinner, the restaurant was a popular eating place not only of well-to-do Hungarians but also a haunt of tourists and the ex-pat professional people and their families who lived in District II. The tables of the *Nagy Neni* were invariably well filled with couples, family groups and parties at all times of the day and week. During the summer and in any reasonable weather in other seasons, especially spring and autumn, the most popular place to be was outdoors in the garden part of the restaurant. The garden area was graced with half a dozen huge oak trees and a number of equally tall chestnuts, towering imposingly above the diners. The tables were covered with red and white tablecloths and the chairs were made of red and white striped material. They were set out under a large canvas canopy which stretched on posts between the trees and extended across the garden adjacent to the main restaurant building. In acknowledgement of the international clientele which the restaurant served, the menu was written in four languages and included dishes such as "Auntie Tercsi's stuffed turkey breast" and "Hungarian black truffle cream soup with goose liver flavoured toast", with notes on the history of the restaurant and how the dishes had come into being.

The restaurant was a place which Paolo had not been to before, not least because he could never afford the prices of the food and drink on offer. He was there that night, however, because his brother, who had invited him, was playing the accordion to the diners. Paolo had accepted the invitation, hoping the distraction might help take his mind off his sadness at the recent loss of his friend. As well as his brother playing to the diners, one of his cousins and a friend had also been working in the place for some years as waiters.

Paolo was seated at a small table in the corner of one of the lounge areas of the indoors part of the restaurant. He was tucking into a large complimentary plate of stuffed cabbage with sour cream and fresh bread, which had been put in front of him by his cousin, together with a litre of draught Hungarian beer.

The restaurant was as busy as usual that night with people talking excitedly, laughing and joking and generally enjoying themselves and the food and drink on offer. A number of large open fires were burning in the grates of the traditional walk-in fireplaces at various points around the dining room areas, keeping the freezing night air outside at bay and lending warmth not only to the rooms themselves but also to the pre-Christmas festive atmosphere of the place.

As he sat in his corner, however, Paolo found it difficult to join in and appreciate the seasonal warmth on offer. He was acutely aware of the sadness he still felt about the death of his friend and ally Michael Butler. He looked up from his food to see his brother Stefan, who was sitting on a high stool in the opposite corner of the room with his accordion in his arms, bow forward deeply and smile in his direction as he launched his accordion into the next piece of music in his repertoire. In return, Paolo raised his glass of beer in salute to Stefan and gave him a weak smile back. But inside he continued to feel a profound loss.

Chapter 24

Paolo awoke early the next morning. He lay in bed for a few minutes remembering the sadness at Michael's loss he had felt sitting in the *Nagy Neni* restaurant the night before. He was not hung over, and indeed felt quite clear-headed. Rather than just accept the situation as he had been told it, he realised that he had a need to make enquiries of his own. He climbed out of bed and washed and dressed himself. He was soon out on the street and jumping onto a number six tram. This took him around the inner ring road of Terez Korut and over the river Danube, crossing Margit Bridge.

Paolo hopped off the tram on the Buda side of the bridge and walked the short distance to the Hév overland suburban railway station. He queued at the ticket office, bought a ticket to the small town of Szentendre and climbed on the first train to leave. The train journey ran north along the west side of the Danube, towards the long leftwards and westwards curve of the river known as the Danube Bend, which carried on upstream to the basilica town of Esztergom and beyond. The views of the river which appeared in the gaps between the trees were breath-taking. The width and majesty of the river Danube was something Paolo never ceased to marvel at, even at this time when he was in mourning for his dead friend.

Szentendre was a very popular tourist spot in the summer. In addition to the suburban Hév train, it could also be reached in the summer months by the frequent river boats which plied their way up and down that part of the river Danube. These could be boarded from one of the many jetties which lined the shores on both sides of the imposing river as it took its place flowing right through the centre of the city of Budapest. On a hot summer day Szentendre was a pretty place to visit, within easy distance of the city and popular for its low-ceilinged period painted buildings, small restaurants with tables in the streets and gardens, and shops. The shops sold mostly craft and souvenir items, such as pottery, paintings and traditional Hungarian clothing. A number of Paolo's family and Roma friends worked in the small town, his sister and some of her friends making and selling clothes and pottery. One of his cousins owned three donkeys and spent his days giving rides around town to both adults and children. During the cold winter months, however, the town more or less shut down as a tourist centre and there was very little else for the men, women and children to do. There was a little farming which went on outside the town, but Szentendre families were pretty much completely reliant on their seasonal summer income from tourism to support them through the rest of the year, including at this time during the long winter months.

Paolo got off the train, walked into the centre of town and made for the community centre where he knew one of the soup kitchens which Michael had helped set up and fund was still running. His friend Peter had taken over the supervision of this enterprise, which was much appreciated by the local Roma families, especially at this time of year. As Paolo approached, there was a line of Roma families, men, women and children, waiting outside the front door for the centre to open for them to walk inside for a free lunch. Paolo pushed open the old wooden door and found Peter inside, laying up the trestle tables for the lunchtime sitting. In the centre of each table sat a wooden board on each of which there was already a large loaf of freshly baked bread, still warm from the town bakery ovens that morning. At other points on the table were plates of cheese and kolbasz sausages, bowls of salads and jugs of fruit juice.

Peter looked up and smiled his big grin. 'Szia, Paolo,' he said, continuing to shine the stainless steel cutlery with a clean tea cloth, as he laid the knives, forks and spoons out around the soup bowls that had been positioned at each place setting.

'Hi, Peter. Good to see you,' Paolo replied, shaking his friend's right hand while holding his shoulder in a filial gesture with his left hand. 'Soup kitchen still going well?'

'Fine,' said Peter. 'We are doing a roaring trade in this cold weather with all the kids now out of school. How was your trip to England?'

His friend Peter knew all about the death of the man called Michael who had been helping them and about Paolo's decision to travel to London to represent them at Michael's funeral. Paolo had got the other members of the Roma council – of whom Peter was one – together before he left for England, to discuss the situation and his determination to make this trip. The council had agreed, and asked him to express their sadness to Michael's wife about his death and say how much they appreciated what he had done for them. They had also offered to pay for Paolo's air ticket from their council funds, for which he was extremely grateful.

Paolo sat down and told Peter about the trip and the funeral, describing the details of that very sombre November ceremony which he had experienced in a wet foreign land. He also spoke to Peter about his feelings of sadness which had persisted since his return to Budapest and about the difficulty he was having accepting the loss of his friend Michael. He explained that he just could not believe that Michael had taken his own life. Peter nodded and sat there quietly, taking it all in.

Paolo looked at his friend. 'When did you last see Michael, Peter?'

'I am not sure exactly,' Peter replied. 'He called in to see how the soup kitchen was going. It must have been only a few days before he left for England for the last time.'

'Did you notice anything unusual about him?' Paolo asked.

'Nothing at all,' Peter said. 'He seemed fine. He was his usual funny self. There was just one thing,' his friend hesitated, 'after Michael left, that Tovabb fellow who has been poking around since we started up stopped me in the street as I walked home that evening. He fired a whole load of questions at me about why we had started the soup kitchen, and who was paying for it. When I told him that it had been started with the help of Michael and his organisation, who had put up the money, he became very interested, not letting me go until he had fired a volley of other questions at me, most of which I just shrugged off with a "don't know".'

Paolo sat in silence listening to his friend Peter. If anything, the information he was hearing made him even more disturbed. Could it really be the case, as he had been wondering, that Michael's death had in some way been connected to the work he had been involved in with the Roma here in Hungary? And what about the work he and Paolo had undertaken to expose the people-trafficking and the sex exploitation trade in Budapest? Had this really been what had led him to take his own life in such a violent way back in England? If this was not the case – and here Paolo could hardly bring himself to entertain this thought as he sat there listening to Peter – was it even remotely possible that Michael had not in fact taken his own life, but had been traced back to his home in London and summarily murdered by those thugs that had perceived him as a threat to their criminal sex-trafficking trade? The same gang that had attacked him so violently in Aradi Street some weeks before? This last thought horrified him more than he could have imagined. He shuddered to himself, but decided that now was not the time or place to share these thoughts with Peter, however close a friend he considered him to be.

After finishing the small glass of beer which Peter had handed him, but politely declining a plate of the food that was being prepared for the customers of the soup kitchen lunch, Paolo bade farewell to Peter, thanked him for his hospitality as well as his information, and took his leave. The afternoon was wearing on, and he decided to see whether he could get on a boat back to Budapest. He walked to the ferry jetty, which seemed pretty deserted as he approached it. As chance would have it, however, a boat arrived from upriver only a few minutes later. He was told by the man at the ticket office that he was in luck, that this was the last boat back down river for the day.

Dusk was falling and the sky lit up with red clouds over the horizon. He sat on the upper deck of the boat and drank another glass of beer as he enjoyed the leisurely journey back to the centre of Budapest. He could understand why this way of seeing the city was such a popular one with tourists in the summer months. As the boat neared its mooring in the centre of the city darkness had already arrived. He could not help but be impressed with the sight of the city, as he always was after nightfall. The Parliament building was flood lit up imposingly and the other famous landmarks on both sides of the Danube, such as the Castle, the churches and the Gellert monument on Buda Hill, similarly illuminated.

As the boat docked at the Batthyany Square jetty, a violent storm erupted from nowhere. The clouds opened and water fell out of the sky not so much as rain, but as heavy torrents of water falling in vertical sheets. Waiting patiently with the other passengers to alight, Paolo supposed that this was what standing under Niagara Falls must be like. The rain was accompanied by vicious streaks of lightning, lighting up the evening sky in every direction and firing in spears towards the ground every few seconds, like a wartime aerial blitz. The weight of the rain which was hitting the decks was enough to cause the boat to rock wildly from side to side and the crew struggled to secure the mooring ropes as the boat pulled up beside the jetty.

Paolo leapt off the boat and ran along the gangway and on to the riverbank, dashing with the handful of other passengers towards the safety and dryness of the nearby Metro entrance. Flashing back into his mind came the memory of a horrible tragedy which had occurred in this very place on St Stephen's

Day a few years before. The large crowds who had been lined up along this part of the riverbank watching the impressive firework display at midnight had panicked and stampeded on the occasion of another such flash storm. There had been horrible loss of life and serious injury as people were crushed in the stampede to get away from the storm. On this occasion, he was relieved to find, the evacuation of the passengers from the boat to the Metro underground entrance was somewhat more ordered, aided in part by the fact that there were many fewer people involved. Having entered the entrance to the Metro station himself Paolo stood looking out onto the scene. He was literally soaked to the skin, every piece of his clothing and his whole body completely dripping with water from this biblical downpour.

Paolo stood at the entrance of the underground station waiting for the water to pour off him. As he did so, he caught sight of a man who was standing at the corner of the Metro entrance looking his way. In the blink of his eye, Paolo recognised the man as the Tovabb party member who had challenged them during their visit to Pecs. The man hesitated, realised Paolo had seen him, and turned and disappeared into the wet black night.

Chapter 25
Following his father's death
August 2014

Jeff sat absolutely still. A cold wind from the north blew straight down onto the north facing slope of the South Downs on which he was sitting. He zipped his anorak up to his neck, secured the buttons over the zip, and wrapped the blanket he had brought with him tightly around himself as well. It was only two days since he had left home, but it could have been two years. He had only just got off the overnight train to Glasgow when he received the news of his father's death on his mobile phone, standing there on the station platform. He had said goodbye to the friends he was travelling with, walked over the passenger bridge to the opposite platform and got back on to the next train leaving for London Euston, heading back home.

The death of his father was something which he just had not been able to accept. He'd had to get away. He was intelligent enough to realise that this was not the first time a man had committed such an act of self-destruction, and would not be the last. But he knew that he needed space to be able to cope with the fact of this tragedy having happened in his life.

The space Jeff needed was not only physical. He needed time to come to terms with the event in his own mind, to think about the reasons why it had occurred and the implications for himself and those around him. He couldn't do this at home with his mother and all the various visitors present. By the time he had arrived back late on the Sunday evening, the house seemed to be full of all sorts of people coming and going. He did not wish to be unsupportive to his mother, who after all was the person most affected by this horror. It was clear to him, however, that she was in the sort of trance-like early stages of grief that would not be very much affected by his presence or otherwise. He quickly realised that he could not cope with this immense catastrophe himself without having the time and space to do so. And without being able to adjust to the situation himself, it was very unlikely that he would be in any state, physically or mentally, to be able to give his mother any helpful practical or psychological support at that moment.

Added to all this, with his elder brother and sister living some way away from the family home, and not likely to be on the scene for a day or two at the earliest, he was the one who had found himself having to manage the situation. This meant he was constantly being required to answer the telephone, respond to the doorbell and deal with all callers. These had included the neighbours, ones who he knew lived nearby and others he could not remember ever having set eyes on before.

Then there were all the people wanting to talk to him in some sort of professional capacity, such as policemen and newspaper reporters. Not wholly unexpectedly, many of the latter had not taken "no" for an answer and had re-appeared at the doors – and windows with flash bulbs – at frustratingly regular intervals, even after he had already asked them to go away and leave them in peace.

Last but not least were the friends who had heard the news

and had come to express their sympathy. Some of these were shocked and supportive, but others inexplicably less so. After a few hours of this, he had handed it all over to Sue, the cleaning lady, and left.

The sun was setting slowly and from his vantage point high up on Firle Beacon he could see the pink light spreading across the English Channel towards France. This was one of the highest points on the South Downs in East Sussex. Hardly a mountain, in the sense familiar to his European friends, but nevertheless high enough to impose itself over the terrain below and aloof enough to be separated from what went on down there. His friend Roger had told him Firle Beacon was a "Marilyn". When he looked this up, he found out that a Marilyn is a mountain or hill in the UK of at least one hundred and fifty metres in height, and that the name had been coined as a punning contrast to the "Munro", a Scottish mountain with a height of more than nine hundred metres. The simile was that of Marilyn Monroe, for obvious reasons. The chalk hills of the South Downs on which Jeff had escaped to certainly did have a voluptuous quality, smooth and rolling, like female breasts arising from the chest wall of the land below them.

As the sun set, the temperature started to fall markedly. He had slept last night on the grassy side of a dew pond, in the armpit of the Downs around it. The large saucer area which had been hewn into the chalk was one of many, quarried centuries before by sheep farmers in order to collect the early morning dew as a source of irrigation and drinking water for their sheep. Surrounded as he was by gorse bushes and a barrier of trees, all leaning in the same direction away from the prevailing winds which had sculptured them into this pose over decades, he had felt warm and protected. He was not against the idea of bunking down in the same way for another night, but felt he was now ready to move down to one of the villages like Alfriston or Alciston and find a pub where he could get some hot soup and bread, a beer and a bed for the night. He still wasn't especially looking for human contact, but felt he could make this move anonymously and still keep his grief to himself.

Jeff pulled himself to his feet, swung his rucksack over his shoulder, and started to walk back down the hill he had climbed earlier the day before. The light was starting to fade and he was aware of the need to watch his step to avoid an ankle strain or worse, if he were to jar his leg down hard onto a piece of flint in the bottom of a rabbit hole or a rut which had been made in the chalk hill by a farm vehicle. After a while he joined the main path which led up to the beacon and walked down it from there to the small road which led to it. At the end of this road he came to the main A27, the relatively narrow South Coast trunk road along which cars were nevertheless flashing by at high speed with their headlights already on in the dusk. He waited until there was a gap in the traffic in both directions before making a dash for the grass verge on the other side of the road once it was safe to do so. Walking along the grass for another few hundred metres, he found the side road to Alciston and crossed over onto it. Here he could walk again with no fear of traffic, even though there was no dedicated pavement.

Jeff was the younger son of Michael and Marion Butler. He had left home to go to the University in Canterbury, where he had obtained a modest degree in town planning. Now twenty-four years old and well in to the "credit crunch", he had not been able to get any sort of reasonable job or to earn enough to keep himself. He had therefore found himself back again living with his parents in Ealing. Understanding though they were about his situation, he could not help but feel humiliated about having to depend on them again, not to mention the social isolation which this put him in. Not being able to afford a car, although he had passed his driving test and had a full licence, this left him dependent on a lift from one of his parents whenever he needed to travel anywhere by road. He was not even able to afford the cost of public transport into London these days, especially on the Underground.

It was true that he was not the only one of his friends and former student acquaintances to find themselves in the same position. Quite a lot of his year remained unemployed or were working in part-time low paid jobs with no income guarantee, not to mention the fact that they were without any sort of long-term career prospects. Many of those he knew who did have employment were working on what had become known as a "zero hours" contract basis. In other words, they had no stability of tenure; had no guarantee of hours available to them from one week to the next; and at any time could be out of work temporarily or permanently with no reason given. Furthermore, there was no question of these tenuous jobs offering employment benefits such as the chance of holiday pay, sick pay or the possibility of contributing to a pension scheme.

All of this applied to his friend Jon who had been teaching

English to foreign students at a language school in Bournemouth. He had emailed Jeff only the week before, desperate about the fact that he had received a message on the Friday evening that he would not be required the next week because the German group who had been expected to arrive on Monday had cancelled at short notice. No work meant no pay, and he had no idea how he was going to be able to finance his recently-acquired mortgage, let alone support his wife and new baby, in this unpredictable situation. And Jon knew that the German students had been booked for a fortnight.

He reached the end of the lane that led down to the village of Alciston. Jeff saw The Royal Oak pub in front of him and caught the smell of burning apple wood. He pushed open the main oak door to the saloon and entered to see the blazing fire in the large open fireplace where the smell was coming from in front of him. The girl at the bar greeted him with a broad welcoming smile and large blue eyes.

'What can I get you?'

'Oh, pint of Harvey's please,' Jeff replied.

He sat on a stool at the bar sipping his beer, looking around the place. In the middle of the mantelpiece above the fire there was a simple jam jar of water in which had been placed a small bouquet of cowslips, the fragile flowers he had seen all around him on the Downs where he had been lying the night before. Their yellow bells reflected the light there was in the room. It came to him that for the first time since his father's death he had had his mind taken off the horror of the recent event. For the first time he'd thought about the possibility that his own life would go on, and that he did have a future for himself.

Chapter 26

Jeff strolled into the bar in Soho. Following the death of his father and his flight from home he had not felt able to go back to his mother's house in Ealing. He had of course attended his father's funeral, where he'd done his best to be supportive to his mother and civil to his brother and sister. But, apart from that, he'd wanted nothing more to do with the whole business of his father's death, and remained very bitter about the fact that his father had betrayed them all by his act of suicide. He still had a mobile phone, which he rarely used because of the cost and was not answering any calls from his brother and sister. He had recently, however, opened a text message from his older brother Martin, who said that he would like to meet up with him and their sister Sophie to tell them what had happened at the inquest. Jeff's first inclination was to delete that unanswered as well, but after a couple of days his curiosity got the better of him.

He texted Martin back: 'OK. Where and when?'

Against his better judgement, when he received instructions from his older brother, he reluctantly caught a train up from Lewes to London to meet up with his brother and sister that evening.

Martin was already waiting in the bar, looking irritated, when Jeff got there. Jeff was thirty minutes late already and there was no sign of Sophie.

'Hi,' was all Jeff said as he sat down.

Martin could only just bring himself to grunt in reply. He had been sitting there going over the events of his father's death as he waited. As the oldest of the Butler children, he had always believed he should be the one to take the lead and be responsible. This was no less the case than now, following the unexpected and tragic death of their father. So he saw it as his duty to help them all cope. He did not have the luxury of imploding like his younger brother Jeff, or exploding like his emotional sister Sophie, who was an actor. He could not imagine what had led to his father taking his own life. His dad had always been such a balanced and seemingly well-organised man, in his work as well as in his private and family life, as far as Martin was concerned. The fact that his father had decided to end his own life in such an unexpected and violent way was completely outside Martin's comprehension, and as far removed from his own rather parochial but well-ordered way of life as an accountant as he could ever contemplate.

If Michael had taken his own life, Martin asked himself, was it possible that his father had made some serious professional mistake or found himself in the sort of severe financial difficulty, perhaps with the tax man, which was likely to affect not only himself but also Marion for the rest of their lives together? He was not unfamiliar with this scenario, which he came across quite frequently in his dealings with his clients. Indeed, in these recent recessionary times, it was a situation which he was coming across very much more frequently. Numbers of clients had come to see him with imminently threatened financial ruin, and more than one of these had expressed to Martin the fact that the loss of their life savings, house, business or whatever made them feel they had nothing left to live for. Martin was not aware that any of them had actually taken steps to end their own lives, however.

Alternatively, was it perhaps, even remotely, possible that Michael had found someone else? Was it conceivable that his father had become involved in a relationship whilst working in Budapest that he was unable to face Marion with, but which he knew she would inevitably learn about in due course? Martin had asked himself all these questions as he sat comforting his mother after he had arrived at his parents' house, having travelled straight down from Newcastle on hearing the news. And he had been going over them as he sat in the bar waiting for his brother and sister to arrive. But he could still not imagine that either of these scenarios was at all likely. Indeed, he found it hard to believe that his father had actually taken his own life.

The two brothers sat there in silence, waiting for their sister to arrive, if she was going to. Martin had not even offered to buy Jeff a drink and Jeff had no money to buy one for himself and Martin, even if he had felt like doing so.

'Martin, Jeff, how are you darlings?' Sophie crashed through the door and descended on them, kissing each of them on both cheeks, in her theatrical way.

Jeff grimaced and Martin smiled wanly, somewhat embarrassed by this public show of affection. He found it difficult to be sure whether this was how Sophie behaved all the time these days, or just something she put on for their benefit.

'Sorry I'm late,' Sophie said, plonking herself down on

the bench next to Martin, but not sounding much as if she was.

Her arrival was at least the impetus for Martin get up and buy them all a round of drinks.

'So, what have you been up to, Sophie?' he asked his sister as he arrived back at the table with the glasses, unable to stop himself feeling irritated and trying to calm himself down with small talk.

Sophie told them that she had been appearing at the Nottingham Playhouse, in a play called "The Savage God", by Al Alvarez. It was a stage production based on his book by the same name, which had been sub-titled "A Study of Suicide", which the author had subsequently adapted for the theatre. As fate would have it, and by an extraordinarily bizarre coincidence, Sophie had found herself playing the role of the wife of the leading man who ended up taking his own life in a contemporary scene which concluded the historical cycle of suicide represented in the play. She had found all this extremely difficult to deal with on a personal level, she told her brothers, causing as it did the recent memories of the death of her own father to flood back to her on a daily basis. During all this Jeff sat looking bored and at the ceiling. He had said precisely nothing since he had arrived.

Martin told Sophie and Jeff about the hearing, and what an ordeal it had been for both his mother and himself. Sophie wanted to know in detail all the events which had led up to their father's death and about the outcome of the inquest. Martin answered all of these questions as best he could.

'But what were the *reasons* which led Dad to take his own

life?' Sophie said.

'I have really no idea. I'm as much in the dark as you are as to why Dad was sent home from Hungary and what could have led to his death,' Martin replied, still feeling a little irritated. He took a large swig of beer, again to do his best to calm down. 'I have to say, Soph – I am not completely convinced that Dad actually *did* take his own life,' Martin said, after he had composed himself. 'In fact I felt quite cross at the end of the inquest by the verdict of suicide that the coroner had arrived at, with not much factual evidence for it, as far as I was concerned. But I did not want to say as much in open court – it would have crucified Mum – and there is nothing more that can be done now. I still can't believe it.'

Jeff looked at his brother incredulously: he had absolutely no doubt about the fact that their dad had killed himself and still felt in a rage with him for having been so selfish for what he had done.

'Don't be ridiculous,' Sophie said. 'Of course he killed himself! You're not suggesting he was murdered by person or persons unknown?'

This was not going as Martin had intended.

'How did you take the news?' Martin asked his sister after an awkward pause, trying to bring things back to a more amicable level.

'Well, naturally, I was very upset,' she replied. 'Hysterical, in fact. If it hadn't been for Guy, I don't know how I would have survived. And I have to say, I was not really surprised. Mum told me in confidence a number of times over the years how worried she had been about Dad. Not only about the stress of his job, and about their enforced separations while he was working abroad, but also that he'd had periods in his life when he had been depressed and sometimes even paranoid.'

'I didn't know that!' Martin interjected.

'Yes,' Sophie went on, 'Mum told me that she had spoken more than once to the GP, who was sympathetic but said he could do nothing to help unless Dad took himself to the surgery. She had tried to persuade Dad to go and discuss his episodes of depression with the GP on a number of occasions when he was home in England, but he always refused to go, saying "it'll blow over".'

'I find that difficult to believe!' Martin said, 'I always thought of Dad as a happy and well-adjusted sort of bloke.'

'That just goes to show how much you knew about him, after all these years!' Sophie replied, rather unkindly. 'But I don't blame Dad for what he did, though. He obviously had a longstanding mental condition which led him to this. If you must know, I have felt a little proud of Dad for actually having had the courage to end his own life if that was the only way out of his depression and grief that he could see.'

Martin sat staring astounded at his sister. How could she think such a thing? All this time Jeff had still said precisely nothing, as the other two continued to bicker away as if he was not there.

Jeff sloped out of the bar, leaving Martin and Sophie to it, and made tracks to Victoria station to catch a late train back to Sussex. He had no doubts about the fact that his father had taken his own life, it was ridiculous of Martin to try and pretend this wasn't how it had happened, as far as he was concerned. He couldn't understand why Martin found it difficult to believe that his father had died by his own hand, and was also disbelieving about what Sophie had told them about their father's depression. When Jeff thought about it himself, this fitted with a number of occasions in the past he could remember when his father had been inexplicably depressed and morose. He had at least learnt during the meeting that Sophie was as convinced as he was that their dad had taken his own life during a further bout of depression. That sadly this had been the case and that there was nothing any of them could have done to prevent it. Even if she had reached the absurd conclusion that this was something to be proud of him for doing.

Chapter 27

Jeff was standing behind the bar pulling pints. This Saturday evening was particularly busy and he was sweating all over his forehead, rushing backwards and forwards from one end of the bar to the other, taking orders and serving customers non-stop all evening. It was the week before Christmas and the atmosphere was good natured, relaxed and with a certain degree of holiday celebration mood affecting customers and staff alike. Mike the pub manager was walking round the bar and candle-lit tables with a huge tray of hot sausage rolls and mince pies, offering a complimentary one or two to all the customers, locals and visitors alike, who were gracing the pub that evening.

Jeff was content with where he was. On that Monday evening in August when he had walked into the pub after a night sleeping out on the Downs above it, he could have had no idea that this would be the outcome. Following the horrific events of his father's death, he had seen the place and its homely open fire as a refuge from the personal tragedy that had gone before. That first evening he had sat there and drunk a number of pints of beer, chatting in a friendly way to Melanie the girl behind the bar in a non-committal way. As closing time drew near he knew he did not want to move on, but was not sure what he should do. Finally, he had overcome his shyness and asked Melanie whether they had a room he might rent for the night. As it turned out, she was the pub manager's daughter. She had clearly taken a liking to him, and was able to find a spare room for him to sleep in for the night.

The next morning – it was actually about eleven a.m. when he started to surface – there had been a knock on the door and Melanie came in with a large tray containing the Royal Oak's full English breakfast of fried egg, two sausages, bacon and baked beans as well as toast and marmalade and a pot of hot coffee.

Jeff sat ravenously eating the breakfast on the little balcony of the room with a lovely view over the Downs. Sunshine was streaming directly onto the balcony and Melanie sat with him sharing his coffee. They exchanged their life stories, although Jeff could not bring himself at that stage to talk about the violent death of his father which had only just occurred. They realised that they were both recently out of university with no careers, let alone a job in Jeff's case, to go to. Melanie told Jeff that she was aware how lucky she was to have been able to fall back into work in her father's pub, which gave her somewhere to live and a living wage at least. She started to tell Jeff about how her family had bought the pub ten years before and the hard work that they had all put in to making it a going concern.

There was a pause in their conversation. Jeff took his chance and looked at her directly. 'I don't suppose there's any chance of a job for me here, too?'

Melanie smiled at him in return, hardly able to suppress her excitement. 'As it happens, we will have a space. The French girl who has been working here all summer told Dad last night that she is going back to visit her family in France for Christmas and hasn't decided what she wants to do after that. I am sure he would be happy to take you on, especially since we were going to be one down from next week!'

Chapter 28

Jeff could not have been happier. He had landed on his feet. He could not believe that it was only a few months since the suicide of his father. He didn't belief in fate, but he began to believe that, if it existed, it had now dealt him a kinder hand, one on which he determined to maximise as time went by. It was true he had to work hard forty hours a week, including most evenings and weekends, but he didn't mind this. He was almost always on the same shifts as Melanie, which also meant that they were off work at the same times together. The casual attraction of that first evening he had met her turned quickly into a close friendship and then into something more intense. On their days off, they would walk together over the Downs above Jevington and Alfriston. It may have been the middle of January by then, but on the crisp sunny days that they were having, the Downs were empty and the views were sublime. Jeff was in love, and he had the certain feeling that Melanie was too.

Christmas passed and the New Year arrived. As an honorary member of the family, Jeff was working hard but was also appreciated. Every Friday night Mike, Melanie's father, would press a wages envelope into his hand containing about £300 in cash. Jeff felt almost embarrassed to accept this, knowing that he was also receiving full board and lodging, a place to live and as much food and drink as he could manage. All this, in addition to the delights of the landlord's only daughter! It made him more determined than ever to earn his keep, which meant he never counted the hours or had a problem with working over shift; and he regularly worked extra hours if the job required. And Mike knew this.

Jeff had a small room in the roof of the pub, which was situated above the first-floor accommodation that was occupied by Melanie and her parents. But Melanie would come up to be with him nearly every night so that, by January, they were practically living in the same small attic room together. He assumed that Melanie's father and mother knew what was going on, but not once did they make any reference to the relationship between himself and their daughter. Jeff was aware, however, that they had taken to treating him like a son rather than as one of their employees. He had no doubt that this was directed by Melanie herself, who had fallen in love with him, and he with her. He could not believe his luck.

The winter gave way to an unusually warm spring. Jeff and Melanie would walk over the Downs above the pub, hand in hand together, striking out across parts of the South Downs Way above Jevington and Alfriston and sometimes into Friston Forest. Jeff fell in love with this part of Sussex for the first time and forever. He also fell increasingly in love with Melanie. During the winter, they had enjoyed a mutually satisfying love life in the attic of the Royal Oak pub, but now they were experiencing an extension of this in the outside. Jeff particularly had developed an increasing urge to make love to Melanie in the open air. There was something particularly satisfying about having sex in the open which excited him more than usual. The cool breeze stroking his naked bum and balls from behind was one factor. The added excitement about the risk they were taking and the possibility of being interrupted was definitely another. He had come to realise that their usual sexual pleasure was increased tenfold by the knowledge that they might be interrupted in the act.

One Sunday afternoon near Easter, Jeff and Melanie were walking up towards Firle Beacon, enjoying the walk in the warm still spring air. Jeff was harbouring ideas about another outdoor lovemaking session. Although he had not been direct enough to suggest his wishes to Melanie as they left the main path, he secretly hoped that she was feeling in the same mood. She was looking particularly pretty that day, with the smell of her freshly washed long blonde hair competing in his nostrils with the grassy smells of the Downs. She was wearing one of his favourite yellow summer cotton dresses with its floral pattern, which he particularly liked. He also knew that, underneath the dress, she would not be wearing knickers, an unspoken agreement which existed between them when they walked out over the Downs together. He particularly fancied Melanie more than ever when he knew she was not wearing knickers under her dress, and she knew that he fancied her in this way and was only too happy to oblige.

They reached a hollow in the Downs on the north face of Firle Beacon, not unlike the one that Jeff had slept in on the night after his father's death. They were surrounded by gorse bushes and a number of spiky trees which were leaning in the direction the wind had taken them over the years. Jeff spread out his coat, sat down on it, and held out his hand to Melanie. They lay together in each other's arms in the warm spring sunshine and in a very few minutes were kissing passionately. As Melanie held Jeff tight with her right arm around his neck, she reached her left hand down and lifted her dress above her waist. Then, with the same hand, she unzipped Jeff's jeans, pulled them down over his thighs and reached her hand down to free his erect penis from his underpants. Jeff was on top of her, breathing fast, and using the mud mound behind him to anchor his feet while thrusting himself up inside her as she lay receiving him on the slope of the natural hollow.

Melanie held Jeff with both arms tightly around him, her left arm straying down to hold his thrusting penis as they enjoyed each other together as they had learnt to do regularly now. They were both about to come, when the sound of a person's voice nearby made them stop in mid stroke. The next thing Jeff was aware of was of an animal licking his anus. He looked behind and saw a black and white border collie licking him enthusiastically. With a sense of delighted amusement and intense heightened stimulation, he felt himself expand and then explode inside Melanie in a way he had not experience before. For her part, she gasped, shuddered deeply and hugged and kissed him like an equally grateful dog as she came herself. They collapsed in laughter together, looking around to see what had happened. The dog had disappeared as quickly as it had appeared and its owner was nowhere to be seen. Suddenly they heard a voice calling its name:

'Freddie! Freddie! Come here, boy!'

The sound of the dog and its owner receded down the hill. They had no idea whether the woman had seen them locked *in flagrante,* and they did not care. They again collapsed in laughter in each other's arms, tears rolling down their cheeks in a happy and satisfied state of contentment that they could not have achieved if they had ordered it.

Chapter 29

Now that Jeff was happy again in his new life with a job and a girlfriend, he started to think about his mother. One Sunday morning he decided to phone her.

'Hi Mum – it's me, Jeff. I thought I should give you a ring to find out how you are.'

There was a pause at the other end of the line. Marion was completely taken aback. Apart from being aware of his presence at the funeral, she had heard nothing else from her younger son since he had fled the scene after Michael's death and had continued to feel very upset that he had not even taken the trouble to contact her in any way. She had not expected to receive this call now, out of the blue. Indeed, she had wondered from time to time whether she would ever hear from her younger son again.

'Jeff!' she said, breaking down in floods of tears. She could not help herself. 'What's been happening to you?'

Jeff was embarrassed. He knew he should have kept in contact, phoned his mother a lot earlier. 'Don't cry Mum – *please* don't cry! I'm sorry I've not been in contact for a long time. I didn't mean to ignore you. It's just that – I was having difficulty coping with Dad's death myself.'

Jeff went on to tell his mother how much things had improved for him. He told her about his job and his girlfriend. He could not hide how happy he was with his life now, and told his mother so.

'But how have you been since Dad died?' he said, feeling guilty about his new-found happiness in the face of his crying mother.

'Not very good Jeff, as you can imagine,' Marion replied, still tearful at the other end of the line.

'Sorry to hear that, Mum,' Jeff said. 'I hope things get better soon.' It was all he could say. He knew it sounded hollow.

'I'll be alright,' Marion said, without much conviction in her voice.

'I'm thinking of you, Mum,' Jeff said. 'I'll ring you again next Sunday, if that's all right?'

After she had replaced the receiver, Marion sat staring at her hands in her lap. She used the handkerchief she was holding in one hand to dry her tears from time to time. She *had* felt cross about the fact that Jeff had completely deserted her, but now she was pleased that he had been in touch at last, and to hear that he at least was happy again. Following Michael's funeral, she had found herself alone sooner than she had expected. She had received many well-meaning words of support from family and friends alike. But somehow practical support from everywhere seemed to dissipate quicker than she had anticipated, although the other members of her family would have protested that this was not their intention if the subject had been raised with them. Martin had gone back to Newcastle the next day to look after his family and his business. Sophie had been offered a part in repertory at the Nottingham Playhouse, following an audition she'd had the week before her father's death. She had been reticent to leave her Mum on her own so early after her father's death. But Marion had insisted she should go for it anyway. As for Jeff, no one had seemed to know where he had taken himself off to. With no further door-answering and other duties still being required, Sue asked Marion if she could revert to her usual two mornings a week cleaning visits, which Marion of course readily agreed to.

She did miss Michael. At first she had a continuous, crushing loneliness which was more or less constant, which she could not rid herself of. This loneliness was present all her waking days and also came flooding back to her during the night-time hours. Some nights she would lie awake thinking of Michael for a long time, with tears which she was unable to quench running down her cheeks. Eventually, she would drift off to sleep in the early dawn, which would be the only way in which the tears would dry physically for a while.

The loneliness which Marion had felt after the death of Michael was not surprisingly mixed with a wide range of other confused emotions. These included grief, incredulity and guilt. She could not understand why this had happened. What had led Michael to take his own life and what, if anything, could or should she have done to have predicted this tragedy and perhaps even to have taken steps to prevent it? As much as she lay awake at night going through their life together, especially the weeks and months leading up to his death, she really was unable to put her finger on a single word or event which she could honestly tell herself had predicted this outcome. But none of this stopped her carrying a heavy weight of guilt that she must have had a major role in Michael's death, or at least in her inability to prevent it. This was in spite of the fact that she knew, logically, that this was not the case. If only he had left her a note or some kind of message to say goodbye and perhaps shed some light on his intended action.

Of course Marion knew that Michael had been under a lot of pressure at work recently. That was why his boss Conrad had kindly suggested that he come back to work at home for a few weeks, as a way of helping him catch up with his mountain of paperwork without the usual day-to-day distractions. As far as she was aware, Michael appeared to have been working hard and productively to use this catch-up time as planned, and he seemed to have been feeling positively about what he was achieving. But neither Conrad nor any of Michael's work colleagues had given her any precise information, either at the funeral or before or after it, as to what had been the specific nature of the pressure which Michael had been under at work recently. They had all seemed to be as bemused and at a loss to explain Michael's death as she was herself.

From then on Jeff made a point of telephoning his mother once a week on a Sunday morning. After a number of weeks phoning to ask the question "how are you now, Mum?" he was pleased to hear the reply:

'Actually, Jeff, I'm feeling a little bit better, thank you.' Marion went on to tell Jeff that she had received an invitation to visit an old friend of theirs, Henry Hampson, who lived in a large house in Normandy.

'That's great,' Jeff could not hide his relief. 'Hope you have a good time.'

Chapter 30

It was true that, following the death of Michael and as the weeks went by and turned in to months, loneliness and guilt had given way in Marion to a more gentle emptiness and her eventual acceptance of the situation. A day came when she realised that she had at last accepted the fact of Michael's death, and had ceased to grieve. A day also came when, as a bit of a shock, she realised that she was no longer just lonely. She was bored. She did not have enough to do. It was exactly at this time that she had received a letter of sympathy from their mutual friend Henry Hampson in France. He expressed his condolences to Marion, said how sorry he was to hear of Michael's death – he had read his obituary in the *Times* – and enquired how she was? Almost as a postscript, he had invited her to visit him in his large house in Normandy and said that she hoped he would agree.

Henry had been a very successful banker and was very rich. A "wanker banker", as Michael had labelled him in his amusing but rather crude and direct way. He had already managed to get through three wives. He was married to his first wife Valerie when Marion first met Henry in their early twenties. Marion and Valerie had been good friends since schooldays. The marriage had ended in divorce, the details of which Marion had not liked to enquire from Valerie. His second wife, Celia, was a very attractive divorced French woman, about ten years younger than Henry, who was in his early fifties by this time. He had only been married to Celia for a few years, when she was diagnosed with advanced breast cancer. She was dead within eighteen months. Henry was evidently a man who could not live without a woman for any length of time, and had very soon moved in with and then married Stephanie. Henry and his third wife Stephanie had visited the Butlers in their house in Ealing from time to time, usually when it happened to be rather conveniently followed the next day by a flight they were taking out of Heathrow. Even though she found Stephanie excruciating, Marion still had quite a soft spot for Henry. Indeed, her affection for Henry was long-standing. She and Henry had known each other for longer than she had been with Michael.

Marion was out of her period of severe post-bereavement depression by the time she received Henry's invitation to visit him in Normandy. She was sleeping well again and waking up feeling refreshed and emotionally positive. The "black dog" had lifted from her. She picked up her pen and composed a letter to Henry on her headed note paper.

'Dear Henry,' she wrote. 'It was so nice to hear from you. Thank you very much for your kind words of condolence. I still miss Michael so much, but I am pleased to report that I am feeling much better now.' Marion paused, and looked up from her desk at the garden which she could see from Michael's study window, before having the courage to go on. 'Yes, Henry, I would very much like to visit you in France. I thought I might get a train down to Portsmouth and come over on Brittany Ferries to Caen-Ouistreham as a foot passenger. If I did, would it be possible for you to drive to pick me up at the port? Let me know if this would be OK by you, and when would be most convenient. With Very Best Wishes. Love, Marion.'

She licked the envelope and sealed it up, feeling a slight frisson of excitement but also satisfaction that she'd had the courage to take the step to write this letter and to contemplate a little adventure such as this. She almost danced out of the house to the post box on the corner of her road, and posted the letter off directly.

The next time Jeff phoned his mother was the Sunday after her return from her trip to visit Henry Hampson in Normandy.

'I had a lovely time, Jeff,' she said, and he could hear that she meant it.

Marion talked on the phone at length, telling Jeff about how welcome she had been made – in spite of the fact that it turned out that Henry had just divorced his third wife Stephanie and was living alone in his huge chateau. She had been wined and dined, she told Jeff, and been to the races at Deauville where she had enjoyed meeting all Michael's horse racing friends. The trip had apparently gone so well that she had stayed on for a week longer than planned.

'Shit,' Jeff said to Melanie after he had put the phone down to his mother. 'Sounds like things are getting serious.'

Chapter 31

It was the middle of February, nearly six months after Michael's death. Martin's wife Jan had taken their two children Adam and Rachel to visit her parents in Scotland for a week over half term. Martin had discussed with Jan the fact that somebody had to go over to Budapest and wind up Michael's affairs there, and that this probably should be himself. Jan had been happy for her husband to take a few days annual leave while she was up in Scotland with the kids, in which time he could fly off to Budapest, close down Michael's accounts and start the process of selling off the apartment there. When Martin put this idea to Marion, she had agreed immediately, saying that she did not have the energy to contemplate doing this herself. Secretly, she knew she did not want to be reminded of her loss by having to face the contents of Michael's flat and the personal memories she would have had to come face-to-face within it. Martin booked himself an airline ticket from Newcastle to Budapest and left home on the same day that Jan and the kids left for Perth, having seen them all off on the train at Newcastle Central Station first.

Martin's flight arrived at Liszt Ferenc Airport in Budapest on time and, having only hand luggage, he was soon out of the airport doors and onto a 200E bus to the beginning of the blue Metro line at Kobanya Kispest. Martin got off the Metro at the main Nyugati Station and walked the short distance to

Michael's flat. He let himself in with one of the two sets of keys Marion had given him, and threw his bag and clothes on the floor, jumping into the shower to get rid of the "travel dirt", as he called it. Luckily there seemed to be plenty of hot water coming through the faucet. He dried himself off from the shower, sat by the telephone wrapped in a clean bath towel and gave Jan a quick phone to let her know he had arrived safely. Her mobile phone line kept breaking up, but she was apparently still on the platform at Waverley Station in Edinburgh, waiting with the kids for a connecting train to Perth. He found some olive bread in the freezer, defrosted it in the microwave and ate the whole loaf hungrily with a tin of pickled fish. He did not mind admitting to himself that he was exhausted, a feeling he usually had when first coming on holiday after a heavy few weeks of work.

Martin woke at a reasonable time the next morning and made himself coffee. Having been shaved, washed and dressed, he started straight away on the task of clearing up his deceased father's apartment. He had to admit that he had not been looking forward to this chore particularly, not because of the work involved – which he was quite up to – but because of the possibility that he might come across letters, pictures and other items of his dead father's life which he might find emotionally distressing. He had prepared himself for this possibility, however, by reminding himself that it was much better that he took on this task rather than leave it to his mother Marion, which was precisely why he had volunteered to undertake the visit. As it turned out, as the day wore on, there was not much to find in the flat which was unexpected or exceedingly emotionally upsetting. He looked through the large library of Michael's books, noting with interest the detailed notes which his father had made in pencil in the margin. Michael's desk contained piles of letters, business matters and bills which took a good deal of time for him to trawl through, but which was no more than he supposed someone might be examining on his behalf one day after he had departed. The unpaid utility and other bills he came across he put aside to be dealt with the next day. He also found a copy of one of his father's Hungarian bank statements which he knew would be helpful in sorting out Michael's financial matters.

Martin walked to the branch of the OTP Bank shown on the heading of his father's bank statement, number six Andrassy Avenue, later the next morning. He stood looking at a ticket machine at the entrance to the banking hall. He did not speak or read Hungarian, so just had to guess which of the buttons to press, hoping that he was in the right queue for account enquiries – rather than for mortgage applications or business banking, or whatever. Having pressed an arbitrary button, he tore off one of the triangular tickets which came out of the machine, much like the delicatessen counter in Sainsbury's which he was familiar with, and sat down to wait his turn. When his number came up in red on the LED screen, he went to the appropriate desk.

To Martin's relief, it turned out that the young man behind the desk spoke quite good English.

'My name is Martin Butler,' Martin said to the man, handing him a page of his father's bank statement. 'I am acting on behalf of my late father Michael Butler, who died in August last year. I am his trustee and have the probate

147

papers here. Here are my identity documents.' He handed the bank official his passport, UK driving licence and one or two other bits of paper including his father's death certificate which he thought would be relevant, passing them through the two-inch gap under the glass which separated himself from the official. 'I'd like to close my father's account and withdraw the balance, either in cash or as a bank transfer in the name of my mother who has probate. I have a letter of authority from my mother to act on her behalf,' he said to the man behind the counter, passing across the letter Marion had written for this reason.

The bank official spent a long time studying the various papers which Michael had handed him. He could see the man had opened the details of his father's account on his computer and was looking backwards and forwards from the screen to the papers.

Finally he looked at Martin and said: 'One moment please, sir. I just need to talk to my supervisor.'

Some minutes passed and the man returned with his supervisor, a person about Martin's age with thick-rimmed brown spectacles.

'Can I help you, Mr Butler?' the supervisor said.

'As I have explained to your colleague,' Michael replied, starting to feel a little impatient by all this bureaucracy, which he had heard was a common experience here in Hungary, 'I am here to wind up my dead father's affairs and just need to close his account on behalf of my mother.'

The supervisor looked straight at him. 'You cannot,' he said. 'The account is still in use.'

Martin was stunned. He looked at the bank official

incredulously. 'What on earth do you mean "the account is still in use"? Has someone been accessing my father's account fraudulently?'

The man was stone-faced and terse in his reply. 'I'm sorry, sir. It is the bank's policy not to discuss the details of its customers' accounts with others.'

'What do you mean "with others"? I have just explained to your colleague that that my father died six months ago. I am the trustee of his estate and have financial power of attorney to enable me to conclude his affairs.'

The man remained implacable. 'I'm sorry, Sir. I am unable to help you further at present. If you have any concerns about the possibility of fraudulent wrongdoing, then I suggest you go to the police. If they believe there is any evidence to support this claim, then we will of course co-operate fully with them, as we always do in such matters. Good day, Mr Butler.'

The supervisor turned and walked back into the inner office, shutting the door behind him. His junior colleague stood staring awkwardly at Martin, moving his weight from side to side, from one leg to the other, in an imperceptibly swaying fashion, but said nothing. Martin glared back at him for a few seconds then, deciding that there was no point in prolonging the discussion with this junior employee, turned on his heel and marched out of the bank. He started walking back up Andrassy Avenue towards his father's apartment.

Martin let himself back into the Eötvös Street flat, put the kettle on and made himself a cup of tea. He needed time to think. Had there been some serious fraud going on, either with or without the bank's knowledge, or was there perhaps some more simple explanation? Perhaps there had just been an error in identifying the correct account? He had no idea what the man had meant by the statement "the account is still in use". He had assumed that this must mean that there had been some recent activity either into or, more likely, out of the account. And if this was the case, they had given him absolutely no information as to what sum or sums might be involved and on whose authority they believed this was happening. Surely, if it was just the fact that they doubted his *bona fide*, then they would have at least asked him to return at a later date with further proof of identity? He seemed to have reached a dead end.

Chapter 32

Martin sat at the kitchen table drinking his tea and realising that he had been given nothing to go on, and nowhere to go next. He decided that he wouldn't discuss this problem with Marion in Ealing immediately. There was no need to cause her anxiety unnecessarily, especially if the whole thing turned out eventually to be a silly bureaucratic mistake. He was even more sure that he was not in a mind to start talking to the Hungarian police about all this at present, unless he absolutely had to. He had not heard Michael ever pass comment on the state of organisation or trustworthiness of the Hungarian police, but he had noticed on his way in from the airport the day before, that they appeared less than professional in appearance, slouching in small groups at the corner of a street and talking and laughing together while sharing a cigarette or three. He could not imagine any police force in the UK, where smoking in uniform was prohibited as far as he was aware, being allowed to behave in this way and get away with it.

After a while, Martin got up and started to wander round the flat in the hope of hitting on some idea as to what to do next. He had already sorted and cleared out all the drawers and cupboards in his usual efficient fashion. All the furniture had been emptied and cleaned by the cleaning lady and was waiting ready to be sold on prior to the flat being put on the market. The soft furnishings like sofas and chairs were covered with sheets to keep them free of dust. He decided to have one more look through those bits of furniture that might give him a clue about all this, and therefore spent some time going through the drawers of Michael's desk again, as well as the kitchen cabinet and the bookcases. But he found no new pieces of paper or documents that would give him any help or provide information that he might have overlooked previously.

Then an idea came to him. He left the flat and locked the front door behind him. He walked down the stairs to the basement in search of the concierge's apartment. He found a door with a sign on it, which he assumed indicated that he was in the right place. He knocked tentatively on the door, which was thrown open to him almost immediately. The concierge was an old lady, rather unkempt with thinning unwashed hair and old clothes. She wore a dirty grey skirt and an equally dirty over-stretched pullover with food stains down the front of it. Martin spoke no Hungarian, and it was clear that this woman spoke no English. As an introduction, he held out his passport to her, opened at the page which showed his name and photograph, and pointed upwards in the direction of his father's apartment. She took the passport and peered at it intently as she looked through all the pages, one by one. Having completed this detailed examination, she looked up and gave Martin a toothy grin, revealing the fact that she had a number of front teeth missing. The rest that were on view were stained brown and in poor condition.

'Igen, Igen,' she said, raising her right index finger and then darted back inside her flat. She reappeared holding a bundle of mail, held together by an old red rubber band.

'Köszönöm szépen' Michael said, taking the bundle from the woman. Those were a few of the only Hungarian words which he knew and he had learnt that they meant "thank you very much".

Martin walked back upstairs to Michael's flat and let himself in again. He threw the bundle of letters on the kitchen table and sat down on a chair to read them, but this time not before pouring himself a large glass of wine. He used a kitchen knife to open the couple of dozen letters in the pile which the concierge had given him. He read them one by one. There were more gas bills, electricity bills and telephone bills, some of which were becoming significantly overdue and needed immediate repayment before the company was to take steps to cut off the supply. Although he did not understand the over-complicated and very bureaucratic Hungarian bills' lengthy wording, he just deduced the need for urgent payment by the increasing amount of red ink which the bills contained. He would go into the post office on Terez Korut in the morning and settle all of these.

Just as he was feeling tired and getting bored with all this, Martin came across a letter containing the most recent statement from the OTP Bank for the last month. This was addressed to Michael in his name and with the account number which he had begun to memorise after the shenanigans of earlier that morning. He looked at it in a rather bored fashion. Then, suddenly, something hit him. There had been more than one withdrawal for amounts totalling about fifty thousand forints during the last month. He had grasped enough about the exchange rate to know that these were not big amounts in terms of pounds sterling – he calculated that they totalled about £150 or thereabouts. What he could see was that these were withdrawals which had all taken place from an OTP bank in Hungary with the same bank code: 8360. Martin went straight to Michael's computer and Googled "OTP Bank". Choosing the English language option, it did not take him long to navigate to the "Find a Branch" section of the website. He looked through the lists of literally hundreds of OTP banks within Hungary and abroad which were shown, but was not able to find anywhere that directed him to each bank branch's code number. He was frustrated, but at the same time excited. He knew that he had found a link to the account which was "still in use", as the bank official at the branch in Andrassy Avenue had put it. He finished the bottle of wine and turned in early.

Next morning, Martin woke up early, shaved and showered, and dressed in one of his more presentable suits. He left the apartment about eight thirty a.m. local time and walked out to the bank. He did not re-visit the main branch at six Andrassy Avenue, where Michael had held his account, but walked down the road to the OTP branch at the Oktogon interchange which was very near the flat. He had to wait until the doors were opened at nine thirty a.m. When they did open, he walked in with a handful of other customers, took a ticket and waited his turn. When his number came up he walked casually to the teller, passed the statement under the glass as he had done the day before and asked whether the girl spoke English. When she nodded in assent he asked:

'I am Mr Butler. Could you just remind me where this withdrawal was made?' pointing to one of the 8360 branch code numbers.

'Certainly, Sir. One moment please.' The girl scrolled through her computer screen and then looked up and gave him a big smile. 'That is our branch in Keszthely.'

'Of course!' replied Martin. 'I had forgotten. How stupid of me!'

'Is there anything else I can do for you, sir?' The girl smiled at him.

'No, thank you very much,' Martin replied, giving her a big smile back. 'Sorry to have bothered you.' He walked out of the bank with a feeling of excitement, his heart beating fast.

Chapter 33

'Hi Jeff, it's me, Martin. I'm phoning from Budapest.'

Jeff was surprised to hear his older brother's voice on his mobile phoning from Hungary, not least after the rather frosty meeting in the Soho bar they'd had following the inquest into their father's death a few months before.

'I think I need your help, Jeff.'

Martin proceeded to tell Jeff that he was over in Budapest sorting out their father's affairs and that he had, quite by chance, found irregularities in their deceased father's Hungarian bank account. He had noticed that cash withdrawals were still being made from their father's account and had tracked these down to having been made in Keszthely, which was a town in the south of Hungary, on the shores of Lake Balaton. Martin sounded excited and a little breathless over the phone.

'I see,' said Jeff, after he'd had a moment to digest what he was being told. 'What do you want me to do to help?'

Martin explained to Jeff that he had decided he needed to travel down to Keszthely to investigate who was using their dad's account and face up to whoever it was in person. He told Jeff he did not feel he could hand this matter over into the hands of the Hungarian police; not immediately, in any case. He was not completely sure he had confidence in them. It could still be, he said, that there had been a simple administrative error which would explain all this. Perhaps it was just the fact that their deceased father's account had become confused with another account of a completely innocent person? A computer error or a one-digit mistake, for instance? At the same time, Martin said to Jeff, if there was any question of fraud or underhand practice, he felt uncertain about investigating the situation by himself. He felt he needed to have somebody with him whom he could trust. He would pay Jeff's air fare for him if he was able to come over this week and support him.

Jeff paused at his end of the phone before replying. This was not so much due to the story that Martin had just told him, but to the fact that, as far as Jeff was concerned, this was the first time in his life that Martin had addressed him on equal terms as an adult. Up to then, Jeff had always felt that his older brother had seen him as a kid and not worth taking seriously. Martin was considerably older than he was, and for most of the last decade Jeff had been either a schoolboy or a student, while Martin had been conducting his career as an accountant, had been married and had children.

'Of course, Martin,' Jeff replied. 'I'd be happy to do whatever I can to help. As it happens, my girlfriend Melanie is away in Reading for two weeks on a course, and I've also got two weeks off from my job in the pub. I will try to be with you as soon as I can get a ticket, hopefully by the day after tomorrow.'

'Thanks very much, Jeff. That would be great. Send me an email when you know your flight details and I will be there to meet you at the airport.'

The relief in Martin's voice was evident to Jeff.

'We can stay at Dad's old flat. It's on the market to be

sold and a lot of the furniture is already packed or covered up waiting to be disposed of. But there are a couple of spare beds and sheets and it would be better if we spent the night there before travelling down to Keszthely. Thanks very much for agreeing so readily. See you on Wednesday.'

Martin put the phone down and felt considerably relieved. Everything he had said to Jeff was possible. He was as sure as he could be, however, that the money being taken from their father's account was not being withdrawn in error. The patterns of the ATM withdrawals were such, as far as Martin was concerned, to be almost certainly due to fraudulent use of the account. It may be, he thought to himself, that somebody had got to hear the news of their father's death, had stolen one of his bank cards, and was using it in the knowledge that he was unlikely to be found out. In which case, the person involved had started by taking modest amounts out but on a regular basis, so as not to raise any suspicion of wrongdoing.

Jeff's plane arrived on time and Martin was at the airport to meet him. They jumped into a City taxi and were very soon at their father's apartment in Eötvös Street in the heart of Pest. They dumped Jeff's bag there and decided to walk the few hundred metres to a nearby restaurant which Martin had found a couple of days before. Although it was a midweek evening, the "étterem" was already pretty busy, nearly full – mainly of Hungarians relaxing after work, with not many tourists in evidence.

They sat down and ordered a litre of Soproni draught beer each. Martin was very relieved to have Jeff there to help him with what might be a difficult situation. As a consequence, he was much more relaxed and communicative than he'd been with Jeff at their last meeting in the bar in Soho after their father's inquest. They chatted easily, getting up to date with each other – Martin talking about Jan and the children and Jeff explaining enthusiastically about his new job and girlfriend.

Once they had broken the ice, Martin started to discuss in earnest the reason why he had summoned Jeff over for his help. Jeff sat listening carefully to Martin's story about how he had found a recent bank statement of their father's, which appeared to be still having withdrawals made from it after their father's death. Martin explained about the visits he had made to the OTP banks and the way in which he had tracked the fact that the activity which was still occurring on the account was originating from this town called Keszthely on the south banks of Lake Balaton. They agreed that they should travel down together to look into this, and that there was no reason why they should not get the train down from Keleti Station early the next morning. They both accepted that the fact that neither of them spoke any Hungarian might pose a barrier, but they hoped that they would not have a problem finding somebody impartial who could help to translate from English into Hungarian for them.

Chapter 34

Jeff and Martin got up early the next morning and on an impulse decided to get the bus rather than the train to Keszthely. They took the Metro to Nepliget and came off the escalator from the underground station straight into the main bus station. Martin bought them a single ticket each to Keszthely, presumably Jeff assumed because he did not have any idea how long this investigation would take them, leaving aside the fact that neither could guess what they might find and therefore when they might be returning to Budapest. At Martin's suggestion, Jeff had thrown a toothbrush and a few spare clothes into the small shoulder bag which Martin carried with him. They boarded the waiting bus, which departed forty minutes later.

The Volanbusz ride to Keszthely took about four hours. After leaving behind the sprawling city, they travelled southwest of Budapest along rather dirty main roads and through unattractive countryside. Scattered along the roadside at intervals were collections of houses, individual convenience stores, builders' yards and an occasional smallholding. After about an hour they could see the beginning of Lake Balaton and very soon the bus was travelling down the northern shore of the lake. As they progressed down it, the lake opened out into a vast expanse of water, so wide by now that they were unable to see the opposite shore on the south side of the lake. The bus stopped frequently, particularly at the larger communities it passed through, although not many passengers got on and off. There were hotels and pensions the whole way down the lake; the tourist towns were packed with souvenir shops, fishing areas, boats and jetties, with an occasional amusement arcade and a small casino. But as they drove past, they could see that the hotels and tourist areas were almost all without exception shut up for the winter. There were barely any signs of tourists at this time of the year, the bus being overtaken by a German or other foreign car only once or twice in the whole course of their journey. The bars, cafes and restaurants were all closed. Martin wondered aloud to Jeff whether, if they were required to stay overnight in Keszthely, it would be easy to find somewhere for them to stay.

The bus finally arrived in Keszthely, pulling up in the town square. Martin and Jeff got off with the remaining passengers, Keszthely being the end of the line for this service. During the journey, they had decided to waste no time and go straight to the local OTP bank. They walked from the square to the main street and very soon found the bank by waving one of Michael's bank statements in the faces of a number of passers-by who pointed them in the correct direction. They reached the bank at a minute past one p.m., after it had just that moment shut its doors for lunch. There was nothing more they could do until two thirty p.m. when the bank re-opened, so they went across the road to a small restaurant, where Martin bought them both lunch.

When the bank re-opened at two thirty p.m., Jeff and Martin were first in the queue waiting for the doors to open. They had anticipated that it would be more difficult to communicate in this small-town bank than it had been for Martin in the large OTP branch in Budapest, and so it proved to be the case. The young man behind the counter clearly did not understand a single word of English. After what seemed to Martin to be an unnecessary delay, he called for help from a young girl who was barely older than her colleague. She spoke a few phrases of rather halting English:

'Good morning, sir. How can help?'

But when Martin started to explain the purpose of their visit, the task in hand became very much more difficult. Having shown the girl one of Michael's bank statements, they presented their passports to her as a way of demonstrating that they had the same surname as that of the account holder and were therefore part of the same family. The girl seemed to understand the word "family", but beyond that they were quite unable to get over the fact that they wanted to know why money was still being withdrawn from their deceased father's account. Jeff tried his best by adopting his Christmas party miming technique, scooping backwards with his cupped right hand in an attempt to demonstrate the meaning of the word "withdrawal", but to no avail.

They were getting nowhere and just as they were on the point of giving up, a man who had been waiting patiently behind them stepped forward.

'Can I help you, sir?' he asked Martin in excellent English.

'Oh, thank you so much!' a relieved Martin welcomed him into the discussion.

Martin explained to their translator the purpose of their

visit in short sentences and in as simple English as he was able to muster. The man relayed these sentences, point by point, back over the counter. The girl was obviously now understanding what she was being told, but as she followed the account details on the screen a frown spread across her face as she bit her lower lip.

'Moment, please,' she said, looking at the two brothers.

She went into the office behind her and closed the door. Some minutes passed, and Martin was starting to have a sense of *déjà vu*. This was beginning to be a replay of the first visit he had made to the main OTP bank branch in Budapest. He hoped that they had not come all this way, only to get nowhere and end up none the wiser. He said as much to Jeff, who just shrugged in his anorak in reply.

After what seemed an age, the girl re-appeared from the back office, this time accompanied by Georg Pasztor, the bank's manager. Luckily, in spite of the long delay, their translator friend had been good enough to continue to wait, whether in politeness or nosiness, but by this time Martin did not care.

'Good afternoon, gentlemen,' the manager said through the interpreter. 'Would you care to step into my office?' He lifted up a hinged section of the counter at one end of the reception desk and guided them through.

As the interpreter hesitated before passing through, Mr Pasztor looked at Martin and raised his eyebrows in an interrogative way.

'What? Oh yes, of course,' Martin replied in English – which was translated back to the manager by the man – in the knowledge that, however personal the information they were

163

about to receive, they would not be able to do so without the continuing help of their interpreter friend.

The manager unlocked the door of his office on the number pad, let them all in, and followed them through, shutting the door behind him. Georg Pasztor walked to the other side of his substantial leather-covered director's desk and invited them to take the seats opposite him.

'I have to give you both an apology,' Pasztor started directly, via the translator. 'There has been an unfortunate error on the part of the bank.' He sat with the tips of his fingers of both hands pressed against each other, his hands resting on the desk in front of him. 'The account which you have seen belongs to a Dr Michael Bütler, who is a retired German doctor living here in Keszthely. Unfortunately, it appears that his recent monthly bank statements have been addressed to your deceased father at his previous address in Budapest. This has never happened before to my knowledge, and I will be conducting an urgent enquiry into how this has occurred. I suspect it has something to do with an error in the OTP national computer database which has married up the name and address of two account holders incorrectly. Again, I can only apologise on behalf of my bank for any inconvenience and distress which you might have been caused.'

Mr Pasztor paused after this statement, and Jeff noticed that Pasztor was looking intently from Martin's face to his own and back, as he waited to receive their reaction.

'So that explains it, then!' Martin almost blurted out his response. Jeff could see that his older brother could hardly hide his relief. 'We are pleased to hear that nothing more sinister has taken place, and that nobody has been using the account in our dead father's name fraudulently.'

'Yes, indeed,' replied the bank manager. 'When my young female colleague came in to raise the query with me, I had feared that this might be the case. But it did not take me long to locate the real account holder's name on our computer and find the mistake that has arisen with the addressing of the statements.' He paused. 'Is your mother still alive, might I ask?'

All this conversation was still taking place via their interpreter.

'Yes, she is,' replied Martin, continuing to show his relief, 'but we decided not to trouble her with this information until we had investigated it for ourselves.'

'That's understandable,' said Mr Pasztor. 'Then I take it there is really no need to upset her in the first place by mentioning this unfortunate error?'

The two brothers could not believe the level of colloquial English the interpreter they had come across by chance possessed.

'No, no. None at all,' replied Martin.

'Very good, then. I will credit your deceased father's account with the amounts that have been incorrectly debited from it and then transfer the balance of your father's account in pounds sterling into your mother's account in the UK. If you will be good enough to leave her account details with my colleague, this can be done straight away,' Pasztor summed up in a business-like way.

'Well, gentlemen, I have other business to attend to so, since you have accepted my apology on behalf of the bank with such good grace, and if there are no other questions, I shall bid you good day.' Georg Pasztor paused as he rose to shake their hands: 'I do appreciate that you have both been put to some considerable inconvenience and expense in order to make this journey. If you would care to drop me a line with a list of your airfares and other travel expenses, the bank will of course not hesitate to reimburse you.' He handed Martin and Jeff a claim form and one of his address cards each.

'Thank you very much, Mr Pasztor,' Martin said, getting up to shake the bank manager's hand.

Jeff could almost see the travel expenses form already being filled out behind Martin's eyes, in his efficient accountant's way.

Georg Pasztor opened the main door of the bank and saw them out himself, shaking them both by the hand again as they left. The whole interview had taken a little more than about fifteen minutes, and would have taken even less time if it had not been for the fact that the interpreter had had to translate the two-way conversation in both directions. During this time, Martin had done all the talking. Jeff had sat quietly, listening to the conversation which evolved, and silently considering what he was hearing.

On the pavement outside the bank, the brothers shook the interpreter's hand appreciatively and asked for his name.

'I am Istvan Fischer,' the man replied. 'It has been a pleasure to help.' He turned and walked away up the road.

Chapter 35

Martin and Jeff stood on the pavement outside the bank wondering where to go next. Jeff looked at Martin.

'Let's get a cup of coffee,' he said.

They walked across the road to the small restaurant where they'd had lunch only an hour before. As they sat down at the same table in the window which they had only recently vacated, Martin's mobile phone rang.

'Hello, darling. How are things?'

It was Jan on the end of the line, phoning from Perth.

'It's all been sorted,' replied Martin, still obviously relieved. 'I'll tell you about it when I get back. How are things with you all?'

'We've had a great time,' Jan replied, and proceeded to give her husband a report of their visit to the Scottish Highlands.

After he had finished his telephone conversation with his wife, Martin turned to Jeff. 'Jan and the kids are on their way back on Wednesday. Since we seem to have finished here, I think I will make my way back to Budapest and see if I can get a plane back tomorrow to be there to meet them. What do you want to do?'

'Oh, I don't know,' replied Jeff, in the laconic way that Martin was now well used to. 'This is my first visit to Hungary. I thought it might be nice to spend a day or two exploring Lake Balaton a bit, and then head back to Budapest to sightsee the city before taking the plane back home. My return ticket is for Wednesday next week, but I might bring that forward to the weekend or Monday. Melanie is away on a two-week residential catering course in Reading and is not due back until the end of next week in any case. I have got leave from the pub until she gets back.'

They walked back to the bus terminal on the main square to find that there was a bus leaving for Budapest at four o'clock, in less than an hour's time.

'Do you mind if I take this?' Martin asked Jeff, who could see his brother had already made up his mind in any case.

'Of course not, brother,' replied Jeff. 'I think I will check in to that hotel we passed by just now for the night, and see what tomorrow brings.'

They waited together for the bus to arrive. Martin opened his shoulder bag and handed Jeff the toothbrush and spare clothes which he had put into Martin's bag before they left Budapest and Jeff stuffed them all into various pockets of his anorak. Before getting on the bus, Martin wished Jeff a good break and gave him the spare set of keys he had for Michael's apartment in Eötvös Street, so that Jeff would have somewhere to stay when he got back to Budapest himself. The bus was starting to rev its engine. Martin slapped Jeff on the shoulder rather over-enthusiastically, still showing his relief at having sorted the problem of their father's bank account statement. Keen to get back to his wife and family, he jumped onto the bus.

Jeff raised his arm in farewell to Martin who was waving from the bus window as it pulled out of the square, and headed for the Keszthely Hotel. As he did so, for some reason, perhaps because he was now on his own in a foreign place, he took to glancing back behind himself from time to time as he walked. Twice, as he turned the corner of a street back to the hotel, he thought he saw a man disappear quickly into a shop entrance or out of sight around a corner. Perhaps he was just imagining things, he told himself.

Chapter 36

The fact was that, in addition to wanting to play the tourist, as he had indicated to Martin, Jeff had decided to stay on in Keszthely on his own to give himself the opportunity to investigate things further. For some reason he had a hunch that something wasn't as it should be. He checked into the Keszthely Hotel. The middle-aged woman behind the reception desk spoke no English but was pleasant and welcoming. He guessed it was probably one of the only hotels or guest houses in the town which remained open at this time of the year, still in the off-season. The lady showed him to his room, which was clean and very pleasant, with a balcony view looking over Lake Balaton. He thanked the woman in English, and hesitated, not sure if he was expected to tip her. But the woman acknowledged his thanks and left discretely, after inviting him by sign language to come down later for his dinner in the restaurant, if he wished. After she had left, Jeff collapsed on the bed and within a few minutes had fallen asleep for an early evening nap. The long bus journey and the unpredicted stress of the encounter with the bank manager had exhausted him.

Jeff woke again about seven p.m. He felt ravenous. He pulled off his clothes, jumped in the shower and washed his hair and himself all over. As he stood drying himself with the large white bath towel, he felt completely refreshed. On reflection, he was pleased he had decided not to take the long and rather wearying bus trip back to Budapest with Martin that evening. Martin would only be about halfway back by now, he guessed. He dressed in clean underclothes and a clean shirt, put on some deodorant and a squirt of aftershave, and felt good. He walked down to the hotel's restaurant. There were one or two customers in the bar, but the restaurant itself was almost empty. He was hungry enough not to mind. He started to think of Melanie, and wished she could have been there with him. He sent her a text on his mobile phone to her to say so, and waited for her reply. This did not stop him ending up after the meal sitting in an armchair by the fire, drinking a liqueur coffee with a glass of Tokai sweet dessert wine. He finally made his way up to bed, took his clothes off, and, after reading Melanie's text in reply to his, slept soundly that night.

Jeff woke about seven the next morning feeling completely refreshed. He got up, shaved and showered again, and went down for breakfast in the restaurant. While he was waiting to be served, he thought about the events of the day before. Although he had not said anything to Martin before he had left to go back to Budapest, he had not been entirely convinced by the bank manager's explanations. He could not help but wonder whether Pasztor had been involved in some sort of cover up. He realised that, if this was the case, it would be almost impossible for them to prove this, or indeed to investigate the matter further. He had been surprised and, he now realised, not a little disappointed by the way that Martin had jumped on the explanation that they had been given, accepted it at face value and dashed back home. He understood Martin's wish to get back to his wife and family – he might have felt the same if Melanie had not been away herself – but why come all this way from Budapest to investigate the question of their father's bank accounts if he was prepared to accept the first excuse he heard? He knew Martin had previously been almost certain that there had been some serious wrongdoing going on. He had heard it in his voice when he had first telephoned him and asked him to come over to Hungary and support him in the investigation. He knew that Martin would not have asked him to come all this way if this had not been the case.

After breakfast Jeff took a walk down to the lake. Even at this time of the year the view was impressive. The water was grey and somewhat foreboding, but the enormity of Lake Balaton carried with it a sort of majesty. He walked for a few hundred metres along the shore of the lake, but since a light drizzle had started to fall, he decided to turn inland and head for the shelter of the town. As he turned back from the lake, he saw a man in a long black coat standing a little higher up the slope, watching him through the trees. He could not be certain, but thought it could have been the same man who he thought might have been following him the day before. As he stared back, the man turned and disappeared quickly out of sight up the hill to the road.

Am I really being watched? Jeff thought to himself. *Who is this guy and why is he interested in me?* He stood and pondered this question further. Could this man have some connection with his dead father? Could it also be that he might have had something to do with his death? For the first time, after all these months of raging against his father's act of suicide, he considered the possibility that his father's death had not been by his own hand. He remembered the same doubt Martin had expressed to himself and Sophie when they met together in the pub in Soho to hear about what had happened at the inquest. Was it possible, after all, that Martin might just have been right?

Jeff soon found himself back in the High Street and wandered back into the small restaurant where he been twice with Martin the day before. It was just before eleven by this time, and he ordered himself a cup of coffee and sat at the table in the window, looking over the High Street to the OTP Bank. He was not clear in his mind why he had come back there, but as he sipped his coffee, he realised that it was a good vantage point on the High Street from where he could see but not be seen from the street. Time went by slowly and he ordered a second cup of coffee.

Jeff spent the rest of the day back at the hotel, reading a book he had got into on the flight over and exchanging a few more texts with Melanie. About six o'clock in the evening he gravitated back down to the bar of the hotel, where he sat and had a drink next to the open fire, and then moved on to the restaurant where he had an equally enjoyable meal as the night before. Although he was missing Melanie desperately – and told her so on a number of occasions in his texts to her – he was in one sense rather enjoying his reversion to a bachelor life. He had done nothing yet to think about returning to Budapest, let alone seeing whether there might be a flight he might get on to. He knew he could not afford to live in a hotel for too many days, even though the bill for this was going to be far less expensive that the equivalent stay in a UK hotel would have been. But he also relaxed in the certain knowledge that, as far as he was concerned, Georg Pasztor would cough up, whatever the total might be, with no questions asked.

*

The next morning Jeff woke up, texted Melanie to say "Hi darling, I love you", and had breakfast in the hotel restaurant as he had done the morning before. He walked along the High Street for a wander around the shops. He looked behind himself quickly on a number of occasions to see if there was any sign that he might be being followed again, as he had thought was the case the day before. But this time he saw no one suspicious. By mid-morning he found himself drinking coffee again in the window seat of the small restaurant across from the OTP Bank. This was not something he had planned, but just seemed to be an acceptable way to pass the time. He was casually sipping his coffee and watching the Keszthely world go by outside.

Suddenly Jeff sat up straight. Walking into the bank opposite he saw a man he knew. Just before the man pushed open the front door of the bank, he turned slightly to the side to allow Jeff to see he had a small growth of beard. But there was no hesitation in Jeff's mind. He knew at once, by his appearance and by his walk, that this was his father. He had no doubt who he was watching. He was stunned by this revelation, but could not have been more excited. Jeff put the money in payment for his coffee on the table and continued to sit there waiting expectantly for his father to re-emerge from the bank.

After only a few minutes, his dad came out of the bank and looked over towards where he was sitting in the restaurant window – although Jeff was sure he could not have seen in through the window from the outside across the road – turned and walked briskly up the road to his right. Jeff jumped up, waved to the waitress, pointing to the change he had left on the table, and hurried out of the restaurant. He could see his father already disappearing about a hundred metres up the road. Jeff followed quickly but on the opposite side of the road, doing his best not to draw attention to himself. This was not difficult, because his father walked straight on in front without looking back at any time, and anyone else in the street who might have been interested would have been too busy with their own affairs to take a second look in Jeff's direction. There was very little traffic passing backwards and forwards, and he was able to walk on the side of the road without problem.

His father was following a road that led out of town. As he left the houses behind him, Jeff felt very much more exposed and started to drag his feet and do his best to appear like just any other pedestrian on the roadside if his father chose to look behind. But he need not have worried. His dad continued to march on, presumably making for home, without a single backwards glance. About two kilometres out of town, by which time Jeff was a considerable distance behind his father in his attempt at achieving anonymity, Michael suddenly left the road and disappeared down a track in the direction of the lake. When Jeff reached the top of the track he stared at the overgrown steep path that his father had just disappeared down. About two hundred metres through the trees he could see a small plume of smoke that he guessed must be coming from the chimney of the house that Michael had been making for.

Chapter 37

At the same time as Jeff was sitting in the window of the restaurant across the road, Georg Pasztor was sitting at his desk in his office at the back of the Bank. He had arrived at work very early that morning on the day after the visit of the two Butler bothers. He had not slept well during the night, his sleep being frequently disturbed by anxiety dreams. At about five o'clock he knew he was not going to get back to sleep again, and decided to get up. He did so quietly without disturbing his wife who was sleeping soundly beside him. He pottered around for a bit, made himself a cup of coffee, ate some cereal, and finally left early for work, arriving at the bank before eight o'clock. He was now sitting there at his desk in the middle of the morning, with nothing pressing to do, but was going over in his mind the events of the previous afternoon.

The fact was that Jeff had guessed right. When the young girl came in from the desk to tell the bank's manger about the enquiries that two Englishmen were making about their dead father's account, Georg realised he had to make a quick decision. He was quite sure that the man called Michael Butler, who called in to make withdrawals from time to time, was who he said he was. In any case, he had presented his British passport to confirm his identity the first time he had called into the bank. A photocopy of the page with his details and a photograph was there in his account file. And although

Georg did not speak English and Michael Butler spoke no Hungarian, he had no doubts that the man had his full mental capacity. This being the case, he thought to himself, there must be a good personal reason why he was choosing to over-winter there in Keszthely. It may be that he did not wish others, including even members of his own family perhaps, to know his whereabouts. In a sort of telepathic way, although they were unable to communicate by word of mouth, Georg had decided that Michael seemed a pleasant chap. He was a man of his own age who appeared to be of a professional and intelligent demeanour. The girl had told him that the two men outside had explained that they were Michael Butler's sons, and an examination of their passport identities was certainly consistent with this.

Georg knew that, since Michael Butler may not have wanted his sons to know that he was living in Keszthely, he would have to tell them that he was sorry, but he was not at liberty to discuss the details of the accounts held by customers of the bank with other persons for confidentiality reasons. This was the reply that Martin had received, correctly, from the bank official in the main OTP branch in Budapest the week before, of course. But it had not stopped Martin from coming all the way down to Keszthely to investigate the bank withdrawals further. Georg also knew that, were he to give this proper but stalling response to the sons again, this was bound to increase their suspicions about the possibility of foul play and to make them even more determined to get to the bottom of the matter. They would likely demand to be given a reason for the continuing withdrawals from the account following their father's death, which they knew to be the case from the recent monthly statement they had come across. They would also almost certainly insist on a response from the bank's head office in Budapest if Georg Pasztor was not able or willing to answer their questions satisfactorily himself. If this was to occur, Georg knew, the fact that their father was still alive and living there in Keszthely would come to light eventually.

Georg felt very uncomfortable about being the person who would have been responsible for divulging Michael's secret and the uncovering of his identity and whereabouts. He reasoned that, if the man wanted to hide from his family (and his wife, or the tax man? – whatever), he felt very uneasy about being the one to be responsible for breaking his cover. If he had insisted on not giving them details on the grounds of confidentiality, this would only delay the truth getting out. In any case, in addition to respecting his customer's confidentiality, he had quite grown to like the man.

Georg therefore made a decision on the spur of the moment. He would explain that there had been a simple administrative mistake to do with the identities of two different customers having been mixed up. Not something that had ever happened in his branch before, but which he believed must have been caused by a computer addressing error. He would undertake to conduct an immediate enquiry as to how this had happened and put the problem straight at once. He would invite the men into his office and start with an unreserved apology on behalf of his bank. He would also personally see to it that any expenses they had incurred were paid by the bank in full. This process of thought and plan of action had occurred to Georg in the space of only about five minutes as he sat in his office and made his decision as to how to handle the situation. He had never in his professional banking life been deceitful to any visitor to his bank. But he had made the snap decision that his professional loyalty should be to the Englishman, Michael Butler, and that this was the only way he could maintain this loyalty.

As soon as Georg walked out of his office, he could see that the two men at the counter were clearly Michael Butler's sons. He did not need to see their passports to confirm this. They had enough family resemblance to their father to leave him in no doubt. He invited them back into his office not only to have their discussion in private, which is what they had assumed, but also so that he was out of earshot of his two young male and female colleagues at the desk, in addition to any other customers who may have been within hearing. He knew very well that, if his colleagues had heard and understood the explanation he was giving to the Butler sons, they might have had difficulty believing the story, or at least would have later asked Georg questions about how this mistake could have happened and what they could do to help to rectify it. He knew that these would have been questions that he would not have been able to reply to to the satisfaction of his own staff. One important blessing, as Georg saw it, was that the sons spoke no Hungarian and his staff spoke essentially no English. There was, however, the question of the volunteer interpreter. He recognised the man vaguely, knew he lived locally, but on the spur of the moment Georg was unable to put his finger on who he was. He would just have to take a chance on the man not breaking any confidences, and on him keeping the discussions he had been responsible for translating to himself.

Georg sat with the two sons in his office delivering his head-on apology, followed by an explanation of the administrative computer error which had occurred, and ending up with an open-ended offer of repayment to them of travel and other expenses incurred. He watched them intently as he did so, and could not believe how well his plan had gone. The older brother, who was the leader, had accepted his explanations completely and at face value, as well as accepting his unreserved apology on behalf of the bank. The younger brother was silent most of the time, but had not asked any additional questions or raised any objections before they both left, seeming perfectly reassured. The whole interview had lasted less than fifteen minutes, and he had felt a profound sense of relief as he saw them cordially to the door. Sitting there in his office the next morning, however, he continued to feel very uneasy as he went over in his mind what had transpired, the snap decisions he had made and the way in which he had dealt with this enquiry.

Georg Pasztor had at all times throughout his career acted as a consummate professional in his dealings with customers and bank matters alike. He had certainly never lied to anyone before. And it was this last fact that had caused him a sleepless night after the interview, and had continued to make him feel very uneasy as he went over events the next morning. He knew he had acted wholly out of respect for Michael Butler's confidentiality. But he also knew he may have jeopardised his whole career and his family's future. The fact that the decision he had taken was based on a lie which could blow up in his face at any time bothered Georg greatly. And it would continue to do so.

Chapter 38

Jeff hesitated at the top of the track leading down to Michael's house. He felt immensely excited and yet fearful. Fearful that there was a possibility, of course, that he was chasing rainbows. That, in his loss and bereavement of his father, he had imagined that the man he had seen going into and coming out of the bank was somebody who fitted with his memory of his dead dad. But he had spent the last two kilometres walking up the road behind this man to confirm that this was indeed his father. He now had really no doubts about the matter. The hesitation and fear he felt now was rather more centred on the possibility that his father might not want to see him again. Perhaps that he might even slam the door in his face, and exclude him from his life once more, now and forever.

The longer he stood there at the top of the track, Jeff knew he had to accept this possibility. He had come too far to turn back now, and he could not turn around and go back to his own life without being certain whether or not his father was indeed still alive. In one sense, his rejection of his father's death at the time had been the reason why he had run away from home, and had ended up shivering on the side of Firle Beacon in the South Downs that night. He had not been able to accept his father's death then. But he had also not been able to believe it. It appeared now that his rejection of the event at the time might have been correct.

Buoyed by these thoughts, Jeff turned off the road and climbed confidently down the track to the house. As he got nearer, the place came clearly in to view, situated as it was in a clearing on the slopes just above the lake. When he was within a hundred metres or so of the house, he felt less confident and stopped still for a moment, taking the scene in. The building was old and pretty run down, but at the same time homely enough, with the smoke from a wood fire which could be seen and smelt rising out of the main chimney. Jeff crept down towards the house and edged hesitantly around to the front, as if he was in some way planning to burgle the place, or at least visit it as an uninvited intruder. The front door was open on the jar. Jeff was not sure whether to knock on the door or call out to the occupant. Instead, he coughed loudly and gave the door a gentle push. 'Come on in,' he heard his father's voice say. He walked through the door, into the living room area, and stood at the entrance to the room as his father, who was sitting in front of the stove, turned to face him. Jeff was unsure what he should do next, but the decision was made for him.

Michael jumped up from his chair and threw his arms around his younger son. 'Jeff! Good to see you!! How *are* you?' Michael appeared surprised and excited to see his son. But his welcome could not have been clearer or more sincere.

'Dad!' was all Jeff could say, putting his face on his father's shoulder and bursting into tears. 'We thought you were dead!'

Michael held his younger son in his arms and was pleased and relieved to see him. 'Well, I'm not Jeff. It's so good to see you!' was all he said.

The two men, father and son, stood like that for more than a few minutes and then came apart. Michael held Jeff by the shoulders at arms' length as they looked directly at each other for the first time in what had been more than six months.

Michael put the kettle on the stove and made them both a cup of coffee. He poured a large slug of whiskey into each mug, handed one to Jeff and sat down beside him in front of the stove with the other.

'How have you been?' he asked Jeff.

'I'm OK, Dad,' his son replied.

'How's Mum?' Michael asked his son, somewhat hesitantly.

'She's OK,' Jeff answered again in his monosyllabic way.

Michael was well used to Jeff's economy of speech and knew that this camouflaged a sensitive and thoughtful young man underneath.

'What *happened* to you?' Jeff looked up at his father, a mixture of blame and concern in his voice.

'It's a long story,' replied Michael. He sat next to his son and told him his recent life story, from beginning to end.

Chapter 39
Michael's story
August 2014

Michael was sitting at his desk working back home in Ealing that Saturday evening. Jeff looked in at the door.

'I'm off now, Dad,' he said.

'OK, son. Hope all goes well. Have a good time,' his father replied.

Jeff was leaving to get the overnight train from Euston station to Glasgow. From Glasgow he was meeting up with some of his friends to walk the West Highland Way and over to the Isle of Skye. The weather forecast was not great, but in spite of this Michael envied his son. It was a long time since he and Marion had spent a lovely holiday travelling around the Western Isles, staying in remote hotels and guest houses and taking trips in boats out to the islands. In addition to the Isle of Skye itself, of course, one of Michael and Marion's favourite spots was the inland Loch Morar.

Michael would always remember the peacefulness and tranquillity of walking with Marion around this small loch on a sunny late summer day in September. As they stood hand in hand looking over the water from the path at the edge of the loch, the tranquillity was abruptly disrupted when they suddenly realised that Marion's red collie dog, Tag, had disappeared and was in the field above them sprinting with joyful enthusiasm towards a large gathering of sheep that were grazing on the hillside. Marion screamed in terror at the dog, ordering him to come back. Michael, who was used to this sort of emergency with one or other of Marion's dogs, nevertheless froze as he looked out onto the lake to see one of the men who were fishing in a boat stand up and raise his shotgun to his shoulder, aiming towards the dog. A split second passed during which, as he turned back to look at the dog, he saw it wheel around and start to run back towards Marion's imploring cries. Out of the other eye, Michael saw the man in the boat lower his gun, hesitate, and the then sit down again in the stern of the boat. Close call as it had been, this episode had not spoilt what was a blissful interlude for himself and Marion alone together, something that not even the ever-present midges could detract from. It was not just this holiday which Michael felt a sudden desire to re-visit, but also the wish that he could once again have the freedom to roam wherever he liked that Michael envied in his son.

Jeff hesitated at the door, then came back into the study and sat down on the brown leather armchair next to Michael. 'Is everything OK, Dad?' he said, leaning forward.

'What do you mean, Jeff?'

'I was just wondering why you came home last weekend before you were due to and why you are now working here at home,' his son replied.

Michael looked up at Jeff and turned in his swivel chair to face his son. 'Nothing major, Jeff,' he said, looking down at his hands which were clasped firmly in his lap. 'Things have been a bit difficult for me politically in Hungary in the last few weeks and Conrad gave me leave to come over and work from home until they cool down. I'll probably be back in Budapest again by the time you get back.'

Jeff stared into his father's eyes in an unusually intense

way. 'That's all right then,' he said. And then, leaning forward towards his father again: 'You would tell me if there is a problem, even if you can't talk to Mum about it, wouldn't you?'

Michael looked up in surprise at the adult directness shown by his younger son. 'Of course I would, Jeff.' He paused. 'It's just that there are some things that are best not discussed, even in families, from time to time.

'Put it this way, if you don't know, then I don't know either, if you get my meaning. Things not discussed can never be recorded and therefore have never taken place.'

Jeff hesitated, and then rose from his chair. 'OK Dad, I understand,' he said.

But when he looked back later on this discussion Jeff was sure that he hadn't understood and, as events transpired, continued to be unable understand what it was his father had been trying to tell him for a long time after.

Jeff reached forward and put out his hand to his father in an uncharacteristically gentlemanly and filial gesture of affection.

Michael took his son's hand, shook it and said: 'Thanks, son. Have a good trip. Let's talk more about this when you get back.'

Jeff picked up his rucksack, heaved it on to his back, and raised his arm to his father in a salutatory wave as he went out of the door and left the house in the direction of Ealing Broadway station.

Chapter 40

Later on that Saturday night, after Jeff had left for the station, Michael was still in the same place at his desk in his study at the back of their house in Ealing. The fact was that the situation in Budapest following the attack on him had become of so much concern to his organisation that he had been sent back to the UK on leave for his own protection. It was true that he did have a vast amount of paperwork to catch up with and reports to write, so he viewed it as an opportunity to get all this done working in peace from home. Angie had managed to persuade Michael that this might be a good idea for the time being. Conrad was in agreement with the idea and had readily allowed him unlimited leave from the Budapest office in the present situation. Indeed, had Michael known, it was Conrad who had suggested that Angie should put this plan to him in the first place. Since his arrival back in the UK the previous Saturday, Angie had been emailing him daily and he had been sending her back his reports for onward transmission as frequently. As a matter of fact, he was that evening in the process of completing his report on the Roma in Hungary document, ready for Angie to send on to the OSSE Head Office in Brussels on Monday.

Marion was delighted to have him back home earlier than expected and secretly relieved that Michael was no longer having to bother with all the stresses and strains that her husband had been exposed to in his present post. Marion was a not unintelligent woman. She had herself been an honours graduate senior civil servant in her own right. But her reaction to Michael's situation was based on the problems as far as he had discussed them with her, which was a significantly watered-down version of reality. And this was how Michael wanted it. He had always sought to protect her from the harsher aspects of his job and certainly did not wish to reveal anything of his involvement in bringing the criminal people-trafficking gang to justice. Because of this he had also chosen not to tell Marion about the threats he had received from the sex-trafficking ring he and Paolo had been investigating, and especially about the attack he had suffered in the street in Budapest.

Having gone out to the kitchen to make himself another cup of coffee, he returned to his study and got his head down again. Ignoring the outside noises of passing traffic, he got on with his report.

A sudden louder noise made him look up from his laptop. He could have sworn he'd heard a man's voice shouting in objection. As he sat still listening carefully, wondering what this could have been and where it had come from, he heard their garage doors being slammed shut. He jumped up and ran into the front room. As he parted the curtains a fraction, he saw two men in dark clothing jumping into a black Mercedes saloon which then sped off down the road. He only caught a glimpse of them from behind in the dark, not enough to identify them in any way. Nor did he have time to see the car number plate or make out any other details. He let the living room curtain fall back into place and stood there deciding what his next step should be. He walked into the hall, opened the front door and walked slowly towards the garage.

Michael opened the right-hand garage door with trepidation, expecting perhaps some sort of booby trap, or at least a surprise. What he did see before him was certainly an unexpected and unpleasant surprise. At the back of the garage was the body of a man swinging from a rope which was hanging from one of the wooden garage ceiling beams. The man was clearly dead already, but the case that he was only just dead was supported by the fact that his body was still swinging gently from side to side in peaceful but macabre evidence of what had just taken place. Fresh urine was staining his trouser crutch and dripping on to the floor below. The smell of human faeces came to Michael. A wooden box was on its side on the floor, not far from the man's dangling feet, from where it had been kicked away.

Michael stood staring at this dead man's body, swinging there in his own garage, for a number of minutes. Who was he, and what was he doing there? The picture was so distressing, he had to look away for a few seconds, to give himself time to take in what he was seeing. He looked back again and, even though the body was in the early stages of death, he was as sure as he could be that this was not somebody that he had met before. Although the body was of a man about his own age and a similar build to himself, it bore no resemblance to anyone else he could think of. It did not take him long to ask himself the question: whoever this man was, was it possible that he had been summarily killed here in his garage in mistaken identity?

It came to him in an instant. The body which should have

been hanging there was his own. He felt a chill running down his spine at this thought. Was it possible that this was a poor individual who had perhaps been walking by at the time – even if he had been found on their drive or in their garden on anti-social business – and had been attacked and murdered in mistake for himself? He had no idea who the men who had carried out this murder were, but he was pretty certain that this was the warning that Alistair had given him. That the people-trafficking criminals in Hungary had been out to kill him because of what he knew. That they had now traced him to his home here in England and followed him there to "take him out" before their racket could be exposed.

Michael looked up and down the street. Not a single person was to be seen. The curtains of all the windows of the houses opposite were closed for the night, only one or two upstairs lights still on. He was as certain as he could be that no one except himself had seen what had just happened in their garage. He closed the garage door as quietly as he could and walked slowly back into the house. He was shocked and afraid, but at the same time completely clear-minded. He realised at once that it was his life that was still in danger. Unless, of course, it was "his" life which had already been ended. The more he thought this out, the more this seemed to him to be a logical way out of his immediate predicament. Who was there to contradict this theory? If he was not there to do so, it was highly likely that, by morning, nobody else would. That was it. He certainly did not want to expose Marion as well as himself to further danger, if the men were to realise their mistake and come back for him later. Therefore he had no other choice, as far as he was concerned.

He had to get away from the scene of "his" murder.

Michael walked silently upstairs, opened the door to their bedroom and looked inside. Marion was in bed, soundly asleep and breathing quietly. She obviously had not been disturbed by the immediate events. He very quietly reached into the wardrobe and removed a shoulder bag and one or two essential clothing items, leaving the majority of the rest undisturbed. Closing the bedroom door softly, he walked downstairs and back into his study. He opened his desk, took out his passport, one credit card for his Hungarian bank and some cash in pounds sterling and Hungarian forints from his wallet, and placed them all firmly into the inside pocket of his jacket. Taking care to leave behind the rest of his credit cards, driving licence and a good deal of money, he replaced the wallet back in the drawer where he normally kept it.

He left the house as quietly as he could, closing and locking the front door behind him without a sound, and walked down the street towards the Broadway and Ealing station.

Chapter 41

The underground journey from Ealing Broadway to Victoria late on that Saturday night took no time. Most of the overground train services at Victoria had finished by this hour and the station was quiet, apart from a few late stragglers like himself who were walking through the station. Coming off the up escalator, he crossed the main station concourse and exited onto Buckingham Palace Road. A few taxis and night buses were still operating outside but the streets were almost empty. He crossed over and walked the short distance along the road to Victoria Coach Station.

In spite of the lateness of the hour, he found himself in a small queue at the coach station ticket office. He had no clear plan as to where he was heading. He looked up at the departure board. There were coaches departing to Brussels, Lille, Cologne – all cities well-known to him. Looking further down the list, he saw Vienna, Bratislava, Budapest. When it came to his turn at the window, he paid in cash for a single ticket to Budapest. There was a Eurolines coach leaving at two a.m., via Brussels where he was told he would have to change. He had made a snap decision that, if it came to light that it was not his body hanging there in their garage, then the last place that the criminals who wanted him dead were likely to look for him was back in Budapest. He was also honest enough to admit to himself that he was having trouble coping with the stress of the threat to his life and had a strong wish to seek comfort from Zita again. He knew he could use this as an excuse to do so.

Thirty minutes before the coach was due to depart Michael heard the announcement on the public address system. He found his coach waiting at bay fifteen and made his way to a seat in the corner of the back row. Placing his travel bag between his feet, he settled down to endure what he knew was going to be a journey of something like twenty-six hours. He had never done this before, always having travelled from the UK to Europe by plane in the past. He knew people who did this journey by coach regularly, however. These included one or two of the secretaries in the office, their boyfriends or visiting family members who were prepared to tolerate the privation of a long coach journey across Western and Central Europe for the sake of economy and what they claimed was a chance to meet all sorts of interesting people. This type of sardines-in-the-tin fraternity was said by those who enjoyed it to be a definite bonus. As far as Michael was concerned at the moment, however, the possibility of meeting other people was the last thing he wanted. He felt very uncomfortable with all these strangers around him. But having chosen this anonymous way of fleeing for his life, he was just going to have to bear the fact that he was surrounded by people who he had no wish to engage with. Judging by the two rather drunk men who had sat themselves in the back seats next to him and were already asleep, he felt it unlikely that he was going to have to engage in much conversation from their direction.

The coach was filling up fast. Michael sat in the back of the coach peering anxiously at each of the other passengers as they climbed in at the door at the front. He knew rationally that – even if his attackers were eventually to realise that they had killed the wrong man in his garage – they would not learn this immediately. Nevertheless, irrational though this fear was, he could not stop himself examining every new face for evidence that the person might be one of his predators, joining him on the bus to keep him under surveillance. Any one of these men now boarding could be one of the Hungarian thugs Paolo had described to him from their visits to the Budapest brothels. He knew this was completely illogical, but still could not stop these paranoid thoughts raining in on him as he sat there sweating in fear.

As Michael sat waiting for the coach to depart, he could feel that his heart rate was starting to settle very slowly towards normal and his sweating to ease. He wiped the sweat off his forehead and tried hard to relax a little. His fear had not left him, but he just had to accept the fact that it was most unlikely that any of these particular fellow travellers could have boarded the coach to cause him harm.

The coach was about twenty minutes late leaving. The ride through southeast London and into Kent seemed to be painfully slow, even at this early hour of a Sunday morning. He must have dozed off eventually, because when he awoke they were all being shepherded off the coach and through the emigration channel at the port of Dover. The coach drove off empty to wait for them at the other side of the checkpoint. The majority of his fellow passengers waiting in line were clearly not UK citizens. There were Czechs, Poles, Dutch and North Africans, not to mention a handful of Hungarians whom he recognised from the conversations he heard around him. The woman at the passport desk was not interested in his British passport and did not even bother to scan it. Michael realised vaguely that, if it had been found not to be his body hanging in his garage and attempts made to trace his true whereabouts, there would be no record of his departure from the UK by the port of Dover. They were bussed on board the ferry which was about to depart.

The ferry crossing was unpleasantly rough, but they reached Calais and were bussed off the boat. The French immigration woman was even less interested in his UK passport than her colleague on the English side had been, and again waved him through without hesitation and without scanning his passport. She was however spending a large amount of time processing the passengers from other nationalities, some of them in great detail and with protracted questioning, delaying the onward passage of the coach. When the coach did finally leave the port of Calais, he noted one or two empty seats that had not been present before, their occupants having been removed by immigration at Calais. The coach sped along the E40 motorway making good time to Brussels. At the central coach station in Brussels they were required to get off the coach for more checks but eventually were allowed back onto the same coach, not having to change coaches there for their onward journey to Budapest as his ticket and the woman at the ticket office at Victoria Coach Station had indicated would be the case.

From Brussels the journey continued through Belgium before crossing the German border at Aachen and then proceeding on to Cologne, where they had another protracted stop for reasons that were not obvious. By this time Michael was exhausted and, drifting in and out of consciousness, was not able to remember much of the detail of their journey down through Germany. There had been a number of stops, mainly it seemed to allow passengers who needed to to jump out and light up, dragging on their cigarettes in the cold damp air as if their lives depended on it. Which of course they did, Michael mused to himself. There was a toilet on the coach but it stank and the seat and floor around it were covered with urine and excrement. This in spite of the driver's admonition to only use the on-board toilet for "small business not big business". Most of the passengers, especially the women, chose to hold on until the next coach stop.

After travelling for about eighteen hours they entered Austria near the town of Passau. Night was falling again, but Michael woke up and started to feel both hungry and thirsty. At the popular hotel-restaurant coach stop at St Valentin, he got out with the rest of the passengers. He stood at the restaurant serving counter and ordered himself a cheese omelette. He was impressed to find the large cheerful Austrian lady standing behind the counter cook the omelette on a stove in front of him, asking him how many eggs he would like, and what kind of cheese he would prefer, which she then melted in folds into the expertly cooked, thick omelette. The simple meal was one of the tastiest he could remember for a long time. He bought a box of individually wrapped Mozart chocolates to suck for the rest of the journey and joined the other passengers who were starting to drift back onto the coach.

The rest of the journey through Austria seemed much less wearying. They by-passed Linz and arrived in the outskirts of Vienna where they stopped briefly. The last one hundred and fifty odd miles from Vienna to Budapest passed quickly, the coach seeming to accelerate towards its final destination as it got nearer. The brief stop at the Hungarian border was even more casual than at any national boundary they had passed already. They drove into the outskirts of Budapest, arriving there only some three hours since they had left Vienna.

Chapter 42

On arriving at Budapest Nepliget coach station, Michael got off the coach, stretched his limbs and wandered into the park, unsure where he should go next. During all the time that he had lived and worked in Budapest he had never found his way into Nepliget (literally, the "People's Park"). He was surprised to find such an extensive and beautiful park in this otherwise unremarkable part of the city. He idled through the acres of grassy parkland looking up at the beautiful trees. It was about five a.m. and he was completely alone in this peaceful place. The ground was covered with dew, and the early morning sun that was shining through the trees was warming the dew into the mist that was drifting up from the ground, bestowing an almost mystical appearance to the whole scene. Scattered around the trees were islands of interesting-looking mushrooms, thriving in this dank grassland park. He was wondering whether these were worth gathering up with a view to eating later, when he came across a marble plinth in the middle of a clearing in the trees. Laid on top of it was a single mushroom; next to it some public-spirited person had scrawled a note on a piece of paper: "*Gyilkos Laloca!*" – "*Deadly mushroom!*". Michael thanked his unknown advisor and actually laughed to himself, albeit a little hysterically. In spite of his continuing fearful and paranoid state even he could not envisage that he was at risk from death by deadly mushrooms.

Michael sat on a park bench and considered his situation. He felt sad and tearful about the fact that he had run away from his family and home. He understood completely the grief he must have left behind him in Ealing, Marion and his children thinking it was himself who was hanging dead there in their garage. He could not banish the fear for his own life and the threat to those he loved, however, which had been the trigger for his decision to make himself scarce. He sighed as he sat on a park bench in the dawn and told himself that he'd had no choice in the matter. He knew his temporary absence would be for the best for them all in the long term. He was also honest enough with himself, nevertheless, to admit that the circumstances had given him the opportunity to consider the affair he'd recently been having in Budapest with Zita. This self-imposed absence would give him time to decide whether he wanted to be with her or Marion in his life ahead.

In spite of the fact that he had just completed a coach journey lasting more than twenty-four hours, he'd not given any time during that journey to consider what his next step should be or where he should go from there. He knew that he had to continue to hide from his attackers, and that he should not make his presence known to any of his friends or colleagues here in Budapest. He counted out going back to his own flat, even for a brief visit, for the same reason. He also decided reluctantly that he could not to go and see Zita at the moment. That would put her in danger too. He understood he had to remain *incognito* for the time being. He knew at the back of his mind, however, that even if the death of the man in his garage was recognised not to have been the death of himself, it was unlikely that any party choosing to look for him would start to do so by searching for him back in Hungary. This was the best place to be as long as he kept his head down.

Almost by instinct Michael walked back to the ticket kiosk in Nepliget coach terminal and stood looking down the departure board. Rather as if he was pinning a tail on a donkey, he chose his destination. He bought himself another bus ticket in cash with Hungarian forints to the southern town of Keszthely, which was situated on the southwest shore of Lake Balaton. The simple reasons for which he chose this destination was that he had heard that it was a very pleasant place to live; that he'd never been there before; and that it was a long way from everywhere else.

Chapter 43

Michael sighed to himself and cursed loudly. He had taken to talking to himself out loud, since he had nobody else to speak to. He was sitting on the balcony with a cup of coffee for his breakfast, looking out at the beautiful view of Lake Balaton. In spite of the lovely scenery – or perhaps because of it – he was feeling very sad. He had not stopped feeling deeply unhappy since he had left his wife and family behind in England, thinking he was dead. He did have insight into what grief this will have caused them. At the same time he had not lost the fear for his own life which he'd felt on that Saturday night when he had found a stranger's body hanging in his garage where he should have been. He still had the firm conviction that the decision he'd taken on the spur of the moment to make himself disappear had been the right action to protect his own life and perhaps even the lives of his wife and family. But knowing this did not lighten his mood, in spite of the beautiful view and lovely weather the morning was bringing. He had not felt so utterly depressed for a long time.

In addition to the sadness which he could not throw off about leaving his wife and family behind, Michael also felt unremitting guilt. Guilt about the affairs he'd had with other women, without Marion's knowledge, while living away from home over the years. Now that he was truly alone, he'd had time to think back on his life and realise that his affairs over the years had been unfair on Marion. Most of all, was the guilt he now felt about the most recent of these affairs. He had not forgotten Zita – in fact he thought about her every day – and in spite of his guilt could not bring himself to decide that he should never see her again. But he was still too frightened to consider travelling up to Budapest to visit her at the moment. In the meantime, he had chosen to live in a lonely self-inflicted personal hibernation.

Michael had found this old but rather charming house on the shores of Lake Balaton, which he'd rented from a widow who lived in the town. It was a traditional wood-built lakeside residence, with only two bedrooms, but with the advantage of a long balcony over-looking the lake. The place was somewhat timeworn and the paintwork weathered and chipped, especially on the outside, but everything worked. There was a large wood fired boiler which gave him plenty of hot water for his bath or shower as well as heating the living room and most of the house pretty efficiently. Outside under the low over-hung roofs were stacks of chopped wood reaching high into the eaves, enough to heat a family for a year or two, he estimated. He guessed that the house had probably been used as a holiday let in the summer, but had become more than the old lady could afford to keep up without renting it out at other times of the year as well. He could imagine how idyllic the place must be in the hot summer months. In the meantime, he had taken steps to improve his security there in the event of an attack by the brothel mafia, by fixing the broken shutters, putting locks on all the windows and upgrading the door locks.

He was expecting the severe continental freezes, which he

knew from living in Budapest often occurred in Hungary, to arrive soon. The first snow should be arriving before Christmas. He had noticed that the cars on the road had already changed their tyres over to winter tyres, as the law required, in preparation for the snow and ice that was expected imminently. These winter tyres were much thicker and heavy duty, with rubber studs on them to give increased purchase on the ice and snow when it did arrive. He had found some snow shoes and snow clearing equipment in the old shed on the far side of the house. He cleaned the snow shoes up ready to be able to put them into service as his personal winter tyres when the time came.

Chapter 44

There was one other way in which Michael had been "unfaithful" to Marion over the years. He had not been open with her about the extent of his income. Early on in their marriage he had opened an account in his name with a foreign bank in whichever city he found himself working, and deposited a regular monthly amount into it. Right from the start, he had justified this behaviour to himself as his way of creating some "rainy day savings". He never thought in much detail what this really meant, but as the years went by these foreign bank accounts had accumulated pretty significant amounts, attracting high interest savings in deposit accounts as they sat there waiting. Apart from buying gifts of silk and lace underwear and small items of jewellery for Zita, he'd never had any occasion to raid these accounts. He excused the fact that he had opened the accounts by telling himself that he would never use all the money without telling Marion about the accounts' existence. He'd always intended to discuss with her what they should spend the money on, should the need arise.

The account he'd saved into most recently was with a branch of the Hungarian National Bank OTP in Budapest. Now that he found himself living in Keszthely on the southern shores of Lake Balaton, where there was a local branch of this bank, it was easy for him to call into the bank and withdraw cash from his savings account as he needed.

He was using the account as his subsistence account while over-wintering there, as he saw it. After a month or two of hiding up in Keszthely, as a fairly regular customer, he had got to know the staff and manager of the small OTP branch. To say that he'd got to know them was perhaps somewhat of an exaggeration. Georg Pasztor, the bank's manager, spoke no English and Michael had only a few words of Hungarian, a language which he continued to find insurmountably difficult in spite of his time in Budapest. He had achieved a reasonable degree of competency in the languages of all the other countries he had worked in previously. He spoke good French, reasonable German and Portuguese, and even managed to get by in Polish. But Hungarian remained opaque to him, as he knew it did to many of his friends and colleagues who also found the Magyar tongue more difficult than most. Therefore, whenever he had occasion to visit the bank in Keszthely, he would just nod to Georg or touch his cap, and the manager would nod back to him. On one occasion, Georg held the door wide open for him as he left and patted him fraternally on the shoulder. And that was how the rapport between them had continued.

Chapter 45

After a couple of months of almost complete solitude, Michael eventually had to admit to himself that he could not survive with no human contact whatsoever. At the same time, he still lived in the fear of his presence being found out by those who had tried to kill him once already. Once or twice a week he would walk the couple of kilometres into the centre of Keszthely, continually looking up and down the road, fearful that he might be being followed. Usually on a Monday and a Friday when the main market was in full swing, he would walk round the stores filling an old linen bag which he'd found in one of the cupboards in the kitchen with produce of all sorts. On the early trips he had stuck to his basic needs, stocking up on potatoes, lettuces, green beans and some cheese and fresh eggs. After a while he started to branch out, trying produce which he had perhaps not eaten before or not cooked before. He would buy himself some very large local mushrooms, a hand of salsify, a bunch of rocket and a plastic bag full of avocados. He had read that Keszthely was particularly known for paprika, cherries, walnuts and caviar, and made a point of trying all of these local foods. In the process of shopping he would duck in and out of the different stalls and repeatedly look over his shoulder in an attempt to reassure himself that there was no-one following him in the crowded environment.

After a number of trips he had got to know the various

store holders and had decided which of the market stores he preferred. This was not easy at first, because there were such a large number of stores selling the same type of produce, with a choice of exceptionally fresh and high quality products on offer. He began to re-visit particular stores based on the fact that one of the greengrocers was particularly pleasant; the cheerful woman on the cheese counter he used was always more than generous in the size of the portions she gave him; and the man on the meat counter he preferred always tried hard to communicate with him in broken English, proud that he could communicate with Michael a little in his language.

While his visits to the market stalls provided Michael with some human contact, as time went by he realised he was also missing the opportunity to talk in his own tongue and have a reasonable conversation with another person in English. After completing his twice weekly shop at the market, he took to visiting one of the food and drink stalls which were situated at the far end of the market. These food and drink stalls existed in every street market in Hungary he had ever visited, as well as in the railway stations, the Metro subways, the bus stations and virtually every other public place you might wish to visit. He would sit on one of the high stools and order himself a beer or local brandy, drinking slowly for a bit before ordering some kolbasz sausage, a slice of langos – fried dough with toppings of sour cream, cheese and garlic – or other snack on offer.

Late one Friday morning, having finished his shopping, he was sitting sipping a warm brandy when the man next to him started talking to him in English.

'You are English, aren't you?' the man asked him with no hint of an accent.

Michael froze, fearful of entering into a discussion with a stranger. He still remained frankly paranoid about meeting people, in case the person in question might be from the party wanting him dead. He looked at the man who was sitting beaming amicably at him. He could not believe that this fellow represented anything malign. In spite of his fear about being discovered, he decided to take a chance.

'Yes, I am,' he replied hesitantly, without giving his name. He leant forward and offered his hand to his neighbour at the bar.

'Hi,' said the man. 'I'm Istvan. Istvan Fischer. I've seen you in the market over the last few weeks, but only realised you were English when I heard you replying to the man on the meat counter over there when he tried to talk to you in English.'

Once the ice had been broken in this way, Michael felt a huge relief to be able to communicate with somebody in his own language at last. The two men sat and talked freely with each other. It turned out that Istvan was a carpenter. He had been born and brought up in Keszthely, where he still lived, but had spent ten years living and working in Croydon, in South London. This was the reason he spoke English not only fluently but also colloquially. He was only a couple of years younger than Michael. He was married and had a house on the southern side of Keszthely, not so far from Michael's house. He knew the widow that Michael had rented his house from.

Michael and Istvan hit it off well. Michael told Istvan that he had been staying there in Keszthely on vacation over the winter and Istvan accepted Michael's statement at face value without asking him any personal details. On the subject of his own life, however, Istvan was voluble. He told Michael how he had been born in a small village not many kilometres from where they sat. His father was a woodsman and joiner, cutting and preparing the wood from the nearby forest, which he then turned into windows and doors, or any piece of furniture his customers might have commissioned from him. Istvan described how he would sit for hours as a boy and watch transfixed as his father crafted pieces of wood into shapes he would never have thought possible, and then fix them together with dry joints and without modern day screws or brackets. He considered his father a "sculptor in wood", he told Michael. He mentioned a spiral wooden staircase which his father had made in elm wood for the local Catholic Church. This was still in everyday use for those climbing up from the knave to the organ loft and gallery, as sturdy and secure as it had been on the day his father had put the finishing touches to it. If you were to inspect it carefully, Istvan explained to Michael, you would find that there was not a single piece of metal used in its construction. Screws and other such fixings were made unnecessary by the wooden joints and pegs that held the whole structure solidly together.

Istvan's mother was a laundress and they had four other children in addition to Istvan, who was the eldest. Istvan's siblings were all alive and still living in the local Balaton area. The family had lived in a very small house near to the lake – not far away from where Michael was now living – which had originally been a modest wooden hut. Over the years Istvan's father had steadily worked on it, enlarging and upgrading it, until it grew to a well-maintained four-bedroom family house, with all modern amenities. Istvan's older sister Marta and her husband had taken over the house following the death of both their parents, and lived there with their four children. Istvan and his wife also lived in a house which Istvan had built a little bit further along the southern shore of the lake.

They sat and had a few more drinks together, and Istvan introduced Michael to a particularly delicious type of cheese roll which the woman who owned the stall baked on the premises. It was clear that Istvan was not in a hurry to get back to work, or anywhere else for that matter. Before they left, Istvan told Michael that he had enjoyed their meeting, and hoped that they could have lunch there again together very soon.

'In fact,' Istvan said before he got up and left, 'why don't you come and visit us at home sometime? We would love to see you.'

He wrote down his mobile telephone number on a piece of paper, and Michael gave Istvan his house telephone number in return. Istvan shook Michael by the hand and got up and left. Michael had also very much enjoyed the meeting. He felt he had made a good friend and looked forward to the opportunity of meeting Istvan again himself. He finished the last piece of his cheese roll, emptied the glass of brandy, picked up his shopping bag and made for home himself.

Chapter 46

It wasn't difficult for Michael to decide that he would like to meet up with Istvan again, and a few days later he phoned him on his house landline. He had never used the telephone in the house he was renting before – he had nobody to phone – but the telephone was installed in the living room and the monthly rental payments for the line generously paid for by the landlady. He picked up the handset and dialled Istvan's mobile number.

Istvan was at work on a job when he answered his mobile. He told Michael that he was in the middle of installing window frames on a three-storey house in town that was being refurbished. He was up on the third floor hanging out of the window frame that he was fitting when Michael called, he told him. Nevertheless, he took time out to greet Michael, told him he and his wife would be delighted to invite Michael for supper, and asked Michael if he would like to come round the following evening?

'Thank you very much Istvan, that would be great,' Michael said, pleased to be invited out and to have the chance to have an evening in the company of others.

He wrote down the address and instructions how to get to their house, and rang off. He sat in front of his stove thinking about the solitude which he had been thrust upon him by events, but was pleased that this was about to end in some small way.

The next day Michael went back to the market in town and looked around for a present to take for his hosts that evening. If he were in the UK, or even in Budapest, he might have bought some flowers. But he was aware that, if he had done so, these might well have been flown in refrigerated from Kenya, or some other similar tropical location, irrespective of the damage that the aviation-fuelled air miles journey might have inflicted on the climate that had nurtured the flowers in the first place. Michael looked around thoughtfully at what was on offer from the usual abundance of local produce in front of him. He wanted to show his appreciation for the kind hospitality his hosts were offering him while at the same time presenting them with a gift which might have been a little different from their usual fare. After searching around all the stores in the market, he went back to his friend the greengrocer and bought a large bag of succulent and not over-ripe aubergines. He hoped that these would be acceptable as a gift.

Michael was not disappointed by the impact his gift of aubergines made. Katalin, Istvan's wife, was delighted by the contents of the plastic bag he held up to her in greeting when he arrived at their house. He could see that her response was completely genuine. Michael was ushered into the living room by Istvan, his coat and snow hat having been removed and hung on a hook in the entrance hall. He was sat in front of an open fire and offered a glass of chilled Tokai sweet wine as an aperitif, which he accepted gratefully. Istvan sat beside him on the sofa, leaning back in a relaxed fashion with his glass held in his lap, while Katalin perched on a less comfortable chair on the other side of the fire, friendly but perhaps a little embarrassed and less relaxed by this visit of a strange Englishman to their home.

Michael enjoyed his evening getting to know Istvan and Katalin. He learnt about their home town, their lives and their children – they had three grown children, two boys and a girl – and their newly born granddaughter, without them asking any questions about Michael's personal life and family. At first, Michael had felt uneasy about the difficulty he was having in not wishing to discuss current family details on his side, but compensated for this by telling them a little about his upbringing and life as a child and young man. He talked a lot about the state of the UK as it was at the present time, and Istvan and Katalin were enthusiastic to hear about how things might have changed since they had made the decision to come back to Hungary after having spent nearly ten years living and working in Croydon. They had enjoyed living there, where their kids had spent a great deal of their childhood. They were grateful that their children had acquired the benefit of becoming bi-lingual, fluent in both English as well as Hungarian. Istvan and Katalin were proud of the advantages that their life in England had brought to them and their family, but explained to Michael how, in the end, they had become homesick for their motherland and had decided to come back home to Hungary. Istvan's income was not as secure as the one he'd had in the UK, and his self-employed trade certainly did not pay as much. But against that, the cost of living was so much cheaper in Hungary than they had found it in the UK, especially living in Greater London, and they were content to be home.

Perhaps stimulated by this talk of their love of their

motherland, after they had finished dinner Istvan reached up and took down his violin from the shelf next to the bookcase where he kept it. Lovingly taking it out of its case, he passed a yellow duster over the instrument before raising his chin to accommodate the chinrest. Holding the instrument steady with his chin, he adjusted the strings with both hands before starting to play. Istvan played beautifully, and Michael was transfixed. The sound of a well-known Hungarian rhapsody filled the house, the violinist demonstrating perfect control over the pitch, the phrasing and the rising and falling volume of the music. How is it that a mere carpenter can play the violin as beautifully as this, Michael found himself asking? But in truth, he already knew the answer to his own question. He knew enough about Hungary, and had lived there long enough, to know that this love of music, and the playing of the violin in particular, was in their blood.

Michael had been to enough concerts at the Liszt Academy in Budapest, and many other concert halls in the city and outside, to hear scores of different violinists play with equal virtuosity. Indeed, he had also sat in restaurants or passed musicians on the streets or in the Metro subways, where he had heard gypsy violinists play with such talent and passion that it had often made him wonder how these amateur players differed in any way from the nationally acclaimed maestros. Hearing Istvan playing his violin so naturally in his own living room, in the presence only of his wife and visiting friend, was what gave the music a special charm in itself. Istvan took a drink of wine before launching into a series of wistful gypsy melodies, playing on into the night.

The time with Istvan and his wife seemed to pass very

quickly, as far as Michael was concerned. They had all been very relaxed and enjoyed each other's company, not to mention Istvan's music and a good deal of Hungarian wine. When Michael next looked at his watch, he realised it was past eleven p.m.

'I really must be going,' he said. 'I know you have to get up early, Istvan. Thank you so much for a lovely evening – and a delicious meal.' The last comment was directed to Katalin. 'Thank you especially for the beautiful music,' he said to Istvan.

With this they embraced, wished him a safe journey home and invited him to come again soon. Michael hesitated to invite them back to his place, basic as it was, but said he would be delighted to accept their offer to visit them again very soon.

Chapter 47

The expected winter snow had arrived with a vengeance. The local roads around Keszthely were virtually unpassable and very little traffic could be heard moving along the road at the top of the track which led down the hill to his house, certainly not in the early morning until the snow ploughs had passed by and completed some clearance. In spite of the weather and his continuing paranoia about being discovered, Michael had started to venture out farther afield as the days and weeks went by.

He would strap on his snowshoes and tramp with a high stepping gait down from his house to the lake, and then either left or right along the water's edge. The cold was so intense, made even colder by the wind chill factor, that his face would feel as if it had a mud pack on it, his facial muscles being literally frozen and making him unable to smile. The hairs in his nostrils stuck out, frozen solid. He had dressed himself with as many layers of underclothes and over clothes as he could lay his hands on, zipping and buttoning up his quilted coat to his chin, over a number of thick woollen sweaters. On his hands he wore linen gloves, on top of which he pulled thick leather gloves, so that he could barely close his fingers to grip onto nearby braches to steady himself from slipping over on the ice. But even with this layered clothing he could feel the frozen wind as it seemed to enter and pass right through his body. He felt as if he was a character in the films he had seen of Canadian trappers on the banks of Hudson Bay.

The shore of the lake was frozen solid, the mud as hard as concrete under his feet. The water was no longer lapping up cheerfully onto the lake sides, as it had been on the day he first arrived at the house and had walked down to investigate the lakeside for that first time. The twenty or thirty feet of water closest to the shore was frozen solid, the water beyond that looking grey and unusually still. It seemed as if it would be frozen hard far out, and perhaps even right across to the other side of the lake, if he were to come back again in a day or two. He started to hatch a plan that, if the winter freeze were to continue for another few weeks, he might try to walk from one side of the great Balaton Lake to the other. On further thought, he admitted to himself that this was pretty unlikely, not to mention a foolhardy project.

Michael had a go at trying his hand at a bit of fishing. He had found an old axe in the shed, which he kept by his bed at night in case of intruders. He took this out to the lakeside, but even after swinging it repeatedly, he found it impossible to make any real impression on the ice. He spent some time attempting to break up an area of ice large enough to make a hole which would be big enough to fish through. But the thickness of the rock-hard ice resisted him. After about half an hour of swinging the axe above his head and crashing it down on the solid surface, his breath freezing in the air before it hardly left his mouth, he had to admit defeat and give up the attempt. He had thought that a few meaty fresh fish cooked on the wood stove might be a healthy option, supplementing his diet. Instead, he trudged back into the house through the balcony, threw the door to the wood stove open to get some heat back into his body before even considering removing a single piece of his thick clothing, and poured himself a large brandy. He understood now how severe and threatening Mother Nature could be, and how human beings still had to treat her with respect, in spite of all their modern technology.

His snowshoes were now essential for any trip that he made, up to the road and beyond. The track from the house to the road was only a few hundred metres, but in this weather the uphill walk had him expending a significant amount of energy. With each step he made his feet would sink deep into the snow drifts, in spite of the tennis racket-like snowshoes attached to his boots. And with every further step he made he had to struggle hard to lift his foot back up and out of the foot hole into which it had sunk, only for the foot to sink back down again into the next hole it made in the snowdrift. He realised with fear that if he were to be pursued by an assailant in these conditions, it would be virtually impossible for him to make a "run" for it. By the time he did reach the road, he was panting for breath and had to rest for a few minutes, hyper-ventilating from the effort he had made just to reach the top of the track.

Once he was on the road, the going was easier but by no means straightforward. It was difficult to make out the exact course of the road and, since there was no pavement, he would very often find himself caught up in the snow-covered undergrowth that he had wandered off course into. The snow on the road itself would sometimes be compacted by the wheels of the few cars that had managed to travel down it earlier in the day, and he would find himself slipping around on an ice rink and in danger of a broken bone. At other times when he found himself to be the first human being to be passing down the road that day, either by foot or machine, the snow could be as high as his knees. If he did come across footsteps in the newly minted snow, he would immediately start to worry who it might have been that had made these footsteps, and whether they had been coming in the direction of his house.

One evening he ventured out up the snow-covered track to the road to look for a drink and some company at the small bar that was a few hundred metres along the road from his house, on the outskirts of the town. He had taken to visiting there regularly before the winter weather descended and felt he should not let a bit of snow deter him now. While he had not exactly made friends in the place, because of his very limited ability to communicate in Hungarian, he found the atmosphere comforting. He had become on nodding terms with a number of the regulars and had been befriended by some of the bar girls who would sit down beside him and whom he bought a drink for from time to time. It was a warm and friendly place, with a wood fire in the corner of the main bar and a busy trade of customers. It made a change for Michael from the loneliness and familiarity of his rented lakeside house.

That night he had only just sat down at the bar when a man he did not recognise came in and sat down beside him. The man ordered himself a beer and then, unexpectedly, turned on his stool to face Michael and addressed him directly.

'English?' the man asked in a heavy accent.

This time the question did not come over in the friendly manner that had been the case at his first meeting with Istvan. Michael froze in fear. Was this one of the people traffickers come to get him at last?

'Work here?' the man asked again.

There was a pause while Michael took a long drink of his beer, willing his hand not to shake as he did so.

'Holidays,' he said looking directly back into the man's rough face.

They sat there next to each other with no further words being exchanged. Michael drank his beer slowly, feeling frightened and exposed. The man finally finished his beer, put the glass down loudly on the bar, and wiped his mouth with the back of his hand. He nodded curtly to the barman and got up and left, without another glance in Michael's direction. After the man had left, Michael took another drink of his beer and looked at the barman whose expression of barely disguised fear mirrored his own.

'Tovabb,' the barman replied.

Michael felt his heart beating fast. He knew that the man had made a point of seeking him out, to let him know that he was aware of Michael's presence in the town. He was consumed by the fear that his end really might have come at last. He finished his beer and a few minutes later got up and left the bar himself, with an attempt at a cheerful arm wave in the barman's direction. As he turned off the road onto the track down to his house he stopped and looked to see if he was being followed. He peered along the road in both directions in the dark but could see nobody who might be watching him. He switched on the torch he had brought with him for the return trip in the dark, turned and continued down the track to the house. When he arrived at the house, he closed and barred the shutters across all of the widows and locked the door behind him as he went in. He hardly slept that night.

Chapter 48

The concert hall was packed. The people coming in from the freezing night outside were stamping snow off their boots and clapping their gloves together to shake the ice particles off them. Once inside, the hall was nice and warm. The heat coming from the radiators along the walls was kept inside the building by a huge insulation curtain hanging down across the main entrance door. This consisted of thick, rough blanket-like material on the inside with dark brown leather hide on the outside. All those entering had to struggle to push the curtain aside to gain access to the entrance of the hall, the weight of the curtain causing it to fall back into place after each entrant. The hall itself was tastefully but unpretentiously decorated for Christmas, with holly and ivy and poinsettia plants on the windowsills and small twinkling lights framing each of the windows.

Michael came in late, just as the concert was about to begin. This was the first time he had dared to venture out since his brief meeting with the man in the bar. His renewed fear for his life had not subsided, but he knew he could not stay locked inside his house permanently. He had seen the concert advertised by a poster on the wall of the market a few days before and decided it would do him good to have a Christmas treat in the company of others with the chance to hear some live classical music. He could not believe that his life would be at risk amongst all these other concertgoers. He had left the house early, but had only just made it to the hall on time because of the atrocious weather conditions which had meant that the walk into town had taken him much longer than usual. Although he was near the back, he was sat in a seat to the left side of the hall from where he had a good view of the grand piano which was placed in the middle of the small, raised stage. From his vantage point he could see the keyboard well.

The concert began in the usual Hungarian fashion, with a rather excited middle-aged woman dressed in a crimson silk blouse and black skirt introducing the proceedings. She stood on the edge of the stage and started reading a pre-prepared script from an open folder, not looking up at the audience as she read. Michael's small amount of Hungarian was not enough for him to understand the detail of her speech, but she was obviously welcoming the audience, introducing the pianist and his achievements and going on to discuss the programme notes of the pieces they were about to hear. Not being able to understand what was being said, Michael was relieved when she finished, to applause, after only about five minutes. He knew that these introductions were sometimes apt to go on much longer. Indeed, he had attended a concert in Budapest a year or two before which had been preceded by a similar welcoming introduction which had lasted at least thirty minutes. During this rather painful process, an American tourist in the front row had unfolded a large map which he had proceeded to hold up in front of himself and study during the protracted preamble. But even this had not given the woman on the stage a hint, and she had continued to drone on for far too long, much to the boredom of himself and most of the others in the audience.

The soloist was a young man named Laszlo Farkas. He was dressed not with the traditional black bow tie and tails but with a more modern and relaxed open-necked laced white shirt, black waist coat, black trousers and patent leather shoes with rather long pointed toes. He entered the stage to warm applause and bowed low to the audience, holding on to the edge of the piano as he did so and flicking back his large mop of hair as he stood back up again. He was a local boy whose success on the keyboard had taken him to study piano at the Liszt Academy in Budapest and from where he was gaining a rising reputation for his performances. Michael remembered having seen the pianist's name on a number of concert programmes in the last year or two, but was not aware that he had heard him play before that night.

The first half of the concert consisted of a rendition of the Four Impromptus by Franz Schubert. Michael knew the music well and sat back prepared to be transported. The first impromptu opened with a beautifully sustained chord, which the pianist hung on to exquisitely, before leaning into the haunting music which followed. The second impromptu gave way to cascading runs in the right hand answered by firm military chords in the left. The beautiful melody of the third impromptu was music which Michael loved and knew very well. Before the movement had finished, he became aware that tears were running freely down his cheeks. He realised that these had been triggered not only by the beauty of the music but also by the thoughts that were going through his mind of the family and home that he had left behind in

England and would be away from this Christmas. Even now, although he still believed he had done the right thing in fleeing from home, he continued to feel a deep remorse about the fact. Sitting there in this emotional Christmas concert, he also admitted to himself that over the past few weeks his yearnings for the relationship he'd had during his recent affair with Zita had increased. Throughout the time he had spent alone his memories of her had continued to haunt him. The feeling of her hand in his as they walked home after a concert, the warmth of her body next to his in bed and the pleasures they shared there. The glissandos of the fourth impromptu, racing towards its finale, shook him back into the present.

At the end of the concert Michael rose to his feet with the rest of the audience and clapped in loud appreciation of the performance. They all clapped initially in the conventional random style, before giving way to fevered stamping and clapping in unison in the Hungarian fashion. This was not something that the soloist could ignore, and he returned to the stage a number of times before seating himself at the piano again and providing the hungry audience with a beautiful Chopin nocturne. As the concert wound up, Michael buttoned up his coat to his chin, pulled on his gloves and walked out of the hall with the crowd of chattering happy people. The air was still freezing cold outside, so that his breath came out into the air like a small snowstorm and the hairs in his nose froze instantly, like mini-icicles in his nostrils.

He trudged back home alone, looking warily behind him at regular intervals to ensure that he was not being followed.

He had locked the house securely before he went out, left the lights on and the wood burning stove alight: the house was welcoming and warm when he returned. He poured himself a small glass of brandy and sat down with it in front of the stove. It was Christmas Day in three days' time and he would be on his own. He had bought some pieces of turkey, sprouts and pickles in the market and a bottle of red wine. He would eat them alone on Christmas Day, but Istvan and his wife had kindly invited him for dinner on 26th December and he was very much looking forward to their company again. In the meantime, he locked and bolted all the doors and windows once more.

Chapter 49

When he heard the two men in front of him in the queue in the bank speaking in English and having problems explaining what the reason for their visit was, Istvan volunteered to help them with translation without hesitation. He was not in any hurry. He had the afternoon off and his wife was not going to be back home until about five o'clock. It was not the first time he had come to the assistance of English-speaking tourists who were struggling to communicate because of a lack of knowledge of the Hungarian language. During the summer months, he had become accustomed to help out in this way quite frequently. Very often it was just a word, a phrase or a direction that was required, but occasionally, as was the case now at the bank, the situation was a little more complicated. He knew enough about translation to be aware of the importance of not putting his own interpretation on what was being said or asked. To keep to this rule, he was always careful to attempt to translate the English into Hungarian *verbatim*, and not embroider the conversation in any way or express his own opinions about the wrongs and rights of the situation during the conversational exchanges. That was why, as the older of the two men spoke clearly and in simple sentences for him to translate to the female bank clerk, he did his very best to translate his sentences into an equally simple Hungarian alternative.

As he conveyed the Englishmen's enquiries to the bank

teller, Istvan knew that his translation was being clearly understood, that the men were starting to get their message across with his help. But he could also see from the girl's face that the initial exchanges he had translated for the two men had caused complications in some way. She clearly was beginning to have a problem not with their questions, now that she could understand them, but with something she could see on the computer screen which she was scanning in front of her. When she left the counter in order to seek the manager's help, Istvan was happy to wait patiently and, when he was politely invited to accompany the party into the manager's office, he was equally happy to agree to continue as their interpreter. It was obvious to him in any case that the Englishmen were not going to get any further with their enquiries unless they had the continued help of his translation services.

It was only as the conversation in the manager's office ensued, with the manager appearing to be particularly apologetic and polite in his explanation to the two men, that it suddenly dawned on Istvan who they were talking about. The "Michael Butler", who they were referring to as if he was dead, was his friend Michael he had met in the market. Istvan came over in a sudden cold sweat. He had realised that Michael was over-wintering alone here in Keszthely, a long way from his home country. But he had no idea of the reasons for this, and why his own sons might think him dead and were having a problem with their father's bank statements. Michael had told Istvan nothing about his recent personal or family life, even during the evening visit that he had spent with Istvan and his wife in their home. And Istvan had always been polite enough not to enquire.

Istvan was suddenly not sure what to do. Should he interrupt to tell Michael's sons that their father was here in Keszthely, that he knew him and that he'd been a visitor in his house? As the conversation progressed, he could not understand why Georg Pasztor was telling them a story about an administrative error on the Bank's behalf. This was clearly a lie – although the two sons seem to be accepting Pasztor's explanation at face value – but Istvan sensed that, if the bank manager was indeed lying to them, then he might be doing so for a good reason. Could he even be trying to protect his new friend Michael? He went on with his interpreting, concentrating even more than usual on attempting to keep his translation exact and succinct, while thrashing around in his mind what to do for the best. The longer the conversation continued, the clearer it became to Istvan that he should keep his counsel and not divulge what he knew to either party. He also knew that he had to alert Michael about this meeting, which he had become involved in by pure chance, as soon as possible after it had finished.

The three men stood on the pavement outside the Bank at the end of their meeting with the manager. Michael's two sons shook Istvan's hand and thanked him sincerely for his help. They were obviously genuinely grateful to him for the way in which he had come to their aid. Istvan shook both their hands in return, accepted their thanks graciously and turned and walked back up the street. It was only when he was about a hundred metres up the road that he remembered that he had not conducted his own small business with the bank. That could wait for another day. He walked on straight in the direction of his house.

When Istvan reached home his wife was still out and not due back for at least another hour. He picked up his phone and called Michael at home.

'Hello?' Michael's voice sounded cautious.

Istvan was aware that his friend was unlikely to be receiving many calls on his telephone these days, if any at all. As soon as Michael realised it was Istvan calling him, it was apparent to Istvan that his voice relaxed.

'Michael, it's me, Istvan.'

'Oh, Hi Istvan, good to hear from you again,' replied Michael. 'What's wrong?' he asked, sensing urgency in Istvan's voice.

'Something's come up,' Istvan said. 'It's better not to talk about it over the phone. Can I come round and talk to you at home?'

'Be my guest. I'm not going anywhere!' Michael chuckled, doing his best to lighten the conversation.

But Istvan could not fail to sense uncertainty in his friend's voice.

Istvan did not exactly run the couple of kilometres to Michael's house, but certainly walked quickly. He did not want Michael's sons to find out the whereabouts of their father without him alerting Michael first, even though this seemed pretty unlikely after the way that their interview with the bank manager had finished. It seemed to him that Georg Pasztor had put them well and truly off the scent. When he reached the end of the track down to Michael's house he walked around to the front door and saw that it was ajar. He knocked on the knocker and walked in.

'Come in Istvan. Good to see you.' Michael jumped up with a mug in his hand as Istvan entered the living room. 'I've just made some tea. The kettle's only just off the boil. Would you like a cup?'

'Thank you Michael, I would,' replied Istvan.

When Michael came back into the living room, he handed Istvan a mug of tea and they sat down together on the chairs in front of the wood stove.

'So, what's up?' Michael asked, looking at his friend.

Istvan proceeded to relate to Michael the events in the bank that afternoon. How a chance offer to help two Englishmen translate an interview they were having with the bank staff turned in to Istvan's realisation that these two men were in fact Michael's sons. And that they had come to Keszthely to investigate some irregularity about a bank account of Michael's. A bank account which they thought should be inactive in view of the fact that their father was dead.

As he was talking, Michael sat quietly, saying nothing, but Istvan could see his friend was looking pale and alarmed by what he was telling him. When he had finished his account of the meeting, Istvan looked apologetically at Michael.

'I hope you don't mind me barging in with this news, Michael. Am I right in concluding that these were your sons?'

'Sounds like it,' Michael replied, doing his best to shrug, but clearly agitated by this news. 'Oh, *bugger*, I suppose I should have expected something like this!' Then, after a pause: 'Did you say they went off convinced by Pasztor's story?'

'I believe so,' replied Istvan. 'The older brother Martin seemed completely convinced and perhaps even relieved. The younger one – Jeff? – did not say much at all. But he did not have any questions for Mr Pasztor and did not raise any objections about the story they'd heard.'

'Bloody hell,' sighed Michael. 'Forewarned is forearmed, I suppose. Thank you for coming to tell me about this, Istvan.'

From then on Michael did all the talking. He told Istvan every detail about his posting in Budapest; his work for the Roma and his investigation into the people-trafficking trade; the attack in Aradi Street; and the finding one night of a man hanging dead in his garage in London while he was on leave working there. He was sure that he had been targeted by those in the people-trafficking and sex exploitation trade in Hungary because of what he knew, because of what his investigations had uncovered. He also told Istvan that he now feared that his whereabouts here in Keszthely had recently been discovered and that he was under surveillance. He believed his life may still be at risk.

Istvan sat and listened to all this in silent amazement. He was not expecting Michael to divulge all the secrets in his cupboard, and was frankly astounded that he had done so in such detail and with such openness to a man with whom he had become friends only a few weeks before. He wondered silently whether the man was deluded, seriously paranoid perhaps. At the same time, it became clear to Istvan as Michael spoke, that he had a need to share these events at last with somebody he could trust, after all these months. Istvan was also perceptive enough, however, to realise that Michael had not shared with him the reasons why he had chosen to keep his self-imposed exile from his wife and family up to now.

Chapter 50
February 2015

As father and son sat together in the house by Lake Balaton, Michael continued telling Jeff his story. He started by explaining to Jeff about his work in Budapest. He told Jeff what he had been doing to support the Roma community in Hungary and the way he had stumbled upon an international organisation for people-trafficking which involved the sex exploitation trade of young Roma girls; about how he had been attacked in the street in Budapest and his organisation's concern that this might have been something to do with the violent men running the sex trade in the country wanting to kill him before he was able to expose them, which was why he had been sent back to England on leave by his boss; and how later on that Saturday night – after Jeff had said goodbye to him and left to catch his train to Glasgow – he had heard a commotion outside the house following which, when he investigated what it had been caused by, he'd found the body of a man hanging from a rope in their garage; and, finally, how he had come to the conclusion that this man had almost certainly been murdered in mistaken identity, and that the dead man in their garage should have been himself. That they were indeed trying to kill him for what he knew.

Michael explained to his younger son that, when he had discovered the body of another man hanging there in their garage, he knew he had no alternative but to flee the scene of the murder. He told Jeff that he realised that this was the only way that he could perhaps save his own life and, at the same time, protect Marion from the possibility of a further attempt being made to harm them both.   He had realised almost immediately that there was a chance that the body in their garage would be mistaken for the body of himself. He had also calculated that, if this were to have been the case, running away from the scene would protect himself and Marion from harm, perhaps forever. He had not wished any harm to Marion or to his three children, he told Jeff. On the contrary, he believed at the time that he was making a difficult decision to remove himself from his wife and family for a while in a way which he hoped would protect them all from future harm. He believed that the fact that no harm had come to them subsequently was proof that his decision had been the correct one. Nevertheless, he had been desperately lonely and missing them all ever since he had been living here in isolation in the south of Hungary. When he had finished recounting this story, there was a pause.

'Christ, Dad,' Jeff said, after listening to all this. 'You must have been shit scared.' And then, after another pause, 'But why have you been hiding up here ever since without making any attempt to get back in touch with us, or at least sending Mum a message to let her know that you were OK?'

Jeff did not ask this question in any sort of accusatory way. It was clear that he truly did not understand and just wanted to know why. Michael looked down at the floor. The truth was that he was not precisely sure of the answer to this question himself either. He had known that he needed to hide, he told Jeff. And that any attempt to contact Marion or Jeff might blow his cover and lead to them all being put at risk again, perhaps even of their lives. He told Jeff that he was certain he was now under continued surveillance even here, and he described the encounter he'd had with the man in the bar there in Keszthely only a few weeks earlier.

He also knew, he explained to his son, that he needed time out from life as it was. He knew that, as time had gone on, he had decided to remain *incognito* not just from Tovabb or any other party that may have been wishing him dead. He had also reached a time in life when he needed a break from the whole of his life. Call it the "male menopause", if you want. It was a fact that he had hardly been able to articulate, even to himself, but had just gone along with. The piece of the jigsaw that Michael did not tell Jeff was the subject of his recent affair with Zita and the fact that he still remained uncertain about whether he wished to go back to Marion or start a new life with this other woman.

'I don't know, Jeff. I just needed to stay in hiding without putting myself or my life in any more risk.' This sounded pathetic as he said it, and he knew that it was.

Jeff gave a twitch of his head, but otherwise sat completely still. 'What did you mean on that last Saturday evening when you said, "if you don't know, I don't know"?'

Jeff was not exactly interrogating his father now, but Michael could see that he wanted more answers. He wanted to be able understand a little more about why Michael had put them all through this agony and grief.

'What I meant, Jeff, was that it was better that you did not know the full gravity of the situation. Since I had chosen not to share this information with you then, it would have been as if it had never happened. The same for your mother, which as it happens, continues to be the case. There was no way that I felt able to burden Marion with those details, and in many ways I still do not wish to do so.'

'But, Dad... did it not occur to you that when you left like that you would leave such a lot of *pain* behind you? We loved you, you know – we still love you,' he corrected himself, 'but since you left no note or sign that everything was actually all right, would continue to be all right – none of us has had any reason to believe that it was not all right. And that you were dead.'

Michael swallowed hard and looked miserably at Jeff. 'Believe me, Jeff. It was never my intention to hurt you, or your mother or the rest of the family. It was just... it was just the only way I was able to cope with the situation. And has been the only way I have been able to cope with it since. I am so sorry, Jeff...'

Chapter 51

Jeff spent the rest of the day with his father, sitting there in front of the wood fire discussing all manner of things. For a while the discussion left the events of the last six months behind and they spent a few enjoyable hours remembering family outings and holidays that they had spent together. They reminded each other of all the different places around Europe where they'd lived. Some had been like Lisbon, in palatial accommodation with sunshine and an easy access to the sea and an outdoor life. Others, like Warsaw, had required them to live in a cramped apartment in a high-rise building, in a city which was both dirty and polluted at the time. They both agreed that the city was lacking in character, largely consisting of concrete and glass in spite of an attempt which had been made to re-create the old town. This was perhaps not surprising, since the city of Warsaw had been virtually razed to the ground during the Second World War, and had had to be completely re-built as a consequence.

Jeff could only remember the smoky fogs which came down out of nowhere at any time and were the start of his asthma. During their time in Warsaw he had experienced very bad attacks and, although these were never quite severe enough to land him in hospital, they caused him a lot of pain and distress, he remembered, and were the reason for him missing a good deal of schooling at the time. Luckily he was rarely bothered by the problem these days – an occasional bit of wheezing and coughing during the pollen months or if he got a viral illness during the cold winter air – and he had been told by a doctor that it was not unusual for children to grow out of the problem as they became adults. Jeff was sure however, he told his Dad now, that it was leaving the Warsaw smog behind that accounted for his recovery from the condition.

At about six o'clock Michael poured them both a drink and fixed them a bit of supper. He served up some cold smoked mackerel with Hungarian kolbasz sausage, cheese and fresh dark brown bread. They both agreed that the cheese was more like a block of waxy rubber. Michael admitted that, as far as he was concerned, all the cheeses he had ever eaten in Hungary were equally boring, and they had a laugh about the fact that the Hungarian word for cheese, "sajt", was pronounced "shite", however it was spelt! But the fish and sausages were excellent and, with some beers to go with them, they eat well and felt full after having had an enjoyable meal together.

After supper they got up from the table and sat down in the front of the fire again with a glass of brandy. The discussion came back once more to the present situation which Michael had found himself in, and what he wanted to do about it. Michael told Jeff that he had known all along that he could not stay hidden up on the shores of Lake Balaton forever, and that he would have to make his way back home sooner rather than later. At the same time, he acknowledged, he should have taken steps at the outset to have at least sent a message to Marion to tell her that he was still alive, and well. (Jeff did not have the heart to tell his father about the funeral that had taken place and all the details of the closure of his financial affairs and so on. It must have occurred to his father that this would have been the result of the dead body hanging in the garage being mistaken for his own? But he felt that it was not the right time to go in to all these details at that moment.)

'How do you want to break the news to Mum, Dad, and who do you want to do it?'

'Oh, I'll do it myself, Jeff,' his father replied. 'Just give me a couple of weeks to get myself and my plans together. When I've done so, I'll return to Budapest and book a flight back to London. I think it would be best if I tell Marion what has happened myself. But I won't just turn up at the house. I'll probably give her a ring before I do so, to give her time to get over the shock.'

They both agreed that, in the meantime, they would keep the news that Michael was still alive and well in Hungary to themselves. Jeff concurred with his father that if he were to tell Martin or Sophie, the news might come out by mistake, and that this would not be fair or kind to Marion. He also had enough sense to understand that, should the news of his father's "return to life" reach the media, it would very likely become an international headline. If this were to happen, Jeff acknowledged, then Michael's life and the safety of Marion and his family might once again be put in jeopardy.

The talks had gone on late into the night and it was about eleven p.m. when Jeff took his leave. He said goodbye and embraced his father one last time, before leaving to walk up the track towards the road back in to Keszthely. Michael gave him his spare torch so that he could pick his way safely up the overgrown path.

As he climbed up the track, Jeff looked up at the moonbright sky. Suddenly, he was sure that he could see the silhouette of a man, lit up by the moonlit night sky behind him, standing at the top of the track looking down towards where he was. He hesitated as he saw the man but, a second later, the silhouette had disappeared. He finished his climb to the top of the track and stepped out onto the road. He stood on the roadside peering left and right into the dark, using the torch to try to penetrate further into the dark night and undergrowth on both sides of the road.

There was nobody to be seen in either direction and Jeff assumed that the man must have disappeared into the deep woods which covered the lakeside hill which he had just climbed up. He turned onto the road and started to walk the couple of kilometres back in to Keszthely and his hotel.

The next morning Jeff woke up early, paid his bill and said goodbye to the woman at the desk. He decided to return to Budapest by train. When he reached the station he was lucky enough to find that there was a train leaving in fifteen minutes and he bought a ticket and got on. The train journey back to Budapest was faster than the bus trip had been, even though the train was not exactly an express and stopped frequently. The train took him back to Budapest along the southern shore of the lake, passing through Siafok and other towns he had not seen before. The journey gave Jeff the opportunity to see the lake from the opposite side from that which he and Martin had travelled down only a couple of days before. The train line was on the other side of the road from the lake, but the view of Lake Balaton was at times even more impressive than it had been on their journey down by bus. This was on account of the fact that the train track was higher than the road for much of its course, allowing Jeff a view over the lakeside buildings and trees across to a wide uninterrupted panorama of the lake itself.

When the train arrived at Budapest Keleti Station, Jeff got off and caught a tram back to Michael's apartment on Eötvös Street. He let himself in and looked around. Now that he knew that his father was still alive, the flat somehow took on a different appearance. He went online and booked himself onto the easyJet flight to Gatwick for the next afternoon. He then sat down and wrote out a list of his travel and hotel expenses, with an accompanying letter in English to Georg Pasztor at the OTP bank in Keszthely, giving his UK address. He left the flat and walked round the corner to the main post office in Terez Korut and posted the letter off.

By the time he got back it was early evening. He poured himself a drink and phoned Melanie. He told her that he had finished his business there in Hungary and would be at home to greet her when she arrived back from her catering course in Reading. She was excited to know that she was going to see him the next evening and started to ask him questions about how he had got on. He told her a little bit about his meeting up with Martin and their visit to the bank in the town of Keszthely, but said that he would tell her the rest of the story of his trip when he saw her the following night. Michael had given him permission to tell Melanie about the fact that he had found his father still alive, but Jeff decided that this was best not done over the phone, even to her.

The next night they were back in each other's arms again.

Jeff told Melanie the whole story of his trip to Hungary, and the amazing news that he had located his father alive and well. They hugged each other, happy about the news and even happier to be back together again. The following morning they were both hard at work once more in her parents' pub.

*

At about the same time, in a small town in Fife, on the East coast of Scotland, the local police inspector had closed the missing persons' file on a man who had disappeared about three years before. The man had had no close relatives, but he'd been known to spend time travelling round and living rough on the streets of Edinburgh and Glasgow and other cities. He'd had several convictions for petty theft and burglary. Had the police inspector known, the man bore more than a passing resemblance to Michael Butler.

His case was now placed in the "inactive" file.

Chapter 52

'Oh, *Christ!*' Jeff's voice exploded unexpectedly across the kitchen.

It was only about three weeks since he had returned from his trip to Hungary.

'What is it, Darling?' Melanie turned to look at her boyfriend, with concern in her voice.

Jeff was sitting at the table looking pale. He was holding the cream velum envelope which had arrived in the post addressed to him that morning. She had picked it up from the doormat and placed it on the kitchen table so that he would see it when he finally got up late to have his breakfast. In his other hand he was holding a white card with a gold border which he had at that moment removed from the envelope. Melanie leant over and took the card from Jeff's hand. She read the gold wording in a sort of whisper, mouthing the words as she read, which was a habit of hers:

Mrs Marion Butler & Mr Henry Hampson
Request the Pleasure of:
Jeffery Butler + Friend
To Celebrate Their Marriage
11 a.m. Sunday 12th April 2015
Le Mesnil
Near Thury-Harcourt
Normandy, France

The Marriage Ceremony will be followed by a Reception
and afterwards
by Evening Dinner & Dancing till late
Dress code: Smart
R.S.V.P. Tel. (0033) 02 31 41 51 99

The wording of the card was very formal, but there was no doubt about the message it contained.

'I see what you mean,' breathed Melanie, biting her lip.

'What the hell are we going to do?' Jeff asked her. 'That's only four weeks away.' Jeff jumped up to face Melanie, in a demonstration of his agitation, as he asked the question both to her and to himself.

They stood there looking at each other, neither of them being able to find any words to answer Jeff's question adequately.

Finally Melanie said: 'We have to tell Marion, Jeff.'

Jeff gave an uncomfortable wriggle as he stood face to face with his girlfriend. 'Don't you see, Mel, if we tell Marion that Michael is still alive that will lead to the wedding being cancelled and will shatter all the dreams she has been making for her future. She seems so happy at present. Perhaps happier than I can ever remember her being when Dad was "alive". But if we don't tell her, the marriage will go ahead and sometime soon or in the future the truth will come out and the marriage will be proven to have been bigamous, although obviously not intentionally so on Mum's part. Nevertheless, that will lead to her marriage to Henry being annulled in any case. We're damned if we do, and we're damned if we don't!'

They sat down at the kitchen table simultaneously, suddenly feeling physically exhausted by the news that they had just received and the dilemma which they both fully understood this had put them in. After a moment's silence, Melanie looked at Jeff.

'There is one other option, Jeff. You could tell Henry about Michael's re-appearance and let *him* decide what course of action he feels it is best to take. Marion has got to be told, and it would probably be kindest if he were to break the news to her himself. It would be a gentle way of them accepting together that their marriage cannot go ahead. If he decides not to tell her, then he does so knowing the secret, which will be bound to come out in the future. But it will mean that he really wants to be her husband, for the moment at least. He will have decided to live for that moment. Either way, I think it will be a true test of whether he really does love your mother.'

'You're right, Mel,' Jeff said. 'I'll do it now.'

He went into their bedroom, where the computer was sitting on the table in the window. He turned it on and logged into his email account. He composed an email to Henry Hampson, typing the words "urgent – please read" in the subject box.

'Dear Henry,' Jeff began, 'I am sorry to email you with this news, which I know will come as a big shock to you. I have recently arrived back from a trip to Hungary. My brother Martin asked me to fly over to help him investigate an apparent irregularity in a bank statement of our father's from his account in Budapest which he had come across. The long story short, Henry, is that, after Martin returned to the

UK, I located my father hiding up in the south of the country. Michael is alive and well and asking after Marion. Marion, Martin and the rest of the family do not know about this yet. I knew you would want to be the first to know, and assume you would wish to be the person to break this news to Marion. Let me know what you decide. Regards, Jeff Butler.'

After Jeff had composed the email, he called Melanie in. She leant over his shoulder, read the email, and nodded.

'Send it,' she said.

Jeff hit the "send" button.

Chapter 53

It was about ten days since Jeff had received the wedding invitation. At first, he had felt a little upset that his mother had not told him about her plans before sending him an invitation to the wedding. But now he had accepted the fact and was relieved that she was finding happiness again. He'd had no other contact yet from his mother, apart from the wedding invitation, but felt that it was not easy for him to phone her first to congratulate her about her upcoming marriage without giving anything away. And if he were to phone her, he had discussed with Melanie, the difficulty would be that he would have no idea what, if anything, Henry Hampson might have told her. He had also received nothing in reply to his email from Hampson. He might not have told Marion the news that Michael was still alive. Or he might have told her everything. If it had been the latter, he thought that it was almost certain that by now the telephone lines would have been buzzing not only from Marion to himself, but also that he would have received excited phone calls from both Martin and Sophie.

Since his return from Hungary, Jeff had also heard nothing at all from his father. He had been expecting to receive a call or a text any day saying something like: "All sorted here, flying back on Wednesday". But there had been only silence from Michael's end. After about two weeks had elapsed since their meeting in Keszthely Jeff had tried to telephone his dad a number of times, both to the house land line number which he had made a note of and to his father's mobile. But both phones continued to ring with no reply. Over the last few days, he had taken to ringing the phones at different times every day. He was starting to be very concerned about his father's well-being.

'I'm worried about Dad,' he had said to Melanie at supper the night before. Somewhat to his surprise she had replied:

'Why don't you pop back over to check on him, then?'

It was apparent that she had understood and shared Jeff's concerns. Within a week of his returning from Hungary he had received a cheque in the post from Georg Pasztor in Keszthely for a rather large amount in Euros. Without working out the details and the exchange rate, he could see the total was considerably in excess of the expenses claim he had submitted, and that had contained every last item he had spent on the trip including not only air fares and hotel bills but every bus, train and Metro journey he had made. So he was quite able to afford another trip and, as it happened, he also had some leave still owing to him.

Jeff got a last-minute return flight from Gatwick to Budapest. Arriving at Liszt Ferenc Airport late in the evening, he took the bus and Metro to Michael's flat in Eötvös Street to stay the night, as he had done on his previous visit. He turned the key in the lock, opened the door and took a good look around. Everything appeared to be as he had left it the last time. But there was nothing he could see which indicated that his father had been back to the flat, making plans for his return to England perhaps. The boxes all around the floor remained packed and undisturbed and the sofas and other pieces of furniture were still covered with dust sheets. It was exactly as he and Martin had found the place when they had first come over.

The next morning Jeff got the Metro to Keleti station and took the train back to Keszthely. When he arrived at Keszthely station, he walked straight out onto the main square and took the road out of town, heading for Michael's house. The weather was dry and the traffic passing on the road was light. He reached the track off the road and started to walk down towards the house. He could not explain why, but he found himself approaching it as tentatively now as he had done on the first occasion he visited. As he got near, he could see no smoke coming from the wood stove chimney, which was unusual, since Michael always kept the stove alight all round the clock. He had explained to Jeff that it was actually more efficient of heat to do so. The front door was closed but not locked, which also was unusual. Jeff walked straight in without knocking.

The house was as he remembered it. But there was no evidence that his father was still living there. There were no knives and forks on the table or dishes still on the draining board. No evidence of meals being prepared and eaten. Surely his father would not have moved on and left the house unlocked? No, he would have locked up, returned the house keys to the landlady and paid up his rent before leaving. He thought he might try and find out where the landlady lived in town and check this out, just to be sure.

Jeff sat on the veranda steps thinking about what might have happened to his father. He felt very uncomfortable to have found the house empty and his father nowhere to be seen. He could not help but wonder whether some harm had come to his dad, that he might now have finally met his fate at the hands of the gangsters who had been searching for him and found him here on the southern shores of Lake Balaton. If this was the case, Jeff pondered, the realisation also came to him that Michael was in any case still officially dead. The funeral had taken place, the life assurance money had been paid out and his mother had gone through her grieving process, whatever the outcome of her relationship with Henry Hampson. If his father had really met his death "this time", would he really want his mother, and the rest of the family come to that, to have to go through all this again? It also occurred to Jeff that he was the only person still to know that Michael had been alive for these past few months. Apart, that is, from Melanie and Henry Hampson.

The more he thought about it, Jeff was sure that Henry, if he had cancelled his marriage to Marion, would be unlikely ever to mention to anyone why he had done so. That he had cancelled the wedding on the basis of an uncorroborated email from one of Marion's sons claiming that Marion's late husband was not in fact dead! It was more likely that Henry would decide that this had been a ploy on behalf of the sons, a story they had invented to steer their mother clear of a union which they disapproved of or were unhappy about for some reason. In that case, Jeff calculated, Henry would never have the gall to mention to anyone that he had used this as an excuse not to go ahead with his marriage to Marion. And having completely severed his relationship with Marion, it was very unlikely that Henry would ever come to learn whether or not Michael had in fact ever re-appeared in her

253

life.

But the fate of his father remained a mystery. It *was* possible that the criminals who had pursued him to Ealing had realised they had got the wrong man and had now tracked his father down here in Keszthely. During that last reunion he'd had with his father, Michael told Jeff about his brief encounter with the man in the bar and the fact that he was sure that he was under surveillance. He believed that his presence in Keszthely was now known to the men who had tried to kill him before. And that because of what he had uncovered about their people-trafficking and the sex exploitation trade here in Hungary, they still wanted him dead before he could make his findings public. Perhaps it was his father's fears which had caused Jeff himself to develop ideas that somebody might also have been following him, during the couple of days he had spent on his own in Keszthely?

It was also possible, Jeff knew, that these fears of Michael's had been baseless and had arisen out of his father's history of paranoia and depression. It could have been that his father's fears had been completely imaginary. That Michael had decided after all to end his own life, perhaps because of a bout of severe depression and a feeling of worthlessness. Jeff remembered the meeting he'd had with Martin and Sophie in the pub in Soho following the inquest, and that Sophie had told him about their father's history of recurrent episodes of depression and paranoia, which neither of the brothers had been aware of before. In the light of this, Jeff decided that he also could not rule out the possibility that his father *had* taken his own life, here on the shores of Lake

Balaton. But in the absence of a body how could he be sure?

The only way forward for him was to return to Budapest and perhaps make contact with someone who knew his father. Remembering those who had attended the funeral, surely there was at least one confidante amongst them? He considered returning to the bank to talk to the manager again or seeking out the man Isztvan Fischer who spoke such perfect English, but dismissed these options immediately. The fewer people he spoke to here the better. Similarly the landlady. She would find out sooner or later that her tenant was no longer there.

Jeff left his father's empty house and returned to Keszthely, from where he took the first available bus back to Budapest, arriving late in the evening at his father's flat. He sat on the sofa with a glass of wine, chatting on his mobile phone to Melanie for a while. She was disappointed to learn that he would not be returning to the UK immediately, but understood his need to discover what had happened to his father.

He had just finished his conversation with Melanie when he was startled to hear the door of the flat being opened from the outside by keys in the lock. He jumped to his feet and saw a dark-haired young woman entering the flat. At the sight of Jeff, an expression of shock and disbelief crossed her face.

'Who are you and what the bloody hell are you doing in my father's flat?' Jeff demanded.

Chapter 54
August 2014

As soon as the word of Michael's death in London came through, Paolo was the one who went to see Zita to tell her what had happened. He sat on the sofa in her apartment with his arm around her, in spite of his own embarrassment, and broke the news of Michael's death to her as gently as he could. Zita had been sad and lonely when Michael left for the UK, despite his assurances that the separation would only be temporary. But nothing could have prepared her for this. Even before Paolo had finished telling her the details of Michael's death, Zita collapsed into hysterics. Paolo felt poorly equipped to be the one to have to console her, but did his best, out of his own love and respect for Michael. Once she had digested the news, Zita was to spend the following days weeping and in such inconsolable grief that she could not even muster the strength to leave her apartment. She felt that her life could not go on without Michael, she told Paolo.

After his first visit to break the news to her, Paolo was so concerned about Zita that he returned on an almost daily basis to see how she was. He took it on himself to bring her food and the other essential items she needed at each visit. He sat with her as she told him her happy memories of her time with Michael, the concerts they had gone to and the music that had played such a part in their lives together. The utter grief that she now had to cope with was an unbearable sorrow, she told him. Paolo was worried that she might even take steps to end her own life.

Zita's friends and family also despaired of her ever regaining any purpose back into her life. After a few weeks had passed Paolo persuaded her to return to live in the safety of her parents' home in Nagymaros, the small town on the banks of the Danube, where he hoped the peace and beauty of the forested hills and the calm lapping of the river by their little house might restore in her some sense that her life would continue despite the loss of her love.

Chapter 55
February 2015

After a few months, Paolo was pleased to learn from Zita's parents that they had eventually persuaded her that she needed something to occupy herself, as a way of bridging time between the tragic events of the past and the future, in which she must re-build her life without Michael. She had studied English language and literature at university and had now been offered a post as teacher of English at the local Gymnasium, which her parents encouraged her to accept. As she prepared the lessons for the new term, she remembered that many of her books remained in Michael's flat. She still had a set of keys and a quick call to Paolo assured her that the flat remained empty and unsold. She would find all her books there where she had left them if she cared to re-visit, he told her.

So Zita took the train to Budapest and walked the short distance from the station to the flat. The familiarity of the street caused tears to prick her eyes but she made every effort to compose herself. She reached the flat, opened the door with her keys and was shocked to find a young man sitting there in Michael's armchair. He jumped to his feet and shouted:

'Who are you, and what the bloody hell are you doing in my father's flat?'

*

Whoever this young woman was, Jeff could see that she was shocked and distressed to find him in his father's flat. He immediately felt embarrassed that he had shouted at her in such an aggressive way. Perhaps she was merely a cleaning lady or the concierge who Michael had given keys to? He introduced himself to her as Michael's younger son, offered her a glass of wine and went to the fridge for the bottle he had already opened. He turned to see Zita getting glasses out of a cupboard.

'She certainly knows her way around the place,' he thought to himself. He poured two glasses of wine and invited the young woman to sit opposite him on the other armchair.

Without any prompting from Jeff, Zita started to explain to him why she was there in his father's flat, and how she had got in. She had come to retrieve some English language books she needed for teaching the new term. As sensitively as she could, she went on to tell him about her relationship with Michael, and how it had developed. She tried to convey how much she had loved his father but also was honest enough to acknowledge to Jeff that she knew he and the rest of Michael's family would have good reason to feel antipathy towards her when they found out about their affair. She knew they would now accuse her of being the *femme fatale* in their father's life, the marriage breaker.

Jeff's initial response to hearing Zita's account of her affair with his father was one of utter silent indignation. What a master of deceit his father had turned out to be! He had been pleasuring himself with this young woman while masquerading as the epitome of the faithful husband and family man. And here was his "bit of stuff" letting herself into his father's flat with her own set of keys and proceeding to relate her grief to him over his father's death. He was dammed if he would give *her* any cause for hope that his father was still alive! No, he would certainly not tell her that he had recently found his father alive and well.

In spite of the convivial reunion he had spent with his dad in the house on the shores of Lake Balaton only a matter of a few weeks before, the betrayal of his mother by the revelation of this affair Michael had been conducting now incensed Jeff unspeakably. Marion had kept the family home in Ealing as a welcoming place whenever Michael returned on furlough from his job in various European countries. She had supervised their children's education and supported them with their studies as well as sacrificing her own career in support of her husband. The anger he now felt was compounded for Jeff by the knowledge that a few days before he may just have blown his mother's chances of future happiness with Henry Hampson. What a fool he'd been! His father did not deserve to be given a second chance.

Jeff's stricken face moved Zita to tears again. She sat in front of him weeping uncontrollably. When she had recovered sufficiently, she told him that she now regretted her decision to come to the flat, and still more to have told Jeff about her love of Michael.

'I'm sorry, Jeff, I shouldn't have told you all this,' she said as she stood up to leave, smoothing down her skirt, replacing her handkerchief in her purse and finally bringing her own emotions under control. 'It is not my wish to upset you and your family further. I do understand how you must all be going through your own bereavement at the minute. Perhaps it is best that you do not pass on what I have just told you to your mother? I shouldn't have come.'

As she walked to the door Jeff's resolve to remain aloof from this girl crumpled. He called out to her as she reached for the door handle:

'Wait, Zita, I'm sorry. This has been a lot to take in. Please come back for a moment.'

Zita hesitated and then turned and sat back down on the sofa again. Jeff sat down next to her, pausing for few minutes while searching to find the right words to say next. He was trying at the same time to put his own feelings about what she had just told him into perspective.

'I do understand why the recent news of my father's death must have come as a shock to you as well. It certainly was for my mother, myself and the rest of our family, not least when we heard about the way that he had died. In spite of my initial anger about your revelation of your relationship with my father, I can see that you have been going through the same sadness as we have. My immediate feeling just now was to hate you, you know, but what good would that do to all of us?' Jeff paused. 'I think it only proper that I tell you the latest news, which I now see you do have a right to know.'

'What on earth are you referring to?' Zita asked.

'Well, the fact is, I came over with my brother Martin a few weeks ago and, while visiting the town of Keszthely on the south of Lake Balaton, I found Dad in hiding, alive and well.

Zita lent forwards and grasped his arm excitedly.

'Michael is still alive? Can this be true! Please tell me everything that has happened!'

Jeff told her the full story, exactly as his father had sat and told him only a short time before.

'But that's not the end of it,' he said. 'Dad was planning to come back to England by now. But I'd heard nothing since and was so concerned about his safety that I flew back to Hungary on Monday to check on him. But when I re-visited the lakeside house he'd been living in in Keszthely yesterday he was nowhere to be seen. I am seriously worried about his well-being, particularly after what he had told me about his fears that he was now being watched by the men who still want to do him harm.'

Chapter 56

Zita's joy at knowing that Michael had *not* died in the UK was now replaced by her realisation that, if he was still alive, his life was in mortal danger there in Hungary. She had not forgotten how agitated he'd been by the possibility that he was being targeted by men who did not like what he had been doing to support the Roma in Budapest. She began to tell Jeff about what she knew.

'If Michael is still alive, we need to find him, and quickly. But we cannot do this without help,' she said, explaining to Jeff what she knew about the danger that Michael could be in. She told him about the man who had accosted Michael during his trip to Pecs and the attack that had been made on him in Aradi Street.

Jeff, who knew nothing about all this, sat astounded by the story of the attack. His father had withheld that part of his narrative from him when they had sat together in the house by the lake.

They discussed the various possible ways they might go about trying to find out whether Michael was still alive, including involving the Hungarian and international police agencies. But they dismissed this last possibility as unworkable because the police would believe that Michael was officially still "dead".

'How about that man Paolo?' Jeff asked. He had remembered the bear of a man whose words at Michael's funeral had given his mother so much comfort.

'You're right!' Zita told him. 'I hadn't thought of Paolo. He was someone Michael used to trust above all others. He has been working with him on Roma affairs for some years and got to know and like him as a friend.' She got out her phone and, despite the lateness of the hour, phoned Paolo and asked if he could come to meet them at Michael's flat as soon as possible.

They waited together in Michael's flat, Jeff telling Zita in more detail how he had found his father in a small house on the southern shores of Lake Balaton, and how Michael had promised to return to England from there shortly. But that when he re-visited Keszthely the day before he could find no sign of Michael or evidence that he was still living in the house.

'I have been very worried myself about what might have happened to Dad,' he told Zita. 'When I was down in Keszthely this week I started to have fears that Dad might have disappeared because he had been "taken out" – as he called it – by these gangsters. But now that I have heard about your own concerns that his life might be at risk again, I am even more worried.'

At about eight p.m. the bell communicating with the huge door to the street rang. Zita pressed the button on the handset by the front door of the flat to let Paolo in. Soon his heavy tread could be heard as he mounted the stairs to the first floor flat.

Chapter 57

Paolo had not been surprised to receive Zita's call. Prescience, or at least a balance of probabilities, had led him to assume it would only be a matter of time before Michael's Lazarus state would become known. He had hoped that his family would find him and initiate a rescue plan, but this was not how events unfolded.

When one of Paolo's Roma friends who lived in Keszthely contacted him to tell him that a man resembling Michael was living in a house on the shores of Lake Balaton, Paolo had initially dismissed the report as a case of mistaken identity, even though his friend had insisted that the man was English and spoke very little Hungarian. Hadn't he been to Michael's funeral and witnessed the grief of his widow and children? But seeing is believing, and the friend managed to get some photographs of Michael and sent them on to Paolo. When he looked at these he realised his friend was right. There could be no mistake. The pictures he was looking at were indeed pictures of Michael. The friend also reported that the man's two sons had visited Keszthely and one had returned and spent time with Michael. Paolo recognised the younger son Jeff – whom he had met briefly at the funeral – in another photograph which his friend had taken surreptitiously.

Once he had been convinced that Michael was indeed still alive, Paolo's first thought was that he should leave Michael alone to lead his life in Keszthely, respecting that whatever the motives he had for hiding out there were – not to mention the fact that he had somehow returned to a country where there were people who wished him harm – they must have been based on a careful consideration of the risk he was taking.

Recently, however, Paolo's friend had reported that there were others who had found out that Michael was now living in the area. A conversation in a local bar had been overheard. A local drunk was boasting about the money he had been given by a stranger to get information about the English man's presence in the town. Soon after that, Paolo's friend contacted him again to tell him that he had heard that several members of a notorious mafia gang had been seen driving around the town in a darkened Mercedes and that it had to be assumed that their presence there meant that they had tracked Michael down in the town. Paolo immediately sent a couple of trusted Roma men to Keszthely and, under cover of darkness, they whisked Michael to safety in a truck under a consignment of cherries which were destined to be sold in Szena Square market in Budapest the following day. He was now living in the cellar of a Roma safe house in the city.

Chapter 58

Paolo entered the flat, shook Jeff by the hand and bowed slightly to Zita with the words "*kezet csokolom*" – "I kiss your hand". Which he then proceeded to do. He accepted their offer of a drink and all three sat down, uncertain of how to begin the conversation. Without preamble, Paolo told them the news that Michael was alive and well and living in the cellar of the Roma safe house there in Budapest, where he was safe for the moment. He told them sternly, however, that Michael's life was in grave danger and that they would not be able to visit him for fear of discovery. He also told them that their lives would be in danger too if the gang responsible for the previous "murder" of Michael were to discover that they knew of Michael's whereabouts. He advised them that they should leave Michael's flat separately that evening. He had reserved rooms for them in a hotel nearby under false names, he told Jeff and Zita, and gave them new mobile phones with new SIM cards in them. He explained that the concierge of the building was loyal to Paolo and would help them by closing up Michael's flat and removing evidence of their presence there. They should only communicate with Paolo using these new mobile phones he had provided, Paolo said, and that they should not use them to make any other calls whatsoever. He promised to meet up with them again at an anonymous meeting the following day, the time and place of which he would communicate by a text message.

With that, he got up to leave.

As he made for the door, Zita ran to hug Paolo. 'Thank you so much, Paolo! Please tell Michael how much I love him,' she begged him.

'I don't need to tell him that, but I will anyway,' he replied with a smile as he left.

Chapter 59

Jeff and Zita sat eating a hamburger in the McDonalds restaurant at Jasai Mari Square. The restaurant was packed with young people and tourists.

'It doesn't get more anonymous than this,' Jeff remarked to Zita out of the corner of his full mouth.

Paolo arrived and sat next to them on the same table. Quietly, in a low voice, he started to tell them what he knew about the situation. He explained that Michael was the target of the much-feared gang of Mirgo Varga. A great deal of the information he had gained had come from the investigations that he and Michael had previously conducted into the people trafficking rings here in Budapest, as well as from police officers who could be trusted. The sphere of influence of this criminal Mirgo Varga spread across Europe and into the UK; some accounts also suggested that he had contacts in USA and Arab states. His principal activity was the trafficking of drugs and weapons, but he was also involved in trafficking young girls to supply the demand for young women to be enslaved in brothels and "massage parlours". Most of these young women, he explained, were from villages in rural Hungary, Moldova and Romania. Many were poor Roma girls with little education. They were lured by promises of well-paid jobs in hotels and as nannies or au pairs in European capitals. In spite of campaigns by human rights groups to warn people via the internet of this trade in human misery, and some widely publicised films depicting the degradation suffered by the victims of the world-wide sex trade, girls were still tricked into leaving their homes, surrendering their passports and identity cards, and joining convoys of other victims in buses and cars across the European Union into the brothels, "nail bars" and "massage parlours".

Europol was treating Mirgo Varga as a person of special interest in their attempts to break up the criminal gangs, Paolo told them, but they had been partly thwarted by the legitimate front that Varga had for his operations. He ran an international modelling agency and had several celebrity models on his books. This generated a great deal of money and lured innocent girls, dreaming of a life as a top model, into the hands of his gang. Eurorpol needed to catch Varga red handed, actively abducting the young women and abusing them on his premises. But this was not an easy prospect. His cronies were always on their guard, with bribes paid to amenable police officers to ensure that their activities continued unabated.

Michael had got closer than anyone to interrupting Varga's crime network, Paolo told them, and for this reason he had been targeted by Varga to be eliminated. The "death" of Michael in Ealing had been mistakenly accepted as due to his suicide by the UK and European law enforcement agencies. But the fact that Michael was still alive was now known to Varga and it was only a question of time, now that his hideout had become known, that another attempt on his life would be made. As long as Varga was operating out there, Michael's life was in danger.

On this depressing note, Paolo stood up, made his farewells and promised to contact them the following day, advising extreme caution in their conversations with each other and their contact with strangers.

Chapter 60

Zita and Jeff returned to their hotel rooms to consider the meeting with Paolo. For Zita, the frustration of knowing that Michael was alive and in the same city was unbearable. Despite the risks to both of them, she felt the need to run into his arms and hold him close. The pain of separation was such that she would even risk her life to be with him. She lay on her bed and contemplated the situation.

For Jeff, there was confusion. His anger at his father's deception had been replaced by what could only be described as filial love and a desire to protect. But there was also his anxiety for Melanie. He could not contact her on his old phone – which Paolo had said might already be being tapped by Varga's men – for fear of exposing his father's safe hiding place. But he knew she would be very worried and disappointed by his sudden unexplained lack of contact. There seemed to be no way of resolving that situation at the moment. Varga's power and vengefulness seemed unassailable. They were all impotent in the face of it.

Jeff poured himself a glass of wine and lay down on the bed with the intention of blotting out his overwhelming sense of failure, when there was a knock at his door and Zita walked in.

I have a plan, Jeff,' she said.

Chapter 61

Zita proceeded to explain to Jeff that she planned to allow herself to be trafficked by Varga's gang and find a way to expose him to the police while *in flagrante*, as she put it. For this she would need a new identity and email address to enable her to respond to adverts placed online by Varga's people. Once they had taken the bait, she would attend an "interview", accept a position, and join a convoy of trafficked women with the intention of exposing Varga to the police and effecting his arrest. As a reward for this, she would ask for safe passage for herself and Michael out of Hungary and for a new identity and a safe house to be provided for them both by the British authorities. This should pose no problem as Michael was already "dead" and would be a recompense for assisting in the arrest of one of the most wanted criminals in Europe.

She told Jeff of a film she had seen a few years previously in which a young female police officer had undertaken the same ruse to entrap a gang of criminals.

'I know there is a very great risk to this plan – and I remember how terrifying the film I saw was at the time – but the criminals were brought to justice. Perhaps in real life it might not work, but it I believe it is the only chance we have.'

Jeff was impressed by Zita's resolve but could immediately see flaws in it.

'These traffickers look out for young girls, Zita, their

currency is youth… but, no offence intended, you are not seventeen.'

'No offence taken! I am twenty-six but can make myself look a lot younger.'

At this she shook her hair from its clasp and the dark waves fell around her shoulders. She opened her eyes wide and chewed her bottom lip in a beguiling manner.

She really can be the part, Jeff thought.

'I think it *could* work,' he said,

'But we will need help,' Zita said.

Chapter 62

Paolo met up with them both again at the Hard Rock Café in the centre of Budapest and listened to the plan that Zita proposed. He did not, as they had feared he would, reject it as unworkable or too dangerous to be considered. Instead, he told them to be patient while he worked out how to secure a new identity for Zita.

Zita in turn told Paolo what she had in mind. She proposed that a girl called Marta, from Maroshelyi in Romania, of dual Romanian and Hungarian citizenship, would like to apply for the job advertised on one of Varga's websites, to be nanny for a family in Brighton, in the UK. She would inform the "agency" that she was an experienced kindergarten teacher whose hobby was gymnastics.

'So they'll think I am sweet and with a great body,' she laughed.

Jeff blushed as he mentally concurred with this.

Paolo made a note of the name and profile she had proposed and promised to get his contacts to make the arrangements.

'Give me forty-eight hours to do this. Meanwhile, do *not* leave the hotel and do *not* contact anyone. And that must include your girlfriend in England, Jeff,' he stressed to him once more.

Feeling that there was at least some hope of removing the threat to Michael's life, Zita and Jeff returned to their hotel to talk about Zita's plan further. By now he had ceased to regard Zita as the opportunist home breaker he had initially cast her and had come to admire her courage. Her love for his father was evinced by her determination to bring his enemies to justice and to protect him from them. He could see she was also determined to break up the criminal networks that were causing so much harm and misery in Hungary and beyond.

When Paolo next returned to the hotel, he had a passport and identity card in the name of Marta Rosza Kelemen, aged nineteen, of Maroshelyi. The photo matched Zita well, despite the girl in the photo having pigtails and a slightly goofy smile.

With Paolo's help, "Marta" applied for the job as nanny to the Brighton family. She attached a college certificate in childcare and a reference from her previous employer, a lady dentist in Debrecen, who was lavish with her praise of Marta's love of children, enthusiasm and sweet disposition. Five minutes later came the reply, inviting Marta to an interview the following day at eleven a.m. at a hotel in District 7.

Chapter 63

The hotel, in Nefelejcs Street, close to Keleti station in the District 7 of Budapest, was not one that Zita would have wished to stay in, with its crumbling façade and the odour of stale cigarette smoke and damp carpets which pervaded the lobby area.

She gave her name to the receptionist and was directed to a room on the second floor of the building. Here she joined a group of around six other girls, all chattering excitedly. She introduced herself and was soon involved in the sharing of their stories of the dream jobs that had been offered to them so unexpectedly. They were all aged between sixteen and nineteen and most of them came from areas of rural Hungary and Romania.

The door opened and a huge man entered accompanied by a kindly looking lady. Zita put the man's age at around the late forties. He was tall with long, greasy black hair, which was held back in a ponytail, a large belly which over hung the belt of his jeans and tattoos featuring lizards covering his arms. He did not introduce himself but welcomed them individually by name from a list he was holding, his gaze lingering over each girl as he spoke to them briefly. He then told them that the arrangements for transport to the UK had been made. They were to be at Baross Square, behind Keleti station, at six a.m. the following day, where a minibus would take them to the airport. They would be accompanied on the journey by a representative from the travel agency which had been recruited for the trip. He then took his leave telling them that his colleague, with a nod to the lady next to him, would be responsible for gathering their documents.

Zita and the other girls handed over their passports and ID cards as instructed, the woman explaining that they were required by the agency for the purposes of booking the plane tickets in their names. These would be returned to them at the airport, they were told. They were also asked to give names and addresses of close family members, 'in case of emergencies, just normal procedure,' the lady said with a smile.

Zita had been warned by Paolo that this would happen. He had heard the same story from umpteen girls he had interviewed in the brothels in Budapest. The gang would use this information, he said, to threaten to harm or kill their families should the girls try to escape. So Zita gave the names of her "parents" and "grandparents" living in Maroshelyi, but knowing that, should the gang have reason to look for these people, they would be surprised to find that they were in fact the names of serving police officers in the town.

She returned to her hotel by a circuitous route, constantly checking for any possibility that she was being followed. Paolo and Jeff were waiting for her and Paolo was unsurprised by what she told him.

'You have just been in the company of Mirgo Varga,' he told her.

Zita shivered as she remembered the man's cold appraising look as he spoke briefly to her.

Paolo then explained to Zita the rest of the plan. He had come ready to insert a surveillance microchip into her upper arm. This would allow her to contact the police when she had Varga in a situation where he could be apprehended and arrested. It was also to be used if she felt her life was at risk and she needed to be rescued urgently.

'But how will it work, and won't it be visible?' she asked.

Paolo explained that the electronic device was no larger than the microchip inserted into a dog's neck for identification purposes. It was innovative technology and very unlikely to be known to the gang. If she was ever challenged about what the small, raised area on her upper arm was where the bug was inserted, she could explain that it was a contraceptive implant.

'This type of bug has been designed to resemble such an implant. It is activated by a code word uttered by the wearer. Should you be in danger or in a situation that would enable us to apprehend Varga, you should raise your arm and say the code word into the bug. The police will receive the message instantaneously and come to your location immediately, wherever you are,' he promised.

'So what is the code word?' she asked.

'Salon Kitty,' he replied.

'Why "Salon Kitty"?' Jeff asked.

'"Salon Kitty" was the name of the Berlin brothel used by high-ranking Nazi officers during the war. Listening devices and two-way mirrors were used by the Gestapo to compromise and report on officers using the salon.'

'I see,' said Jeff.

'All you need to do is say the name and the bug will

recognise your voice. Just roll up your sleeve and I will insert the bug now,' Paolo said.

Paolo took a small package from his bag. He removed a syringe with a short wide bore needle and, having used a disinfectant wipe to clean the area, he injected the bug into her upper arm. Zita felt a sharp pain at the injection site which soon subsided to a dull throbbing sensation.

'Now say the code word Zita,' he instructed.

Zita said the words "Salon Kitty" as steadily as she could, her mouth near to the chip in her upper arm.

'Good. That's all that you need to do,' Paolo said.

Before he left, Paolo congratulated Zita on her courage but, in sombre tones, reminded her of the dangers she would face. He told her that she could change her mind at any stage and request rescue. But Zita assured him that her love for Michael was more important to her than her own life. She would do this!

'Okay,' Paolo said. 'Now get some sleep. You have a difficult day ahead of you tomorrow.'

Chapter 64

At six a.m. the following day, carrying a small holdall with clothing from the teens' department of H&M, Zita joined the other girls on Baross Square. A large Mercedes minibus with smoked windows drew up and two burly tattooed men got out accompanied by a woman of around forty years of age. They told the girls they were from the travel agency organising their trip. They said that the flights had been cancelled unexpectedly and that they would therefore be travelling to the UK in the minibus. Once inside the minibus they were ordered to hand over their mobile phones for "security reasons". Some of the girls refused to do so and were rewarded for this resistance by being punched in the face by the men.

The phones were then handed over in silence; all of the girls had been shocked by such brutality.

'Now we can have a peaceful journey,' laughed the woman, who had introduced herself as Mircalla.

Zita was shaken, but did not object to giving up her mobile to the men. She had been given a used phone by Paolo to hand over. On it there were texts from her "family" to "Marta" wishing her well for the journey and her new life. At that moment, she felt very alone and apprehensive, having witnessed the callous brutality of the gang and the violence that they were capable of. She just tried to hold on to her memory of Michael and the hope of a future with him.

The minibus crossed the border into Slovakia and onwards to Bratislava. They stopped at a service station where the girls were permitted to use the toilet facilities one by one under the supervision of Mircalla.

'Pee pee stop girls,' the men sniggered, and made coarse comments as they returned to the bus.

By now, all the girls had realised that they had been duped. One or two were sobbing continuously.

In Bratislava, the bus drew up outside a dilapidated hotel near the international coach station. Zita noted the name "Hotel Tara".

Mircalla and one of the men called out two of the girls by name. They came forward and were bundled off the bus into the hotel lobby and handed over to a man waiting there. Zita saw a wad of euro notes being passed across in return for the girls. One of them started screaming but was punished for this by a kick in her abdomen. She doubled over in pain and was pulled by her hair out of sight into the hotel. Her companion followed meekly behind. Zita had no doubt what the fate of these poor girls would be. They had been sold to the hotel which was clearly a brothel. They would be used again and again to fulfil the sexual predilections of the customers. They would be exposed to brutality and sexually transmitted disease and imprisoned by fear of threats of reprisals to their family members, should they cause trouble to their captors. Their lives would be expendable, should they try to escape.

The minibus continued its journey across Europe. There were no further stops until the coach reached Brussels at midday the following day. Two more girls were removed from the coach, this time in a deserted parking lot behind a bus station. Zita watched as the girls were taken off the bus and towards a group of leather jacketed men, huddled in a corner smoking. She watched in horror as the girls were told to undress and were shoved from one man to the other as each man appraised and handled them as though they were so much meat at a market. More money exchanged hands and the girls were taken away in an old VW van. Zita noted the number plate but realised that this was probably a waste of time. The girls were now in the pipeline and would be moved around according to demand. They would be hard to trace.

The minibus reached the French coast that evening. Mircalla and the men locked Zita and the two remaining girls in the van while they went to eat and drink. No food had been offered to the girls during the journey, although a bottle of water had been provided. Zita could see that her two companions were numb with fear and hunger but was unable offer any words of comfort. She knew what their fate would be and that she could do nothing to help them, for the moment at least.

Later that night, their captors returned, the men smelling of alcohol and cigarettes. One of them drunkenly suggested a bit of sport with the girls.

'Mirgo won't mind us having a bit on the house,' he said. Looking at Zita he leered, 'This one will do.'

He tried to grab her. Zita cringed and made an effort to escape his grasp. His foul breath caused her to retch and a surge of bile gushed into her throat. She spat it out, splashing the yellow bilious liquid onto his pointed black leather shoes.

'You bitch,' he yelled and lunged towards her with his

fists.

At this point Mircalla intervened, holding the man back with her arm across his chest.

'Don't mark this one,' she warned him. 'Mirgo has special plans for her. Take one of the others.'

To Zita's horror the thug grabbed one of the other girls, threw her across the seats of the minibus and raped her in full view of the rest of them.

When he was finished with her, the girl returned to her companions who did their best to comfort her. Her two companions were now aware of what their "new jobs" would be. No words of comfort would lessen their misery.

In darkness, the minibus drove silently and without its headlights turned on onto a beach a few miles from the port of Calais. A small fishing boat was waiting there and the girls were bundled on board. Mircalla and one of the captors joined them, wearing life jackets. The other man drove off in the minibus, no doubt to pick up another convoy, Zita thought.

The boat was piloted by a short swarthy man who spoke no Hungarian or Romanian. After a while, Zita realised that he was Albanian, as was Mircalla. The boat rocked and heaved in the heavy swell of the English Channel. Both of her companions vomited. They cried out that they could not swim and were terrified of falling into the water. Their captors ignored their pleas. As they approached the shoreline of southern England, the Albanian told them to lie low while he manoeuvred the boat around some cliffs.

Suddenly a wide beam of light illuminated the boat and voices could be heard shouting instructions through a megaphone to the pilot of their boat. Zita understood the English. They were the Border Control coast guards, demanding the right to board the boat and inspect the cargo. Zita held her breath, rescue was at hand, but with that would disappear the possibility of getting Varga convicted. Zita knew well that Mircalla and her accomplices were small fry in his criminal network, that they were expendable. Varga knew they would not betray him to any authority, for fear of the consequences to their own families. The loss of the "cargo" would be written off as a bit of bad luck.

What happened next shocked Zita beyond all the belief she had ever had in basic humanity. The Albanian man grabbed her two companions and threw them overboard, one at a time, shrieking and begging for mercy. As the girls thrashed around in the water, the pilot of their vessel shoved the engine into full throttle and wrenched the wheel, changing the boat's direction at speed along the coast and away from the helpless girls. Zita looked back and could see that the Coast Guard vessel was attempting to retrieve the two girls from the water. She prayed that they would do so, but the water was freezing and a dense fog had now come down in the last few minutes. While the arrival of the fog was helping her captors to make their escape, it would do nothing to help the girls' chance of rescue and survival.

Their boat sped away at speed under cover of the fog but slowed down as they approached a shingle beach further along the coast. The pilot spoke into his satellite phone and, after a time of bobbing in the shallows, lights appeared on the beach and two men materialised and dragged the boat ashore as it grounded on the shingle. Zita, soaking and shivering, was wrapped in a blanket and taken to a large SUV parked near the beach. She was joined by Mircalla and her other captor. The fishing boat chugged off into the darkness.

As the vehicle drove her through the night, Zita tried to read the road signs. She had never been to the UK before and had very little knowledge of any part of the country except for London. She had no idea where she was until a sign announcing their arrival in a town called Eastbourne came into view. Michael had previously told her about how a trafficking gang had been caught there. It appeared therefore that Varga's influence still continued here despite this.

The car entered a narrow street where Zita could see dustbins overturned and large white birds tearing at the contents. She was pulled out of the car and taken into one of the houses. Here she was dragged to a room upstairs and the door was locked behind her.

Zita looked around her new prison. Dingy nylon curtains covered the dusty windows. There was the now familiar smell of damp and stale cigarette smoke she had come across in the other "hotels" the gang had kept her. The windows were barred and she could see that there was no way of escaping from the place, were she to have the need to do so. She could hear her captors playing cards and drinking beer in the room outside. She felt a long way from her life in Budapest, and very afraid.

Exhausted by the journey and the events of the past twenty-four hours, she fell into a deep sleep.

Mircalla appeared in the room the following morning.

'Get up and clean yourself. We have important visitors today and you need to look good for them.' She threw a

286

towel and a bar of cheap smelling soap at Zita and led her to a dirty bathroom that adjoined the bedroom.

After a couple of pieces of bread and a cup of tea, Zita was moved to a room downstairs, where she was instructed to sit on a leather sofa. It was late morning by this time and the sun shone brightly through the windows, highlighting the dirt and bird shit that covered them.

A car drew up outside and two men entered the hall outside. She could hear Mircalla greeting the two men in English. There was a discussion about the loss of the "cargo" and Varga was heard to say:

'But the main item is here, as you will see, my friend,' addressing his companion.

Zita sat up and tried to control her shaking hands. She knew they were talking about her. Her hand went to her upper arm to assure herself that the implanted microchip was still in place.

The two men entered the room. One man was fair haired, tall and of slim build. He was wearing the kind of clothes only available in the fashionable shops on and around Andrassy Avenue in Budapest. The second man was also tall, but big bellied and with a long, greasy ponytail. It was Varga.

Zita was told to stand up. Varga's companion introduced himself as "Charles" and complimented "Marta" on her appearance. Then a business transaction took place, with Varga highlighting the beauty of "Marta" and her potential to attract Charles's clients. At this point, Zita could only assume that these "clients" would be the type of men that she had seen mistreating her former companions. But she listened with heightened interest when "Charles" mentioned the names of high-profile businesses and connections to British politicians she had heard Michael talk about. Whatever was planned for her, she knew she was now close to the dark heart of Varga's own business empire.

Chapter 65

On an unseasonably cold May morning in Budapest, Alistair the OSSE security attaché received a visit from a ghost.

Paolo had phoned him just after he had got to his desk and told him of an urgent matter he needed to discuss with him. Alistair tried to defer the meeting; things were difficult enough at the Budapest headquarters of the OSSE at the moment. Many of the Hungarian employees had left, citing conflicts of interest and family pressures. The truth was, as Alistair knew well, that they were anxious about being on the wrong side of Government policy now that international organisations and NGOs were fast becoming *persona non grata* in Hungary. Non-Hungarian staff were working double shifts to compensate for their departure.

Alistair's PA buzzed him to say that Mr Crusesco had arrived accompanied by another man. Alistair sighed and told her to give the meeting twenty minutes and then buzz through to "remind" him of another appointment.

The door opened and Paolo, accompanied by a tall, bearded man wearing a hooded jacket, walked in.

'Hello Alistair,' Michael said.

Alistair was not a man given to expletives but these were exceptional circumstances. 'What the fuck is going on?! You are dead!'

'It would seem not,' Michael said. 'May I sit down? This is going to take some time to explain.'

As succinctly as he could, Michael told Alistair exactly what had happened over the last few months. He explained that his decision to flee to Hungary following the discovery of the body in his garage was an attempt to protect his family and friends from the gang who wanted him dead. After all, if they believed him to be dead it would be unlikely that they would look for him in Hungary. He knew the country well and had access to funds in discreet bank accounts. He confessed to having no idea of what his future would be. He thought it possible that after lying low for a while, he could eventually make contact with Zita and perhaps have a new life with her.

But his discovery by his son Jeff and subsequently by Varga's gang had changed all of that. And that was why he was here now. Zita was in mortal danger and he needed Alistair's help to find her. Paolo had told him of her daring plan. How could he, Michael, remain hidden and safe in a cellar while she risked her life? His newsfeed had reported the attempted interception of a fishing boat in the English Channel. The bodies of two young women had been retrieved from the water. It was a known ploy by people traffickers to jettison their human cargo as a decoy when they faced interception by coastal patrols. As they had no documentation on them, they were only identifiable at the present time by their clothing, which had been purchased from shops in Hungary. For all Michael knew, one of these girls could be Zita.

'So how can I help?' Alistair said, after a while.

'First we need to make sure that Zita is alive and, if so, I want to help find her. Varga's crime network needs to be destroyed. If Zita is alive and has been able to get close to Varga, we have a real possibility of catching him when he is vulnerable to arrest. He would be a big fish in the net of Europol.'

'But I still don't know how you intend to do this. I'm sorry, Michael, but you are officially dead, your passport has been revoked and there are gang members on the lookout for you.'

'If you don't know, Alistair, then I do,' replied Michael.

Chapter 66

Three days later a Mr Oliver Adams stepped off a Eurostar train at St Pancras Station, London, on the last leg of his journey from Budapest. He went to the nearest public convenience to urinate and freshen up. His beard was now two inches in length and the spectacles concealed most of the upper part of his face. Alistair's friends at Europol had done a fine job with his passport. The photograph matched his current appearance and the details of his address, 11 Parkcroft Road in Lee, Lewisham, London SE12 were plausible enough.

Michael looked around for his contact. The station was a turmoil of humanity in transit. A red-haired lady with a rucksack and a suitcase on wheels accompanied by two Border Collie dogs on leads crossed the concourse in front of him towards the Kings Cross exit. She smiled briefly as she crossed his path, unfazed by the maelstrom around her.

He was watching the woman's progress towards the exit and so did not notice a young man wearing a hooded sweatshirt with the name of Colombia University NYC emblazoned on it coming towards him. He held a street map in his hand. As soon as he saw the man, Michael knew at once that this was his contact.

The young man approached Michael cautiously and asked politely for directions to The Parcel Yard Pub, Kings Cross. Michael made a show of looking at the map and then, seeing that his contact still appeared confused, he suggested that he show the man to the pub.

They found a table on the balcony of the restored King's Cross station parcel depot and Michael ordered drinks at the bar. As he carried them to the table he caught a glimpse of the red-haired lady again. She was now chatting to platform staff next to the Flying Scotsman train which according to announcements was soon to depart from platform four for Inverness. The time was eleven forty-five a.m.

'So,' the young man began, 'we know where Zita is but unless she can make contact at the right moment, we will have little chance to rescue her or apprehend our target. She has had a rough time, but our sources say she is very resilient.' He took a drink of his beer. 'Michael, this is not going to be easy, for any of us.'

Chapter 67

Michael sipped his drink and tried to control his anxiety. He was not allowed to ask the young man's name, he knew the rules. But he had many questions which he hoped the man could answer.

Calmly, the contact told him that Zita was the prisoner of a man called Charles Beaton, a wealthy young man from a titled family but who worked in partnership with a Russian businessman called Roman Solokov. The latter ran exclusive entertainment clubs for the super-rich and hosted corporate events, often under the pretext of raising funds for charity. Drugs were routinely part of the entertainment, as was the provision of beautiful young women for sex. Varga's role in this was to locate and supply suitable women, usually those duped by his model agency adverts, and to provide the drugs. Michael remembered a recent scandal involving the hiring of attractive young women to wait at tables at such events and the fallout that followed. Several government ministers had lost their portfolios and charities distanced themselves from the donors. But at least those women had volunteered for the work and had been paid for it. The women Varga supplied were trafficked and enslaved, the agent told Michael.

'And it goes deeper than that,' the contact continued. 'Solokov is a friend of the Russian government. At these events he has bugs placed at all the tables and the girls are expected to relay any information about business affairs and government policy that they may overhear. This is either used to blackmail the clients or to secure preferential deals. By the time the clients are entrapped, they either pay the ransom or cooperate. Most do the latter because it ensures their continued position in their business or government office. Many of the business deals they have been involved in include the provision of arms to foreign governments. We have intelligence that Mirgo Varga's outfit has been overseeing the delivery of large consignments of guns to help the pro-Russian army in Eastern Ukraine. Our security services have been very vigilant at all the ports and airports, but up to now they have not intercepted any shipments of illegal weapons. For this reason we suspect that these arms are being exported from less likely parts of the UK.'

The PA system was at that moment apologising for the delay of the midday service to Inverness. No reason was given, but customers were being asked to wait on the platform for further announcements.

From their seat on the balcony of the pub, Michael and his contact had a clear view of the train on platform four. It was twelve fifteen p.m. Suddenly, a loud bang was heard, and then smoke and shouting emanated from the rear of the train. A man descended from the carriage, his clothing partly on fire. From what Michael could see, he was wearing the livery of the train company. He drew a gun from his pocket and fired at two police officers who were giving chase as he ran at speed along the platform. The passengers scattered in all directions as panic ensued. Then, from behind one of the platform pillars, the red-haired lady appeared.

The lady calmly manoeuvred herself between the pillars

of the platform holding the leads of her two dogs. The man ran in her direction, but was looking over his shoulder at the police officers who were gaining ground on him. He saw the woman at the last moment and swerved to avoid her. At that instant, she let go of the leads and the dogs ran at the man. He broke his speed to avoid the dogs but, as he did so, he tripped over the large suitcase the woman had pushed across his path. He fell to the ground winded, from where the police officers fell onto the man, handcuffed him and led him away. The woman calmly collected her case, secured her dogs and walked on.

'She's one of us,' the contact said, turning to Michael with a broad smile. 'What you have just witnessed is the result of information Zita has just passed to us,' the agent told Michael. 'She had overheard a conversation between Varga, Solokov and others involving the shipment of arms on the twelve p.m. train from Kings Cross to Inverness. She apparently managed to get hold of a mobile phone from one of Varga's clients, recorded the conversation and relayed this communication to us. It turned out that the weapons were concealed in large suitcases. As there are no security checks at rail stations, it is an easy matter for the gang to load them onto the train, with the help of an insider member of staff, and offload them at Edinburgh and then onto a hired van to the docks at Leith. The red-haired lady's role was to have an excuse to get aboard the train early with the dogs, to find seats – "speedy boarders", if you like,' he said with a grin, 'and locate the gang members travelling with the cases. Unfortunately, the "passenger" saw the police officers arriving and threw a grenade at them. His other accomplice ran off, as you saw, and is still on the run. We have a good description of him so we will find him, believe me.'

'But what about Zita?' Michael asked.

'That is why you are here, my friend,' the man said.

Chapter 68

Without any explanation, Zita was bundled out of the door and into the black Range Rover she had seen Varga and Charles arrive in. She was able to get a glimpse of the street as they drove away. It was a fairly run-down residential area with wheeled bins littering the street. A couple of young girls were pushing buggies, each carrying two young children. The girls were holding loud conversations into their mobile phones, apparently completely oblivious of the cries of the children which went unnoticed by them. As they sped away, the car passed along the promenade, from where she could see the sea and the cliffs beyond.

After around two hours the car reached the outskirts of London. It took another hour to reach an address in what was clearly a very affluent part of the city. Grand houses with white stucco façades rose majestically around private gardens. The car stopped in front of a pillared entrance and Charles got out and punched a code onto the panel of the big black front door. Varga reached into the back of the car and pulled Zita from her seat and up the steps to the house.

She found herself in a marble floored hall, with high decorative ceilings from which an enormous chandelier hung. Charles pressed a bell on the wall and in a short time a man dressed in a uniform appeared. He bowed to both men. He then took Zita by the arm and led her out of the hall, along a passageway and into a lift. She could see from the control panel that there must be at least two floors below the entrance level.

The lift whined to a halt and when the doors opened Zita saw a long corridor with many rooms leading off it. The man opened the door of one of the rooms with a code and pushed her inside.

'Get washed and then change into the clothes you will find here. The master will call for you in one hour.'

The room was furnished only with a single bed and had a small shower unit and toilet behind a door. She checked out the clothes on the bed and was unsurprised to see that they were the skimpiest of garments. A silk thong which would leave nothing to the imagination and a lace bra, barely large enough to cover her nipples. Over this she was to wear a very short black dress made of thin stretchy material and black stockings. The shower was most welcome and, as she towelled herself dry, Zita considered the situation. She was lucky to be alive and she was certainly now at the heart of Varga's operations in London. If she played the game and cooperated in whatever he had planned, and with a great deal of luck, she might be able to bring him to justice. She once again felt for the patch on her arm and its presence gave her courage. She could call for help now but that would achieve little. Varga would have the chance to escape. This house was enormous and would without doubt have plenty of hideouts. He would get away and she would be in even more danger in the future. He knew her face. So she dressed for her part, shaking her hair over her shoulders and applying the cosmetics that had been provided for her use.

Within an hour the door was opened and in came Charles.

He looked at her and whistled.

'Mirgo has done well this time,' he said. 'What a pity we have such a busy evening ahead. I'd like to sample you myself.'

Zita endured his hand groping her crotch as he led her back to the lift. Varga was waiting in the hallway. He too expressed pleasure at her appearance. The car was waiting and Zita was pushed in. A few minutes later they were drawing up outside a large villa with security guards at the gates. Coloured lights illuminated the gardens and a fountain played music as water cascaded over the water feature below. There were several expensive looking cars on the driveway and Zita could see people standing around in small groups with champagne flutes in their hands.

Zita was taken into the house, up a staircase and into a large room with ornate chairs arranged around the room. A long oval table was placed by the windows, with candelabra and glasses on it. There were huge, decorative mirrors on the walls and a couple of framed portraits of nudes.

She was not alone. There were three other girls sitting there. Varga shoved her roughly onto a chair and instructed her to wait and to do as she was told.

'Remember bitch, we know where your family is,' he said, as he left the room.

As soon as they were alone, Zita turned to the girls and asked what was happening. Despite their beauty and party clothes, they all looked miserable.

'Don't you know?' said one of the girls who introduced herself as Anya, from Estonia. 'We are here to entertain Solokov's friends. He's put on quite a show tonight. That lot downstairs are all politicians and filthy rich businessmen. He's invited them to his daughter's eighteenth birthday party. She's a spoiled brat, nothing but the best for Natalia. Or her ghastly friends. One of us will no doubt be lent to a few of them to have a bit of fun with. She got a Porsche and a diamond bracelet for her birthday. All I got for mine was to be sold like a dog to Varga. It was my birthday three weeks ago.' She started to cry.

Zita had no words of comfort to offer her. She had seen too many terrible things over the past week. Her hope was that she could help to get these girls released, but only if she got Varga arrested first. He was a big fish, but so were Solokov and Deacon. Perhaps they could all be caught at the same time.

After a while a waiter brought champagne bottles and placed them on the table by the window. He stood to attention by the door. This opened and in came six very drunken but extremely well-dressed men ranging in age from thirty to seventy. Solokov led them in, promising a feast for their eyes. This provoked a lot of ribald comment and laughter which continued as the men considered the girls.

'Stand up and make conversation or it will be the worse for you,' whispered Anya in Zita's ear.

The waiter poured out the champagne and the men drifted towards the girls.

'And who is this beauty?' said one corpulent older man addressing Zita.

'I believe this is Marta from Hungary, or maybe Romania,' replied Solokov. 'She is new here but a very good worker, as you are welcome to find out.'

'As long as you pay them well, Roman, old boy. That's fine by me.' He stroked her bottom through the thin material of the dress.

Zita realised that all the men present believed the girls to be prostitutes, paid for by their generous host. They would have no idea of the reality of the girls' situation.

The older man, addressed as Hugh, was challenged by another man as he sat Zita on his knee and began to fondle her breasts.

'Come on Hugh, share and share alike and I promise I won't tell Allison.'

Zita noticed the other girls being taken away after the men had selected them. Anya also had two men vying for her.

'I don't mind sharing if you don't,' Hugh said, as the men each took her hands and led her out of the room, picking up a bottle of champagne as they went.

She was taken into a nearby room. A large double bed dominated the room with an ensuite bathroom behind a door. There was a widescreen TV. On the wall there were several switches, presumably to alter the lighting.

Both men were very drunk, which made it easier for Zita. She almost pitied them. Their sagging, corpulent bodies repelled her. Their hands grabbing and snatching at her body hurt her. She was slapped playfully. Hugh seemed to enjoy spanking her which was very painful. But neither man managed an erection. Hugh made a joke about "brewers' droop", which they even found amusing.

After a couple of hours of taking their pleasure both men fell fast asleep.

Zita saw her opportunity and took it. She rummaged in

302

the men's trouser pockets and extracted a phone from one of them. It was a high specification android phone and was ready to use. She guessed that the men had been using their phones during the party, perhaps for taking business calls. She got dressed and joined the party.

As so many of Natalia's friends were wearing the skimpiest of dresses, Zita did not look too out of place. Everyone was very drunk, but merry with it. She asked one of Natalia's friends of the whereabouts of her father.

'I'd like to thank him for such a smashing party,' she said.

'I last saw him in the pool house with that massive friend of his, the Hungarian guy. They've been shut away there for hours. Probably to escape from this lot,' she said with a nod towards the older guests.

Zita recognised some of the guests from news items she had seen on television. She could count at least two politicians, as well as a well-known and incredibly rich businessman.

She looked outside and saw the Olympic-size swimming pool, where some of the guests were swimming naked under the fairy lights that twinkled in the trees surrounding it. A couple of security guards were slouching over cigarettes under the trees. She would have to be careful. She walked out of the open French windows into the garden, around the swimming pool and in the direction of the pool house.

The pool house was a wooden pavilion secluded and close to the shallow end of the pool. She waited until a couple who had been sitting there, dangling their legs and snorting cocaine, got back in the water. She then crept to the door. She could hear a conversation in progress, but it was nigh on

303

inaudible. The two security guards were some way away from her, still smoking under the trees and had their backs towards her. Checking around the pool house, she moved stealthily along the side of the building and positioned herself underneath a window ledge and sat down with her back against the wall. A large weeping willow tree hung over the pool house at this point, also giving her cover. There was no moon, so she was well camouflaged. Even if one of the security men were to look in her direction, they would probably think she was one of the party girls a little worse for wear. She could now hear the conversation coming from inside the wooden building very well from where she sat.

There were four people in the room, Solokov, Varga, Deacon and another man, who had the same well enunciated English as Charles. There seemed to be a discussion about money going on. Varga was being criticised for the loss of cargo, no doubt the poor girls lost in the English Channel, thought Zita. Then the conversation changed and Zita overheard the word "guns". She looked at the phone in her pocket and found a recording app. Very carefully she raised the phone to the level of the window and switched the microphone on to full volume. From her hiding place she was able to record the entire conversation, which ranged from the sale of girls, dealing in cocaine and using the proceeds to buy and sell weapons to pro-Russian rebels in Ukraine.

Zita was astonished. She had not imagined that Varga's interests were so wide ranging. This man was enabling, in part at least, the on-going fighting in Eastern Ukraine. Zita also heard Varga outlining his plan to load weapons, concealed in large, sealed suitcases, onto a train at King's

Cross station the following day, for transport to Edinburgh. From there, the guns would be taken to be shipped from Leith docks. The time and destination of the train she heard clearly. It was to be the midday service from Kings Cross to Inverness.

She had heard and recorded enough. The next thing to do was to phone Paolo and give him the information.

Chapter 69

When Paolo's mobile phone rang with "Caller Unknown" displayed on the screen he hesitated before answering it. Only Jeff and Zita knew this number, so surely this must be bad news? Perhaps Zita's cover had been blown and she had been tortured and forced to provide his number. Perhaps Michael had been caught too.

With shaking hands he answered: 'Hello, Paolo here.' When he heard Zita's voice he wanted to cry with relief. 'Zita, it's you! Are you OK?'

'I'm in great danger. You need to act urgently.'

'Why didn't you send the "Salon Kitty" code through your microchip?'

'Because I need to send you some information urgently which I have recorded on the mobile phone I have stolen, and I don't know how to do this!'

When she told him about the phone recording she had made, he explained how she could send it directly by voice mail straight onto his phone. He would then be able to forward this directly to the police. Zita told Paolo quickly that she believed that Varga and Solokov's names were used sufficiently often during the conversation to incriminate them.

'I'll send it to you now!' she rang off.

As soon as he received the recording, Paolo knew immediately she had got what they needed. He saved the conversation onto his phone and forwarded it straight onto Europol with an explanatory note under the subject heading "urgent – action now".

Chapter 70

Zita carefully made her way back through the gardens to the villa and to the room where her two "lovers" snored peacefully. She deleted the dialled number to Paolo from the phone, as well as the recording, and replaced it in the trouser pocket she had found it. She stayed with the men until around two a.m. when Hugh woke up. He shook his friend awake, looked at the time and said they should call a taxi. They actually thanked her and expressed the hope that they had behaved themselves as gentlemen. They asked her to tell Solokov that they would be in touch about the contracts later that day and slipped her two £50 notes "for our pleasure, my dear", they said.

Unsure what to do next, Zita returned to the room where she had been seated the previous evening. Anya was missing but the two other girls were there, sobbing, with their clothes torn and bruises around their necks and on their arms. Zita said what words of comfort she could muster. She was shocked by their accounts of having first been raped by the men who came into the room and then passed around by Natalia's drunken friends, male and female. They had been abused and beaten. One of the girls, Wanda, had blood running down her legs.

Zita realised that, by comparison, she should be thankful for the treatment she had received from her two elderly would-be Lotharios.

The party went on until dawn by which time most of the guests could be seen leaving in large Mercedes cars and taxis. At around eight a.m. Varga appeared in the room, pulling Anya ahead of him. She looked as if she was in a state of shock, sobbing uncontrollably and very severely bruised.

Varga pushed Anya into the room and told them that they were to stay where they were for the rest of the day. He said he had "business to attend to". Zita could guess what he meant by this. He had a train to catch!

The girls were fed some leftovers from the party. Natalia looked in on them during the course of the morning to sneer at them and threated them that, should they ever tell anyone of the events which had taken place during her party, it would be "curtains" for them.

As midday approached, Zita became very nervous. She was sure that the information she had given to Paolo would be acted on. But what if they police or security forces were too late? If Varga were to escape, he would know that someone had tipped them off. He might find out that she was responsible by examining the images on CCTV cameras around the premises. He was sure to have some of those hidden around the place, including the outdoor swimming pool and pool house. The fact that she hadn't seen any didn't mean they weren't there.

A couple of hours later a black Mercedes drew up outside the house. Solokov followed by Varga entered the villa. From the window she could see that Varga's face was blackened, his clothing was singed and that he was limping badly. She heard the men go into one of the rooms downstairs and decided to risk spying on them again. She moved as silently as she could down the stairs and into the reception hall of the house. She didn't have to wait long to hear raised voices, furious and threatening violence against her.

'That dark-haired bitch. I'll tear her limb from limb when I get her!' she heard Varga shout.

'And that pair of old fools will regret this. I'll ruin them,' said Solokov. 'Where is she, the Marta one?'

'Upstairs. Let's get her now.'

Zita had heard enough. She ran back upstairs and into the room. The other girls looked up startled as she ran in.

'Salon Kitty!' Zita pleaded very loudly and clearly into the device in her upper arm. Warning the girls that there was going to be a police raid, she told them to stay where they were and wait to be rescued.

Zita ran out of the room and up the stairs to the second floor. From there, she could hear Varga and Solokov mounting the stairs at speed. She heard them enter the first-floor room and curse loudly when they realised she was not there. Every second counted if she was going to escape with her life. She had no idea how long it would take for help to arrive. She opened a door and saw a bedroom with a balcony that gave onto the garden. She locked the bedroom door behind her – thanking her good fortune that bedroom privacy was a given, in this house at least. She ran to the balcony doors and tried the key. Her heart was in her mouth as she turned it, first one way and then another. It had not been opened for some time but she persevered. Finally the rusty key turned in the lock and she was out on the balcony. She looked over to see a considerable drop to the garden below.

She took off her shoes and started to climb over. All the time she could hear the sound of Solokov and Varga's voices and footsteps, doors being opened and slammed shut as they searched for her. She could hear Varga shouting into his phone and demanding a search of the grounds. She lowered herself to the first-floor balcony, to see the startled faces of her fellow captives in the room inside. They sat there quietly and did not betray her as she climbed over the balustrade.

From there, Zita climbed over the balcony and jumped to the ground. She landed heavily. A shooting pain shot from her ankle to her knee. She tried to stand, but the pain was unbearable. She could see Solokov's guards running through the trees, radio phones in their hands. Dragging her useless leg behind her she made a dive for some dense bushes that surrounded the lawns of the villa. Crouching low and listening to the commotion, Zita realised that her life could soon be at an end. No mercy would be shown to her. Her body would be disposed of as crudely as they would take her life.

'I love you Michael,' she said out loud, and awaited her fate.

Chapter 71

Michael was still absorbed in watching the aftermath of the events on the platform when he heard his companion draw breath. A bleeping noise was coming from his phone.

'Salon Kitty,' the man said. 'Michael, we have to go, *now*!'

As they rushed out of the station a police car drew up and both jumped inside.

'What's going on?' Michael asked as they sped through the traffic. The roads around King's Cross had been closed off following the incidents earlier.

The man told him that Zita had activated a code word which meant that she was in mortal danger. The police hoped they would be in time to the arrest Varga and his accomplices and rescue Zita before they killed her. Michael started to pray that this would not be the outcome.

It took fifteen minutes to arrive outside the villa, but to Michael it seemed a lifetime. As their car screeched to a halt he was reassured to see police vans and even a military vehicle parked in the grounds. His companion spoke to one of the armed police officers who informed him that girls had been located in the house, but that Zita was not one of them. The girls were being cared for and one of them had told the police that she had last seen Zita climbing down from a balcony window.

'Which window?' Michael asked.

'That one, overlooking the lawns,' replied the officer.

Michael ran off in the direction the officer was pointing.

'Be careful, sir – there are still armed men on the run around here,' the man called after him.

Blue lights were flashing all around the garden. A helicopter could be heard and seen hovering over the villa. Armed police officers were everywhere and Michael could hear shots being fired.

Michael ran through the gardens, calling her name. Hope and fear pounding in his chest. And suddenly, there she was, dragging herself from the bushes, her hair a tangled mane, trailing a broken ankle behind her. Zita. She fell into his arms as he ran to hold her.

'My brave darling! You're going to be okay. Hold on to me and I'll get you out of here.'

'What are you doing here?' Zita gasped. 'How did you get out of Hungary?'

Michael smiled. 'It's quite a story…' he said. And he kissed her.

*

Jeff received the message on his phone late that night. It simply read: "Salon Kitty has closed for refurbishment. Please call to make new arrangements".

He smiled and phoned Paolo immediately. Once he was up to speed on the events of the day, he used his own mobile to contact Melanie.

'I'm coming home darling,' was all he could say.

Chapter 72
Six years later
June 2021

The child held tightly onto the hand of the tall man as they crossed the stream. In the distance, the Cheviot Hills glowed purple as the sun hit their peaks. Close by could be heard the sound of the River Whiteadder as it flowed in full spate towards the River Tweed.

The boy was Mihaly Adams, or Mikey to his friends at the local school in the tiny village of Foulden, in the Scottish Borders. Only just in Scotland, only just out of England.

The woman followed a few steps behind. The waves of her long dark hair were tamed in a plait that fell over her slender shoulders. The boy carried a fishing rod. His first.

'Look mummy, I'm going to catch a big fish for supper,' he said, waving his new present excitedly in the air.

His father turned to smile at his wife. She smiled back, remembering.

Chapter 73
24th August 2014
11.15 p.m.

An item rarely seen in a garage these days is a car. The house at 24 Eversfield Road, Ealing was no exception. Junk mainly, but he had found some useful tools for his trade, as well as items of clothing. As the clothes fitted so well, he took to popping back from time to time to the garage at night to take more. Each time, he would remove his own shabby clothes, dressing himself in the respectable items he had found in replacement. He would throw his discarded old clothes into the first dustbin he came across on his way back down the road.

'Funny how these middle-class types never lock their sheds and garages,' he thought to himself as he walked back out onto the drive in his latest set of new clothes.

Alarms and CCTV everywhere, as well as those sanctimonious "Neighbourhood Watch" notices. Watching what? They should watch their bairns more. Shocking what they get up to.

They were on him before he knew they were there. They threw him to the ground and, with a tattooed fist in his mouth, dragged him back inside the garage. The rope was around his neck and he was being hauled up to the high beam before he could draw his last breath. The language they spoke was not familiar to him but their intention was clear. There was a loud bang as the upturned wooden box he had been standing on was kicked across the garage. Urine dribbled down his leg as he swung like a deranged marionette.

Acknowledgements

With thanks to Cressida Downing for her advice during an early draft of the manuscript.

And with loving thanks to my wife Jan, for all her helpful ideas and editorial additions in the planning and writing of this book.

Finally, with many thanks to my editor Vicky Richards for her professional expertise and patience with me, and to Kirsty Jackson and all her team at Cranthorpe Millner.

The poem *Ode to the Twentieth Century* was written by Lekza Manus (translated by Gillian Taylor) and is from Hancock, Dowd, Duric [eds.] 1998 *'The Roads of the Roma': A Pen Anthology of Gypsy Writers* (PEN American Centers' threatened literature series), p.54.

Author Jeremy Bending spent his life as a hospital doctor and consultant physician. During that time he continued to write fiction and short stories, some of which were brought together in his book *A Listening Doctor*, published in 2018.

His first novel, *In the Shadows of the Birch Trees*, published in 2020, tells the story of a young Hungarian woman and her baby who, by an extraordinary twist of fate, escape the horror of the mass murders being committed within the Birkenau extermination camp in WW2 as they are about to enter there. The book tells of the lives they live following their flight and that of the SS guard, Peter Leahy, who allowed them to escape.